NEVER LET GO

A LAZARUS RISING STORY

New York Times and USA Today Bestselling Author

CYNTHIA EDEN

CHAPTER ONE

She could hear the sound of his strong, steady heartbeat as it filled her ears.

"How am I, doc?" Sawyer Cage asked as he flashed her a wide smile. The dimple in his left cheek winked at her and his dark blue eyes flashed.

Dr. Elizabeth Parker licked her lips as she pulled the stethoscope away from his bare chest. Her fingers slid over his skin, and she felt his warmth like an electric spark against her. "Your vitals are good." Her voice was crisp, and her back was ramrod straight. She put down the stethoscope and moved to grab his chart. "Good...despite the fact that you returned from your latest mission with a gunshot wound to your shoulder—"

"It's barely a graze. Didn't even need stitches—"

"A stab wound to your right arm—"

"Okay, so that needed maybe...four stitches. Five, max."

"And bruising on your ribs that indicate—"

"Things got a little...intense." His smile dimmed. "Nothing that my team couldn't handle, though."

His team. Right. Because Sawyer Cage was one of the bad asses of the world. A SEAL leader who took his team on missions that most folks would never know about—because those folks just didn't have the clearance to know. But *she* knew. Elizabeth knew everything about his missions, and they terrified her. On most days, *he* terrified her, too. "Intense is an understatement," Elizabeth muttered as she dropped the chart and returned to the exam table. His legs were spread apart and she slipped between them as she shined her light in Sawyer's eyes, checking to make sure his pupils responded appropriately.

He inhaled. "You smell good, doc. That a new lotion? Strawberries?"

She froze. The light was still shining right on him, but not aiming straight in his eyes any longer. They were in her exam room, just the two of them, and as per the requirements of his job—and hers—she was running a post mission check on him. He *never* said anything personal to her in the exam room. They'd been doing this same routine for over a year. He barely spoke to her at all when she checked him out.

"Doc?"

She jerked her hand back from him, all too aware that her heart was racing. Sawyer was big, he was muscled, and he was sexy as hell. Tall, dark, and drop-dead handsome perfectly described the guy. And this was *not* the place or the time for her to be having any of those thoughts.

His fingers—with rough calluses on the tips—curled around her wrist. "You okay?"

He had to feel the mad rush of her pulse beneath his touch. Elizabeth notched up her chin and pretended that she was one hundred percent, completely okay. "I'm not the one coming off an adrenaline high. You're the one crashing." She stared straight into his eyes. "And my lotion isn't really your concern."

One jet-black eyebrow rose. He didn't let go of her wrist. He *did* caress her lightly with his thumb. Their gazes held.

"Do we have a problem?" Elizabeth asked him. Her voice was still crisp, and her heart was still racing so hard she feared it would start to make her whole body shake. *No, he's the one doing that – he's making my body –*

His hand slid away from hers. "Not at all." Sawyer's half-smile came and went again as his dimple flashed. A man as tough and dangerous as Sawyer shouldn't have a dimple. That dimple made him seem charming, easy. *Total lie.*

"Good." She turned her back on him. Elizabeth could feel the heat stinging her cheeks. *It is way too hot in here.* Maybe the air conditioning wasn't working. *Yeah, right.* "You'll need a few days to recover. Try to avoid any strenuous activity. If you need something for the pain—"

"No dice, doc. I can handle the pain just fine without any drugs."

Of course, what else would a guy like him say? He thought he was Superman.

She tucked her hands into the pockets of her lab coat. "Then you're done here. You can get dressed."

There was a faint rustle behind her. She reached for the door handle.

"I like the new scent, doc. It's nice. But then, I always think you smell nice." The faintest hint of his Texas accent slipped through Sawyer's words.

Elizabeth glanced back. He was standing near the exam table, and he'd pulled on his button-up shirt. She could see the edge of the bandage on his shoulder, peeking beneath the cotton material. Sawyer had been right. The guy hadn't needed stitches for the bullet graze, but she'd still cleaned the wound and covered it. And she'd thought about what would have happened if that bullet hadn't just grazed him, if it had instead lodged in his heart. Killed him. Her gaze darted up to his blue eyes.

His stare was locked on her.

And Sawyer's eyes burned with an intensity she hadn't seen before.

Oh, damn.

Fumbling, Elizabeth yanked open the exam room door. Then she shut it, fast, as she stumbled into the hallway and—

"Dr. Parker?"

And she ran right into the last man she'd hoped to see at that particular moment. She staggered when their bodies hit, and Dr. Landon Meyer grabbed her arm to steady her. Behind his glasses, his dark brown eyes narrowed with apparent concern.

"Are you okay, Dr. Parker? You're flushed—"

The exam room door creaked open. The tension in the air suddenly seemed to rocket way up, but Elizabeth hoped that was just her imagination.

Landon's gaze jerked over her shoulder.

"There a problem?" The question came from behind her. That was Sawyer's deep, rumbling voice—a voice that contained a decided edge.

Elizabeth shrugged away from Landon. She pasted a smile on her face as she turned to Sawyer. "Just a clumsy moment. I'm glad Dr. Meyer was here to help me out."

Sawyer's face remained tense. "Yeah. Good thing he was here." He sounded anything but thrilled. He moved forward, pushing right in the middle of Elizabeth and Landon. His gaze raked over the other man. Landon was a few inches shorter than Sawyer, and nowhere near as menacing. Landon's features were handsome in a generic, non-threatening kind of way. *The clean-cut guy.*

"How are you feeling, Cage?" Landon asked immediately. "I heard about the firefight that broke out—"

"No big deal. Everything was under control. It always is."

Cocky. Arrogant. That was Sawyer. But...

His fingers slid over her wrist. Such a careful caress. Then he gave a little salute to her and Landon. "Think I'll go crash now. It's been one hell of a day." He sauntered away from them, moving with a lethal grace. That was the way he always walked—controlled, careful, but as if he were poised to attack at any moment.

Because the man is a weapon. And Sawyer is completely aware of just how deadly he is. Again...cocky? Or just confident?

"Don't forget the event tonight!" Landon's voice boomed after Sawyer. "We'll need you and your team there! The boss wants to talk with you all."

"His wounds—" Elizabeth began.

"I'll be there." Sawyer's voice floated back to them as he paused near the elevator. "You said I had to avoid 'strenuous' things, right, doc? A boring black-tie ball won't exactly make me sweat."

Jumping into a warzone probably didn't make the guy sweat, either.

Landon's stare turned to Elizabeth. "I'll need you there, too." His voice dropped as he stepped closer to her. "Our boss is insisting on seeing you tonight. He's excited about Lazarus, and he's ready for action—"

Now Elizabeth was the one to grab his arm. "*Landon.* Not here." Her gaze immediately jerked toward the elevator, and she found Sawyer staring right at her. His gaze glittered. She swallowed and let go of Landon. "Look, let's talk privately, okay?"

"That's why I was coming to get you," Landon shot back, but his voice was low—only for her ears. "For a private talk." Then he turned on his heel and headed for his office. Elizabeth straightened her shoulders and followed him, but with every step she took, she could have sworn that she felt the weight of Sawyer's gaze on her. Her back seemed to burn from the intensity of his stare. She didn't glance over her shoulder, though, not even when she heard the ding of the elevator.

Then she was in front of Landon's office. He stood just inside the doorway, frowning at her. "Is there something wrong?" Landon asked this question as she slipped inside. He hurriedly closed the door behind her. "Did something happen with you and Sawyer during the exam? Because you came running out of that room—"

"Nothing." An immediate denial. "Nothing happened. He checked out fine." Her lips quirked in a faint smile. "He always does."

Landon crossed the room and sat down behind his wide, cherry wood desk. "Of course." His voice was flat. "He's the leader of the Pack, isn't he? Our superstar." There was just the faintest touch of anger in his voice.

The Pack. That was the name given to Sawyer's group. Their team wasn't on the books, not officially, anyway. That way, the government could always have easy deniability if any of the missions ever went wrong.

But what even Sawyer and his team didn't know…the covert facility that she was currently inside of wasn't just used so that the elite team could be mended after their missions. The place was also heavily involved in military research.

She was heavily involved in military research. And Uncle Sam was a very demanding employer. "You shouldn't talk about Lazarus so freely," she chided, and even though it was just the two of them in that office, her voice was hushed. "The program is far from ready for implementation."

Very slowly, Landon removed his glasses. He sat them near the edge of his desk. "That's not good news." The overhead light gleamed on his perfectly cut blond hair.

A rough laugh escaped her. She did that. Laughed when she was nervous. Flushed when she was scared. Her body was always giving her away. Truth be told, Elizabeth wasn't particularly comfortable around other people. She'd always preferred the security of a lab to the randomness of the real world—and to the emotions that bombarded her when she was surrounded by people.

"I thought you'd had positive results with the experiments." Landon tapped his fingers on the desk. A slow, steady tap.

"I *have* experienced good results. But we are talking about working with lab rats, *not* humans. The rats reanimated, they came back, even stronger than they'd been before, but…some of them were showing serious aggressive tendencies—"

"They. Came. Back? Stronger?" His fingers had stopped drumming. He stared at her, unblinkingly for a moment, then Landon surged to his feet. "*Why didn't you tell me immediately?*"

She actually didn't have a ready answer for his question. *Why* hadn't she told him? Technically, Landon was her immediate supervisor but…*I was scared. I was sitting in a lab and I was playing God and I was realizing I was in way over my head.* "We're only beginning the experiments. Those subjects were rats, not people. We have a very, very long way to go before we could possibly—"

In a flash, he was around the desk and right in front of her. "We need to test on a human subject right away."

What? Was the guy crazy? "We *can't*. There are protocols in place, you know that. *Federal* regulations. There is no way we could possibly risk hurting—"

Now he was laughing. Hard. And she didn't like the sound of Landon's laughter. "Oh, my dear Elizabeth…" He smiled. "We're talking about testing on the *dead*. How can we possibly hurt them?"

For a moment, Elizabeth didn't speak. Project Lazarus was absolutely top secret. Only a handful of individuals knew of its existence, and the project was *her* brain child. She'd been the one to first make the breakthrough that allowed her to reactivate the brain cells of dead lab rats. The formula had taken her *years* to create, but she'd done it. Her last series of tests proved that her theories had been correct. She'd finally had her breakthrough. She'd done what so many had said was impossible. And *why* had she done it?

Because I wanted to stop death.

Only…A shiver slid over her skin. *Only maybe death shouldn't be stopped. Maybe I've been wrong.* "Human trials are a very long time away. We are not even close to that point."

The smile stayed on Landon's face. "You know that our team doesn't play by the rules that others have to follow." He leaned in closer to her. "In fact, we can make our own rules." Another laugh slipped from him. "Remember, we're talking about the dead, Elizabeth. The dead. You can't hurt them."

Yes, you can. "I think you didn't hear everything I said before." Maybe he'd gotten distracted by the whole *reanimated* part. She'd try explaining again. Slowly. "The rats are exhibiting improved reflexes and strength, but there are other effects that are not so positive. Some of the rats that reanimated displayed aggressive behavior." Behavior that made her nervous. "We must study them, we have to see *exactly* what short and long term effects could be happening—"

His phone rang, cutting right through her words. It wasn't the phone on his desk that was ringing. Instead, his pocket was vibrating. Landon hurriedly pulled out the phone and frowned down at the screen. "That's all for now, Elizabeth. We'll talk tonight." He waved her toward the door. "I'm *very* pleased with our progress."

Our? Her eyes narrowed on him. "Lazarus isn't ready yet."

Landon put the phone to his ear and turned his back on her. Obviously, he was done with her. "Sir!" His voice was far too loud and jovial. "I've got excellent news for you. The recent batch of test subjects *reanimated*..."

And she knew exactly who was on the other end of that line. Their boss. The man who could make a president sweat. The man who knew every secret in the world and who never hesitated to use his power. Wyman Wright.

"Lazarus is on target," Landon continued brightly. Without looking at her, he waved toward the door once more, tossing his hand over his shoulder in an impatient gesture. "Everything is exactly on target."

Elizabeth flipped her middle finger at him as she marched for the door. A few moments later, she was in the hallway, her body tight with tension. She kept her head down as she walked, and her hands were fisted in the pockets of her lab coat. When she reached her lab, she fumbled with the door, and actually managed to unlock it on the second try. Once inside, Elizabeth immediately headed toward her test subjects. The rats were where she'd left them and—

Blood.

Elizabeth stilled. She'd left three of the Lazarus rats together in one cage. But now, only one rat was still alive in that cage. Its red eyes stared unblinkingly up at her. Around him, she could see the ravaged bodies of the other two rats. It looked as if they'd been ripped apart.

Her breath froze in her lungs.

Everything is exactly on target. Landon's words rang in her ears.

The hell it was.

The rat kept watching her.

***

The ballroom was filled with the rich and the powerful. Men wore elegant tuxes while women smiled as diamonds glittered at their ears and long, elegant dresses clung to their bodies.

A band played some soft jazz music. Waiters drifted through the crowd. Some offered champagne, some carried plates of hors d'oeuvres. Men and women danced. Flirted. And in the background, deals were made. Lives were changed.

"Same fucking shit, right?" The question came from Sawyer's right. "Just a different night."

Sawyer turned his head, and he saw his buddy Flynn Haddox. Flynn was staring at the crowd, disgust tight on his face. Flynn was a member of the Pack, and like Sawyer, the man would far prefer to be in the field, in the middle of a white-hot battle…than to be in that damn ballroom.

But being there was a part of their job. This wasn't some typical event, and they weren't typical employees of the United States government. The charity ball was a sham, as was so many of the other events like this they'd attended in the past. His boss — Wyman Wright — was at that ball. Making plans. Destroying worlds. The usual course of business for the guy.

And private donors were there, people who gave Wright money off the books. Sometimes, those people liked to come face to face with the team who did the dirty work. The rich got a rush from being in the same room with the dangerous.

He didn't get a rush. He just got pissed off.

"Did you get your turn with the big boss?" Sawyer asked Flynn, nodding toward the closed door on the right. Sawyer had already gone inside that room and talked to the man who was supposed to be only a myth.

"Yeah, I did my part. Checked in. Said I was still good to go for whatever mission comes next."

Sawyer had done the same. It wasn't often that he was required to have an up-close interview with Wright, but when he was called up, Sawyer always handled the meetings with brutal honesty. *Yeah, we needed at least five more men. We still got the job done. But we aren't fucking miracle workers. We need more power.*

Wright had promised him more power. Usually, the guy delivered on his promises. *Wyman Wright.* Probably a bullshit name. Wright looked like a pencil pusher, but he wasn't. Though he wasn't listed on the books *anywhere,* Wright was the backbone of D.C., the puppet master who'd seen plenty of FBI and CIA directors come and go, and he was always ready for action, no matter who might be sitting in the Oval Office.

"Since I've done my face time," Flynn added with a slow incline of his head. "I'm ducking out of here. I'm sure I can find just the right something *special* to help me relax." His gaze was directed across the room. On a pretty blonde woman in a long, red dress.

Sawyer lifted his glass—still full of champagne because he didn't drink the stuff—in a small salute. "Have fun with that."

"I intend to." Flynn slapped him on the shoulder. Flynn was just an inch shorter than Sawyer's own six-foot-three frame, and they were both built along the same rough, muscled lines. While Sawyer had jet-black hair, Flynn's was brown. They'd both spent their adult lives working for Uncle Sam, in one form or another. Hunting was second nature to them. Killing… that was far too easy.

Flynn cleared his throat. "Maybe you should look for some fun, too."

Sawyer found his gaze drifting around the ballroom. "Maybe I will."

The door to Wright's office—well, his office for the night, anyway—opened. And there she was. The star of Sawyer's frequent fantasies. Dr. Elizabeth Parker. Her long, dark hair was loose tonight. Normally, she kept it secured at the nape of her neck. Every single time she gave him an exam, Sawyer had to fight the urge to pull down her hair. To touch the soft silk.

Her hair was down, and her habitual lab coat was long gone. Instead, Elizabeth wore a black dress that fit her like a glove, revealing far too much about the curves his hands itched to touch.

"Uh, right…not happening," Flynn announced with a laugh. "You know Dr. Parker wouldn't look twice at you."

Sawyer's gaze snapped back to his soon-to-be *ex* friend. "What the fuck? Why would you say that?" Now he was legitimately insulted. Shit.

Flynn held up his hands. "Sorry, bro, but I don't think she likes fighters. She's more into the…intellectual type, I'd say. I mean, not that you aren't but…" He shook his head. "She's delicate, you know? Dude, you'd break her in two if you got her in the sack."

The hell he would. "Get your ass out of here. Your blonde is getting away." He didn't wait to see how Flynn responded. Sawyer strode through the crowd, his focus on the prize *he* wanted.

At that moment, Elizabeth looked up. Her gaze landed on him—such a dark, deep gaze. Chocolate. He fucking loved chocolate. Her lips were painted red, and they were sexy as hell. Those lips trembled for a moment when she saw him, but then Elizabeth spun on her heel and headed out onto the balcony.

"Told you man…" Flynn's annoying voice called from right behind him. "Not interested."

The asshole had followed him. "Fuck off." Sawyer rolled back his shoulders. "I'm not going to screw the doc. I know the rules." And rule number one in their program was no fraternizing. That had been made clear to him and his team as soon as they had agreed to join Wright's covert group of operatives.

Sawyer shoved his champagne glass at a nearby waiter. He yanked at the neck of his dress shirt and jerked at his tie. He hated having to put on fancy clothes, and he hated having to act civilized at these stupid events. Sawyer was far more comfortable in the field. Working a mission. Holding a gun in his hand and stalking his prey. He hated being in this freaking circus of a ballroom.

He slipped onto the balcony. The doc was the only other person out there. Her hands were curled over the wrought-iron railing, and the wind lightly teased her thick, dark hair. He stilled for a moment, just staring at her. Did the woman have any idea just how beautiful he thought she was? Did she know exactly how many times she'd starred in his dreams? He'd fucked her in them, endlessly.

She glanced back at him. The moonlight fell on her face. To him, she was utter perfection. Oval face, sweet cheekbones and that stubborn little chin. Her lips were sin, and he'd spent far too much time thinking about her mouth. When he'd been in the exam room with her earlier that day, she'd been standing between his thighs, and he'd wanted to lean forward and take her mouth with his.

"You look good." Her voice drifted to him. "Your injuries don't seem to be slowing you down any."

He moved closer to her. The woman drew him in. *Moth to a flame.* "Nope. Not slowing me even a little bit."

Her lips curved in a faint smile. "Do you think you're Superman?"

"Only some days." *Only when I'm close to you.*

Her smile faded. "No one is immortal." She bit her lower lip, and her gaze seemed to look right through him. "I don't...I'm starting to think no one should be."

An odd thing to say.

"Guess it depends on who you are living forever with." He took up a position right next to her on the balcony. His shoulder brushed against hers. When she didn't speak again, he tried to figure out what the hell to say to her. And, of course, Flynn's asshole words rang in his ears. *She's more into the…intellectual type, I'd say.* He should have punched his jerk of a friend. "Big crowd here tonight. Aren't you supposed to be inside? Charming everyone so that the funding keeps going to our program?" The people back in that ballroom were the power players in D.C. Wright liked to take donations from private parties who shared his interests. It was easier to keep his activities out of the government—and media's—spotlight that way.

"I'm not good at charm." Her voice was soft and husky. "That's not why I'm on Wright's staff."

"You do a good job of charming me." He moved even closer to her.

Immediately, she slid away. "Sawyer—"

A man's sharp laughter cut through the night. Sawyer turned his head and saw that a fellow in a tux had wandered onto the balcony. The guy was laughing it up with some redhead. Dammit.

"Meet me downstairs," Sawyer rasped to Elizabeth. "Five minutes. We need to talk. Privately."

Then, taking his time, Sawyer strolled off that balcony. He didn't look back. Maybe Elizabeth would come to meet him. Maybe she wouldn't.

But what he had to say to the doc — it couldn't be said with someone else's eyes on them.

He needed her alone.

And that's how I'll get her.

CHAPTER TWO

She hated wearing heels. She hated the confines of her too tight dress. She hated having to make small talk and act interested in the conversations that arrogant assholes were having. Elizabeth just hated the whole scene. Landon had said the event was a necessary evil. *Wright doesn't function alone. He needs backers.* Not that those backers knew the truth. Wright was keeping the true nature of his program — the truth about Lazarus — secret.

Landon liked the wining and the dining and the charming, and since he enjoyed it so much, she figured he could handle the rest of the night all by himself. Her heels clicked on the stairs as she hurried down to the bottom level of the historic D.C. building. The staircase was spiral, huge, and the air chilled her skin as she descended. At first glance, no one appeared to be on the lower level of the old building. Why would anyone be? The party was upstairs.

But…

Sawyer *was* down there. Somewhere, waiting in the shadows. *Waiting for me.*

The event was being held at an art museum on the edge of D.C. The first floor was full of artwork — high-end pieces of abstract art. Each piece was connected to a security system and when she finally reached the first floor, Elizabeth caught sight of a few security guards patrolling the area. *Not deserted, after all.*

The museum was their cover for the night. If reporters got curious, the story would just circulate that the rich and powerful had been at that location for an art gala — a fundraising ball. And some money *would* be donated to the museum.

More money would go to Wright's pet project. A *lot* more.

In D.C., what you saw was never the real story.

The first-floor galleries were open, though, as part of the cover, so people could walk in and admire the work. No one was doing that, though, not while the real action was upstairs. She gave a weak smile to one of the guards and headed into the gallery on her right. She really wasn't sure exactly *where* on that first floor Sawyer was. The guy should have been more specific with his meeting plan.

Instead, he'd been mysterious. Demanding. And *sexy* in his tux.

She walked past two long, red curtains—

A hand flew out and wrapped around her wrist. "It's been ten minutes, doc. Ten, not five."

Her lips parted, but in the next moment, he'd yanked her through the curtains. Through the curtains and into what she saw was actually a small office. Before she could make a sound, he'd shut the door of that office, locked it, and then Sawyer had pinned her between his rock-hard body and the wooden door.

"You kept me waiting." His words were a growl.

"I—"

"Gonna have to make you pay for that." And his right hand moved down to grab the material of her dress. He pushed it up, and his fingers stroked her thigh. "Feels like fucking silk…"

Her mouth had gone absolutely dry, and her heart was about to burst right out of her chest. She knew he wasn't talking about the material of her dress. He was talking about *her.*

"Are you wearing panties?"

He didn't give her a chance to reply. Instead, he shoved the fabric of her dress up even higher, and then Sawyer's fingers were pushing between her legs and discovering that no, she wasn't wearing panties.

Because I knew I'd be seeing him. Knew, hoped, same thing.

"Fuck, baby, what you do to me..." His fingers slid over her sex. Elizabeth's head tipped back against the door, and she had to press her lips together to stop herself from moaning.

"You're already wet." One finger caressed her clit and her whole body jerked. His mouth pressed to her throat, kissing, licking, and then he gave a little nip. "Did you miss me as fucking much as I missed you?"

More. Her eyes opened, and all pretense dropped. "I need you, Sawyer. *Now.*" It had been torture, absolute torture, to exam him earlier that day and not give in to her need. To pretend that nothing was happening between them. To ignore the wild, desperate desire that she felt for him. A need that had swept her up into a dark obsession of lust and sensual craving *months* ago. The attraction had always been there, burning just beneath the surface for them both, but then one night...

She'd heard a knock at her apartment door. When she'd opened the door, Sawyer had been standing there. His stormy blue eyes had been filled with a stark hunger.

Two minutes later, they'd been in bed together. They'd *wrecked* her bed.

Her hand angled between them. She stroked his cock through the fabric of his pants. He was big and long and heavy, and she didn't want to wait. Her body was in a fever pitch, and she needed him inside of her. "*Sawyer.*"

He pulled back. Dammit, he pulled *back.* But then she heard the hiss of his zipper. A wide smile crossed her face. *Yes.* He came back to her in a rush, his strong hands curled around her waist, and he lifted her up. Her back shoved into the wood of the door even as her legs wrapped around his hips. The head of his cock pressed against the entrance to her body. And—

He sank deep. Her breath choked out, and then he kissed her. His tongue thrust into her mouth even as his cock drove into her body, again and again. He used his iron-hard hold on her hips to lift her up and down, moving her quickly over the length of his cock. And every sensual movement had her clit sliding against him. Her eyes squeezed shut even as her nails bit into the fabric of his tux. Her climax was coming. *Already.* That was how desperate she was for him. Her body was so primed. The climax was building and charging her entire body.

He tore his mouth from hers. "No sound, baby. Remember…"

She wanted to scream. Her sex clenched around him and pleasure burst through her. She bit her lower lip, hard, holding back the cry of release even as she felt him erupt inside of her. His cock jerked, his body shuddered, and Sawyer held her so tightly Elizabeth wondered if she'd bruise.

And she didn't even care.

Gradually, her heartbeat went from a thunder to a slow thud. He was still inside of her, and Sawyer's hands gripped her waist. She licked her lips, cleared her throat, and managed to whisper, "Did I hurt you?"

His head lifted. Oh, jeez, but he was handsome. Not in some clean-cut, carefully styled way. But in a dangerous, predatory way. *Bad boy to the core.* Hard jaw, glittering eyes, razor-sharp cheekbones.

"Hurt me?" Sawyer repeated. "Not even close, baby."

"Your wounds…"

"When I'm in you, doc, the only thing I feel is pleasure."

Her sex squeezed him. Totally reflex. And it *totally* felt good. Amazing. But… "W-we should go. Someone could come by and find us." Having sex at the museum had probably been a colossal mistake. She'd just—needed him. Missed him.

I lost my control.

Sawyer was the only man who'd ever made her lose control.

"Right. Time to go back to being your dirty little secret." He withdrew from her. His words had held a definite edge. *Danger.*

Her heart stuttered as her feet slid down and touched the floor. She'd lost her shoes. Shit. Where were they? "You know it's not like that." She could still feel him, on the inside.

And outside. All over her skin. His scent seemed to cover her.

Maybe she liked it. It was primitive, basic. Like carrying a mark for a mate. She wanted her scent on him, too, and she liked having his scent on her.

He zipped up and straightened his clothes. Sawyer's dark hair wasn't even out of place. Meanwhile, she felt like a wreck.

Elizabeth caught sight of her shoe—one shoe. A good five feet away. She hurried toward it.

But Sawyer caught her arm before she could pass him. "I'm sorry." His words were gruff. "Didn't mean to sound like a dick."

Her gaze cut back to him.

"I want the whole world to know about us. You're mine, Elizabeth. You're in my fucking blood."

And just like that—her heart was racing too fast again. "If our relationship was discovered, Wright would separate us." She *knew* they'd broken the rules by getting involved. No fraternizing—*no sexual relationship*—was allowed in their division. No mixing under Wright's command. She was the doctor, and Sawyer was the Pack leader. Nothing more. That was the way things were supposed to be, but… "I may be going strictly to research soon." The words tumbled from her. Wright had told her that news when she'd gone in for her face-to-face meeting with him. He'd been so impressed by the work she'd done with Lazarus. He'd been practically crowing, but meanwhile, the knot in her stomach had just gotten worse. "Or maybe, um, I've actually been thinking about getting out of Wright's group altogether." *Perhaps doing a whole new kind of work.* "If that happens, there won't be a need for secrets any longer."

He pressed a kiss to her lips. "Baby, I've been thinking the same thing. Maybe it's time for a change. Time to let go of the battles and focus on something else."

His stare was on her. What was he saying? What did he—

"You, baby. I want *you*. If I can't have you *and* the team, then you're my choice. *Always*. Know that."

Warmth spread through her. A giddy warmth that made her want to smile and laugh. She'd *never* felt this way about anyone. A guy like Sawyer—so intense and dangerous—he wasn't her normal type. Not at all. But something had clicked between them.

The attraction had been too strong. The need too fierce. And the connection? She could swear it went soul deep.

"Now get those sexy shoes back on, doc, because I want to get you home. I want you in a bed." He kissed her. "The first climax took the edge off, but I'm gonna need a whole lot more from you."

She'd need a whole lot more, too.

Elizabeth pulled away. She grabbed one shoe. Sawyer found the other. Her knees only wobbled a bit as she hurried out of the room. Her shoes rapped over the gleaming floor as she headed back to the main lobby and the spiral staircase. Sawyer didn't follow, not right away. Another tactic they used. They never left places together, they tried not to *stay* together too long, and—

"Elizabeth."

And Landon was waiting for her near the bottom of the stairs. Sweet Jesus. She put a hand to her chest, startled. Why did the guy just keep popping up in her path?

Landon looked over her shoulder. "Where's Sawyer?"

"I-I don't know." *I can feel him on my skin.*

Landon kept peering behind her. "I saw you two on the balcony together."

Wait, he'd *seen* them? Her cheeks flushed, but…*Landon hadn't seen anything earth-shattering. Just two people talking. We did nothing wrong.* At least, not on the balcony, they hadn't.

"I thought you'd come down here together."

"No." Her voice was flat. "We didn't." Was her hair a wreck? Was her dress twisted? "I'm tired, Landon. I'm going home." She inclined her head toward him. "Goodnight." Elizabeth walked around him and headed toward the glass doors that would take her outside and to the safety of her car.

But he followed. He followed her out of the building, away from the guards, and to the parking lot. He was silent behind her as the valet brought her car around, and every moment that passed made Elizabeth nervous. Her breath came a little too fast. Tension stretched inside of her, until she just snapped. Elizabeth spun around. "What is it?" His silent follow routine had unnerved her.

Landon blinked. He shrugged. "I was just...I wanted to make sure you got to your car safely."

Oh. Crap. That was nice. And also, very unlike him. He'd never cared before. The valet arrived with her SUV, and she forced a smile for Landon. "Thank you. I'm good, though. Everything's okay."

Still, he hesitated.

The valet handed Elizabeth her keys and hurried away. As soon as he was gone, Landon moved closer to her.

"We've got the go-ahead," he whispered, his words coming rapid-fire, as if he just couldn't contain them any longer.

Her brows lifted.

And still, he came even closer. "Wright just gave me approval. He wants Lazarus used on human subjects."

Her heart stopped. Stopped, and then started racing like mad. "It's not ready. I *told* you, it's not ready for human use yet. And the testings don't work like—"

Landon caught her arm. "Wright doesn't follow the rules. He makes them. Our division is off the books, and he wants human testing. *Now.* Before someone else makes the same breakthrough that you did. Increased strength, faster reflexes, *and* reanimation? Are you kidding me? Of course, he's ready to jump on this. We just need the right candidates—"

A motorcycle's roar filled the night, cutting right through his words, and then a blinding light was shining on them.

Cursing, Landon snatched his hand away from her and shielded his eyes. Elizabeth didn't move. The motorcycle's growl grew louder as it headed straight for them. She *knew* who was driving that motorcycle even before the bike braked, and, over the growl of the engine, she heard…

"There a problem out here?" Sawyer drawled.

Landon shook his head, but he'd taken a step back. "Of course not. I was—I was making sure Elizabeth got safely to her car."

Sawyer turned off his headlight. Immediately, the scene plunged into darkness. Elizabeth knew her eyes would adjust soon, but she experienced a few disorienting moments as she stood there.

"Glad you're looking after the doc." But Sawyer didn't sound glad. The guy sounded pissed. Just as he'd sounded earlier that day when he talked to Landon. "Wouldn't want anything to ever happen to her."

Her shoulders straightened. "Yes, well, I think I can manage to get into a vehicle by myself. But thanks." She gave a crisp nod to them both. "Goodnight, gentlemen." But she hesitated. Her head turned toward Landon. He hadn't been walking her out because he was being *nice*. The guy had been working his agenda. *He was waiting until we were clear to tell me about his talk with Wright.* Landon wanted the Lazarus trials to start immediately. She didn't. "We will talk more. Lazarus *isn't* ready." Her low voice was just for him.

She hurried to her SUV. Elizabeth climbed inside and drove away moments later. When she hit the main road, Elizabeth glanced into her rearview mirror. She expected to see the light from a motorcycle behind her.

But there was only darkness.

***

Sawyer's grip was too tight on the handlebars. He needed to settle the hell down, and he knew it, but…

Landon had followed Elizabeth out of the gallery. The guy had put his hands on her — *for a second time that day.* The prick was pissing Sawyer off to a dangerous degree.

"She doesn't want you touching her." Sawyer's words came out low and hard and deadly.

Landon stiffened. "Excuse me?"

"The doc." He turned off his motorcycle and slid off the bike. For this talk, he wanted to be up-close and personal. Sawyer took his time heading toward the guy who'd been sniffing around Elizabeth far too long. "She doesn't like to be touched. You've worked with her for months. Surely you've noticed that trait before now, right?"

"I — yes, I know that she tends to avoid touching unless it's part of an exam or — "

"So why…" Sawyer's voice was clipped. "Why in the hell have I seen you touching her *twice* today?"

Landon stiffened. "Why does it matter to you?"

"Because she takes care of me and my team. And I don't want anyone or anything making Elizabeth — the doc — uncomfortable." *Because I don't want your hands on her, got me?*

"You're misunderstanding the situation."

Sawyer stalked forward, not stopping until he was toe-to-toe with the bastard. He'd never liked Landon. The guy always had his nose in the air. He treated Sawyer and his team like they were weapons, not people. Didn't ever seem to care about what was happening in their lives. *Patch us up, get us out. Aim and attack.* Landon wasn't like Elizabeth. Elizabeth was considerate. She *cared.* Elizabeth talked to the team. She smiled, she teased but...

Elizabeth doesn't like to be touched, not unless I'm the one doing the touching. "Then let's make sure there are no more misunderstandings. Keep your hands off her."

"You're awfully protective."

You have no clue. "Part of the job description, right? You want me and my team to protect and defend. It's what I'm doing." *I'd protect Elizabeth with my last breath.* He towered over Landon, and he entertained the awesome image of knocking the bastard out with one punch. "It's important for us to be clear on a few things."

Elizabeth was long gone. He should go now and get to her place. He'd park his motorcycle a few streets over and be back at her building in moments. Then he'd be *in* her—

Sawyer turned away from the jerk who was just slowing down his night. He'd taken three steps toward his bike when Landon called out, freezing him.

"What if Elizabeth wants me to touch her?" The words were a taunt, and they were one hell of a lot bolder than Sawyer had ever expected the prick to be.

Very slowly, Sawyer turned to face Landon.

"What if…" Landon lifted his chin. *Chin-in-the-air-asshole.* "What if she wants me to touch her?" He actually repeated his idiotic question.

Sawyer laughed. A deep, rumbling laugh. "Never gonna happen." He jumped on the motorcycle. "But that was funny as shit." He turned on the motorcycle and revved the engine.

"How do you know?" Landon snarled.

"Easy. You aren't her type." *I am.* "Remember, hands the fuck off." Then he blasted out of the parking lot and went after the woman he wanted. The only one.

***

"I fucking hate that SOB," Landon muttered as he watched the motorcycle vanish. Sawyer and his Pack—they thought they were the rulers of the world. That they could do anything they wanted. Anytime. Anywhere.

They had no clue. They were the brawn, but he was the brains. Without him—without Elizabeth—Wright's whole unit would flounder.

And did Sawyer *think* that Landon didn't know the guy was hot for Elizabeth? Every time that bastard looked at her, Sawyer's eyes burned. If he could, Landon knew that Sawyer would fucking eat Elizabeth alive.

But you're not her type. You're not, Sawyer. Because Elizabeth would never want a killer. She wouldn't want a weapon. She was meant for more. Elizabeth and her absolutely brilliant mind deserved *more*.

She'd graduated med school when she was twenty. She was the leading expert on bio genetics and cellular manipulation. Hell, she had more degrees than any person he knew. The woman's brain never stopped, and he'd been thrilled when Wright lured her into his program.

Elizabeth was going places, and Landon intended to be right at her side the whole time. She was the perfect partner. An asset that he couldn't afford to lose.

So, no, he didn't plan to screw with her. Sawyer could relax on that score. Landon didn't want Elizabeth for her body, though it was passable enough. He wanted her for her fucking fantastic mind.

We're going ahead on Lazarus. Turning away from the lot, he headed back toward the gallery, whistling as he went. Lazarus would change the world.

It would be unforgettable.

They just had to find the right test subjects…

CHAPTER THREE

His knuckles tapped on Elizabeth's front door. He'd rushed up the stairs at her building, eager to get back to her. His body was burning from the inside. Heavy with need and lust—for her.

The door opened. Elizabeth stood there, still in her sexy-as-hell black dress, but minus her shoes. Her eyes widened when she saw him, and Sawyer didn't even hesitate. He stepped inside, slammed the door shut with his foot, and then his mouth was on hers.

Elizabeth was so sweet. She tasted so damn good. He loved her mouth. Her tongue. Loved the little moans she made when she got turned on by him. His hands curled around her waist and he lifted her up, holding her easily. She wrapped her legs around him and her sex pressed right over his aching cock. He'd had her once that night, but that one time had barely taken the edge off his need. Truth be fucking told, he could probably have her a dozen times, and he'd still want her just as badly.

Always.

Forever.

With one hand, he reached back and locked the door, and then Sawyer was heading through her home. He knew the place, inside and out, just as he knew her. He maneuvered down her narrow hallway, and he kissed her deep and hard. He nipped her sexy lower lip and felt her shudder against him.

Too many clothes. He wanted her naked. He wanted a better taste of her. He wanted *everything* she had to give.

He carried her into her bedroom, not even feeling the pull of his wounds. Like pain would have slowed him down any. He saw that she'd lit a few big, thick, white candles. She'd been preparing for him.

Elizabeth did things like that. Little romantic, feminine touches that made his chest ache. Things that showed they weren't some random hook-up. They were *more*.

The big, four-poster bed was waiting for him. She'd actually bought that bed just a month ago. The full-size one she'd had before just hadn't been big enough for them both, and he liked staying in bed with her. Liked having her body wrapped around his as he slept.

It was the only time he truly felt at peace.

He lowered her to the floor. Her feet touched the lush carpeting and he backed away, moving so that he could strip. He yanked at his tie. Threw his jacket across the room. Sawyer kicked off his shoes and shoved away the rest of his clothes as fast as he could. He wanted to be flesh to flesh with Elizabeth.

She smiled at him as she reached back and unzipped her dress. It slid down her body. Pooled at her feet.

His breath hissed out. "No underwear at *all*." The fact that she hadn't worn panties had been sexy as all hell, but now he saw that she hadn't been wearing a bra, too. Fuck. The woman wanted to bring him right to his knees. "Get on the bed, Elizabeth."

Her smile came, slow and sexy, lighting up her dark eyes, and he wondered if she knew…did she have any clue just how much she owned him?

She eased onto the bed. "As your doctor, I have to say that you need to take things easy. Why don't *you* lay down, and let someone else do all the work?"

His cock jerked. He could feel pre-cum on the tip. She was already pushing him to the edge. He climbed into the bed and spread out, and then she climbed right on top of him.

"I can do the work," she said as her hands flattened against his chest. "Why not just enjoy the ride?" And she took him in. She was wet and hot and his dick slid deep into her. Elizabeth moaned, but caught herself, muffling the sound.

"Screw that," he snarled as his hips shoved up against her. "It's you and it's me, and I want to hear every sound you have to make."

Her eyes had closed, but at his words, they flew open. Her gaze zeroed in on him, and then she leaned forward. Her mouth opened and his tongue slid inside. His fingers rose to stroke her perfect breasts, teasing the tight tips, even as he felt her sex squeeze him in a white-hot grip.

He'd thought the first time with her had taken the edge off. Sawyer realized he'd just been *wrong*.

His hands clamped around her waist. He lifted her up and down, and she was arching to meet him, driving in the same wild rhythm. His heart pounded in his chest. The walls of her sex clamped greedily around him. His climax bore down on him, but Sawyer held back. There was no way he'd let go until she came for him.

His fingers slid between their bodies. He touched her clit, stroked her softly, then harder, just the way he knew she liked. He knew every damn thing about her body. Knew what made her moan. Made her shiver. His thumb and forefinger squeezed her clit, and she erupted, giving a sharp scream of his name — and he didn't give a shit if her neighbors happened to overhear.

As soon as the pleasure overtook her, Sawyer tumbled Elizabeth back on the bed. He thrust into her, even as he lifted her legs high, spreading her even wider for him so he could plunge deeper. Faster and faster, he drove into her. The bed shuddered beneath him and her climax rippled along the length of his cock. Then he was coming—growling her name and holding her tight. So fucking tight.

Sex with Elizabeth. It was the best sex in the world. Because she was the best.

Mine. Always.

***

Sawyer's eyes flew open. He came awake instantly, as was his habit. No slow awareness, no grogginess. Just a flash and he was fully awake and aware.

Aware that Elizabeth is gone.

He jerked upright in the bed, straining to see in the darkness. The candles had been blown out hours ago, and his eyes took a few precious moments to adjust to the darkness.

Then he saw Elizabeth. She stood in front of her window, gazing into the night.

"Baby?" He shoved away the covers and climbed from the bed. "What happened? Bad dream?" She had nightmares, dark dreams that she didn't talk about with him. She'd cry out in fear. She'd cry out and say—

Don't die! Don't! Don't leave me!

But her cries hadn't woken him that night. Her absence had.

He reached out and touched her shoulder. She flinched but kept staring into the night.

"Elizabeth?"

"I think I'm Frankenstein." Her voice was low and husky, and her words didn't make any sense to him.

His hold tightened on her. "Doc, I'm the one covered with over a dozen scars. If anyone looks like a monster—"

She turned toward him. "Frankenstein was the one who made the monster. I don't…I don't even remember…did his monster have a name?"

He couldn't see her eyes in the dark. And her voice held an emotion that he couldn't decipher. "Baby, why are you up at…" His stare cut toward the clock on her bedside table. "At 3 a.m., talking about monsters?"

"Because I think I'm Frankenstein. I think people shouldn't play God because you don't know what you're going to get."

His body tensed. He knew Elizabeth was working on research efforts for Wright. Classified intel that he wasn't *supposed* to be aware of but…

Landon had a big mouth. The guy talked too freely, and Sawyer had picked up enough to know that something very serious was happening in the labs back at headquarters.

"I'm scared of what I'm doing. I'm scared of what I am."

His hand moved from her shoulder to her throat. He could feel the frantic beat of her pulse beneath his fingers. She *was* scared. "You don't need to be afraid. I'll protect you from any threat out there."

"Even if I'm the threat?"

"You're *not.* I know that. You're good, Elizabeth. The best thing in my life." Surely she understood that. He was blood and death and battles, but she was the hope that kept him going. No matter what shit-hole he was in, Elizabeth was his light. He came back from every mission because he was coming home to *her.*

"I...I can't do it. I worked so long and so hard..." Her head tipped forward and her dark hair slid over his wrist. "The formula isn't right, and I'm afraid of what will happen. I wanted to change the world. But I'm afraid—so afraid—it's just going to get worse."

He didn't like her fear. Never had. Never would. "What can I do?" Simple. Something was wrong, so he'd fix it for her. His hand slid up her throat, and he curled his fingers under her chin. He tipped back her head and once again felt the soft slide of her hair over his skin. "I'll make it better."

"You can't. Only I can." She gave a soft sigh. "I *will.*"

He leaned forward and pressed a kiss to her forehead. "Come back to bed." Because the mission had been a bitch, death had been too close — far closer than he'd let her know — and he wanted her in his arms.

Elizabeth didn't argue. She walked with him to the bed. Slid under the covers, and then she curled her body against his. Sawyer was always amazed at how well she fit him.

Like she'd been made just for him.

Or maybe he'd been made just for her.

"I think Frankenstein wanted to help. I mean, that's why he started making his monster in the first place, isn't it? To help the world?" Her voice was sleepy and a little sad.

Sawyer made a mental note to read that freaking book, ASAP. He'd read it before, of course, back in high school — what felt like a million years ago.

"I want to help," she whispered.

"You do." *You help me, baby. You make the world better just by being in it.*

"Everything is just so wrong."

The hell it was. "Nothing about us will ever be wrong."

She didn't speak again, and he realized that her breathing had evened out. She'd drifted to sleep. He kept holding her, and he stared up at the ceiling. He knew what would come next. What *always* came…

***

"*Don't!*" Elizabeth's voice was sharp. Desperate. Terrified. "*Don't die! Don't! Don't leave me!*"

Sawyer pulled her closer to his body. "It's okay. Just a bad dream."

"*Mom!*"

He stiffened. She'd never called for anyone specific before—certainly not her mother. The dreams had never gone this far.

"*Dad! No! Stay with me!*"

The pain in her voice gutted him. Sawyer shook her. "Elizabeth, wake up. It's a bad dream."

She gave a gasp and shuddered. "Sawyer?"

"Right here, baby. Always here." Only, he wasn't always there. When he was out on missions, he'd often think about her. Worry about her waking from her nightmares, all alone.

She's not alone now.

"I had a bad dream." Those, too, were words that she always said.

"I know." His voice was gentle. With her, he found a gentleness that he hadn't realized he'd possessed.

She cuddled close to him, and the sound of her breathing was ragged. She usually drifted back to sleep, and the nightmare didn't come again, not until the next night.

But this time, her body remained tense.

"Sawyer?"

"Yeah?"

"It wasn't a dream."

He swallowed and kept his light hold on her. "I know." He'd suspected the truth for a long time, but she'd never talked with him about the nightmares, not even when he'd asked as carefully as he could.

"They both died."

His hand was on her back. He stroked her spine.

"There was so much blood. I didn't know how to save them. I was left with their bodies…for two days."

Fuck.

"Two days at the bottom of that ravine. Two days while they stared at nothing, and I stared at them."

His jaw ached because it was clenched so tightly.

"Two days."

His head turned. He pressed a kiss to her lips. There was so much pain—in those two words.

She didn't speak again, and he didn't let her go, not until dawn came.

***

One week later—*just one week!*—Sawyer sat on the exam table. Elizabeth stood in front of him, the stethoscope gripped in her hands, and anger fueling her blood. "This is ridiculous. You haven't fully healed from your last mission. You *cannot* go out again now." She knew her voice held a furious edge, but Elizabeth couldn't control herself.

It was too soon. She'd just gotten him back. He wasn't supposed to disappear into the field again. *Too soon.*

But his blue gaze just held hers. "I won't be the one doing the ground work. I'll be giving orders, safely away from the line of combat. Flynn will be the one leading in the field."

His words didn't make her feel better. There was an ache in her chest, and it wasn't going away. The ache came each time he left, and it stayed until he returned.

Fumbling, she put the stethoscope to his chest. She listened to his heartbeat. Strong, fast. It was a beat that seemed to match her own.

"Don't worry, doc, I'll be back before you know it."

She slid away from him. His hand flew out and curved around her wrist.

"I'll always come back to you," Sawyer told her, his voice low.

I love you. Those words were on the tip of her tongue. Elizabeth wanted to say them to Sawyer, but he was leaving. She had a job to do and, dammit, she hadn't even told Landon or Wright that she was quitting. And now she *couldn't* quit. Not until Sawyer was back. She had to stay there so she could remain updated on his mission. If she left now, she'd lose her link to Sawyer.

I can't do that. I have to know he's safe.

While he was gone, she'd continue working on Lazarus. Maybe…maybe she could fix the formula. Maybe it would get better.

When Sawyer returned…*then* she could plan. *They* could plan. They'd stop hiding their relationship. No more secrets.

She pulled her hand away from him. "I'll need to run a few more tests before I give my approval on this mission."

He smiled at her. His dimple winked.

"Be careful," she told him, her voice barely a breath. "I want you returning back to me in one piece." Then she turned on her heel and headed for the door. A nurse was waiting outside, and Elizabeth gave her a list of orders.

Her heart kept racing. Far too fast.

I'll always come back to you. Her lips curled in a smile. One thing she'd learned about Sawyer—he kept his promises.

CHAPTER FOUR

"Lazarus is a go."

It took a few precious moments for those words to register in Elizabeth's mind. She was bent over a microscope, her eyes on the slide, and she hadn't even been aware that Landon was in the lab with her, not until—

"Did you hear me, Elizabeth?" Excitement sharpened Landon's voice. "Lazarus is a go. *Right the hell now!*"

She spun toward him, nearly falling off her stool. "What?"

His cheeks were flushed. His eyes were almost wild behind the lenses of his glasses. "We've got test subjects. They're on the way to lab five now. The bodies are being prepped for the injections." He licked his lips. His breath came in little pants. "I figured you'd want to do the honors yourself, since this is your discovery—"

She bounded toward him and grabbed his lab coat, fisting it in her hands. "I told you the formula wasn't ready yet."

His gaze hardened. "Wright said it's time. We have the perfect subjects. *Lazarus is a go.*"

No, no, Lazarus couldn't be a go. For the last three weeks, she'd been working frantically on the project, but while the rats had reanimated and some had exhibited stable behavior, there were a million unknowns still at work. "There is no way we can experiment on humans—"

"They are *dead,* Elizabeth." That was the argument he loved to throw at her. Impatience flashed on his face. "You can't hurt the dead."

She just stared at him. *This isn't happening.*

Landon raked a hand over his face, then he smiled. "You can't hurt them, but you can try to bring them back to life. These bodies were donated to science—that means these bodies are *ours.* And Wright gave the order. *Lazarus is a go.* So either you administer the injection…" His chest puffed out. "Or I will."

She didn't think her heart was beating. The whole world seemed to have stopped spinning. Landon's voice was too loud. He was too close. She was still holding his lab coat too tightly.

"You worked on this for so long—long before Wright found you. Hell, it's the reason he *found* you in the first place. He'd heard whispers about your early research. He gave you every resource that you could possibly want, and now you're hesitating? Now?" His tone indicated Landon doubted her sanity.

And, yes, she was hesitating. "Because Lazarus isn't ready." How many times did she need to say that line? "The formula has to be perfect. It's not yet. I've *told* you that. The test subjects—forget them. We can get others, later. We don't need to rush."

His gaze glittered down at her. "These are the perfect subjects. Wright wants us to begin the process now, and that's exactly what we're going to do." He turned away from her and marched from the room.

For a moment, Elizabeth just stood there, rooted to the spot. The formula was *not* ready. Why was Landon doing this? Why was Wright in such a damn hurry?

Breaking from her stupor, Elizabeth chased after Landon. "This is insane. You don't rush something like this!"

"We're not rushing a damn thing. You and I both know you've been working on Lazarus non-stop for years. Long before Wright. Long before me."

Truth. *But Lazarus isn't ready. Maybe it should never—*

"I've read over all your work, reviewed everything you've ever done..." He kept walking, but slanted a glance back her way. "And I know it's ready. Despite what you say, I *know*."

He didn't. "No, it isn't, I—"

"You're worried about aggression. Right. Got it. But aggression isn't a minus, not for Wright."

She grabbed his arm, stopping him before he could walk into lab five. "Some of the rats *killed* each other."

He offered her a grim smile. "They're rats. Not people. But, for the record, humans kill each other plenty, too…and they don't need Lazarus to do it."

Outrage had her shaking. "My work—"

"Actually, it's *our* work. Everything you create at this facility belongs to Wyman Wright, and you know it." He pointed toward the lab door. Lab five. "Now, are you coming with me? Or do you really want to miss the single most important moment in your own life?"

He was an asshole. An absolute ass. "Landon—"

He strode inside lab five. She scrambled after him, and when she entered the lab, she stopped short at the sight of the armed guards. *Four* armed guards. "What's happening? Why are they here?"

Landon picked up a chart. "Because in case any of that *aggression* that you mentioned manifests with these test subjects, I want to be prepared. I am taking precautions. I'm not some amateur. I *am* being careful."

A dull ringing filled her ears.

Landon nodded as he read the notes in the chart, and then he looked back up at her. "This is your moment, Elizabeth. Don't back away now."

Her hands clenched at her sides. She eyed the exam tables. Two of them. Two tables with test subjects. She could see the bodies—they were covered with plain, white sheets. The syringes were already out—out, prepped, and waiting on a surgical tray next to each subject.

"There can't be any degeneration to the tissue," she heard herself say. "The subjects—"

"Their bodies were protected," he assured her. "Exactly per your preservation protocol."

Her right leg slid forward. She lurched toward the first patient.

"Glad to see you're getting on board," Landon murmured.

Her hand lifted and reached for the sheet. She wanted to see this man, she needed to see him—

Elizabeth stopped breathing as the sheet slid away from the first test subject's head and revealed his face. Only she wasn't staring down at a stranger.

That dark hair…that hard jaw…the high cheek bones…the lips…*Lips that have kissed mine.* No. No!

"S-Sawyer?" Her finger slid over his cheek. Ice cold. "Sawyer!" Elizabeth yelled his name because Sawyer…he couldn't be on that exam table. Sawyer couldn't be cold, he couldn't be lying there with his eyes shut. Sawyer couldn't be *dead.*

"He was killed on the mission." Landon's voice was brisk. Totally devoid of any emotion. Like he was discussing the freaking weather. "Both he and operative Flynn Haddox didn't survive."

Flynn? Flynn, too? Dazed, feeling numb, she watched as Landon pulled the sheet off the second test subject's face. *Flynn.*

Oh, God.

"Wright knew these two men would be prime candidates for Lazarus, so he immediately ordered the preservation process to be utilized with their remains."

No. No, no, *no, no, no, no.* "Flynn's...dead. *Sawyer's...* dead." And she was breaking apart on the inside. She was touching Sawyer's cold cheek and shattering because this—this was Sawyer. *Her* Sawyer. He'd said he would come back to her. He'd said he would always come back. But his eyes were closed, and his body was like ice. Tears slid down her cheeks.

"Obviously, they're dead." Now Landon was annoyed. "But if Lazarus works, they won't stay that way. We'll start with Sawyer first—"

His words pierced straight to her core. She whipped toward him. "Sawyer...*no!* We can't use Lazarus on him!"

Landon frowned at her. "Why not? He's the perfect specimen."

He wasn't a specimen! He was *Sawyer.* He was her lover. The man who held her when she had nightmares. The man who flashed his dimple to charm her. The man who—

He's dead. He's dead!

"His body is strong, he's a warrior, exactly the kind of test subject that Wright wants in Project Lazarus. Sawyer is the ideal candidate. With his background and training, he'll be the alpha for this group."

She swiped at the tears on her cheeks. "Lazarus isn't ready. You can't—you can't do this to him!"

"Do this?" Landon repeated as he blinked owlishly at her from behind the lenses of his glasses. "Sawyer Cage is dead, Elizabeth. We can either let him stay that way, or we can try and bring him back." His jaw hardened. "You're crying. Look, I get that it's…difficult…because this is someone we both know—"

"*Difficult?*"

"But you had to realize the men here would make perfect subjects for the program. And if they died on a mission, well, isn't this the natural next step for them?"

There was a nervous murmur from the nearby nurses. Two men and a woman. Both looked very, very uncomfortable. *They should.* Elizabeth realized her mouth was hanging open in shock. *Sawyer is dead. He's next to me, and he's dead, and I'm breaking apart.*

Landon edged closer to her. "Sawyer is dead. What we're doing...we're bringing him *back.*"

"What if he comes back wrong?" The question burst from her. "The Lazarus formula is not perfect and it's — *it's Sawyer!*" Pain crashed through her as more tears slid down her cheeks. "No, no, this is not happening. I can't do this to him! I won't — Sawyer isn't some lab rat. He's — "

Everything.

Landon stared at her a moment longer. His gaze seemed cruel. His face too hard. And... "I feared you might respond this way," he confessed as he lifted one brow and studied her. "Once you saw it was him. Unfortunate, but...it is what it is." Then he motioned with one hand. "Guard, escort Dr. Parker out of the lab. She's done here."

Wait — *what?* The guard grabbed her, locking Elizabeth's arms behind her. He yanked her back, hauling her toward the lab's door.

"Stop it!" Elizabeth yelled. "Let me go, right now!"

But the guard only tightened his hold.

Landon reached for one of the pre-filled syringes. He shoved the sheet farther down Sawyer's body. There would be two injections...one in the heart and one in the base of the brain. That was the protocol she'd created. *"Don't!"* Elizabeth screamed. "Not to him!"

But... *I want him back! Sawyer said he'd come back to me!*

Landon put the long, sharp syringe needle over Sawyer's chest. Then he plunged it into Sawyer's heart.

The guard had dragged Elizabeth to the door. *"Sawyer!"* She dug in her heels, fighting with all of her strength.

Landon was already reaching for the second syringe. He moved behind Sawyer, placing the needle at the back of his head—

"Sawyer?" Elizabeth whispered. This was so wrong.

Landon looked up. "Don't you want him back?"

More than anything. But I can't—

Landon gave Sawyer the second injection.

"Stop! Let me go, please!" Elizabeth begged the guard.

Landon was frowning as he peered down at Sawyer. "Nothing is happening."

The guard hauled Elizabeth into the hallway. A nurse slammed the door shut as soon as they were clear. But Elizabeth could see through the nearby glass viewing window of the lab. Landon was glaring down at Sawyer, and her lover—he was so still on that table. *Dead.*

"Stop," Elizabeth whispered to the guard who kept pulling at her. "I need to see…"

The blonde nurse brought more needles to Landon. Landon grabbed one and injected the formula into Sawyer's heart again.

No! Leave him alone!

The guard's hold eased. Wrongly, he thought she wasn't a threat any longer. She broke free, rushing as fast as she could and ripping the lab door open once more. "Don't give him too much!" Elizabeth yelled. "Don't—"

Landon administered another dose to Sawyer. "He's not fucking moving. This doesn't work." Sweat covered his forehead. "I have to tell Wright this doesn't work!"

The guard grabbed her again.

Sawyer was unresponsive. Sawyer was…dead.

Her heart felt like lead in her chest. The nurse shut the lab door once more, glaring, and the guard led Elizabeth down the hallway. His grip didn't ease this time. Instead, it bruised. She looked back through the viewing window, staring at the inside of the lab, desperate for one last glimpse of Sawyer—

He sat up.

"*Holy fuck,*" the guard said as his hold on her tightened even more.

Her mouth dropped. Sawyer—back. *I'll always come back for you.*

Landon was smiling. He was reaching for Sawyer. And Sawyer—

Sawyer threw Landon across the lab. Landon's body smashed into the glass viewing window right near Elizabeth's face.

The guards inside that lab room lunged to attack. They pulled their weapons. They fired.

But Sawyer didn't stop. He ran right at them. He attacked, punching, kicking, taking their weapons—*firing* on them.

The nurses were racing for freedom. They screamed as they fled into the hallway.

Sawyer was still attacking the guards.

No, no, this couldn't be happening! "I can stop him!" She glanced at the man who still held her, frantic. "I can stop him! Just let me go!"

The guard had gone absolutely white. He released her, not even bothering with a token fight. She ran back into that lab. Landon was trying to crawl for the door, and Sawyer...Sawyer had just fired once more at a guard who was on the floor.

"*Sawyer!*" Elizabeth yelled his name.

His head lifted. He still held the gun in his hand. His eyes immediately locked on her. But there was no recognition in his stare. No emotion. Nothing at all.

"Sawyer, put down the gun," Elizabeth told him, her voice shaking.

He looked at the gun in his hand.

She crept closer to him. Behind her, Landon continued crawling toward the door.

"Put it down," Elizabeth urged Sawyer. Her whole body trembled. "I know…I know this is confusing and scary, but I can help you. I *will* help you." *He's not dead, not anymore. It worked. My formula worked. Sawyer is alive.*

He glanced back up at her…and he…he *aimed* the gun at her.

Elizabeth froze. "Sawyer? It's…it's me."

His eyelids didn't so much as flicker. He stared at her with zero recognition.

"Shoot him!" Landon suddenly bellowed.

Her head whipped back as she looked over her shoulder. The guard who'd dragged her from the lab now stood in front of Landon. The guard's quivering fingers held a gun—and that gun was aimed right at Sawyer.

"No!" Elizabeth cried.

But the guard's fingers were squeezing the trigger. Elizabeth threw her body forward, trying to protect Sawyer. She'd just gotten him back. She couldn't lose him…even if…

Even if he's a monster?

I'm Frankenstein, and I made the monster…

Pain hit her, burning right through Elizabeth. She called out Sawyer's name as she fell.

I'll always come back for you.

Sawyer was the last thing she saw. He was staring down at her with his stormy blue gaze—a gaze that held zero recognition…and no emotion at all.

CHAPTER FIVE

Wyman Wright smiled as he watched the video feed. "Excellent test run." He nodded to his guards. "Release the gas. When everyone is knocked out, you can remove the first test subject. Sawyer Cage should be transferred to the Lazarus facility immediately." His fingers tapped against his desk. "Go ahead and move Flynn Haddox, too."

In the live feed, Sawyer was still holding the gun. He was also still staring down at Dr. Elizabeth Parker. Landon and the guard who'd just fired were trying to back out of the lab.

"Sir…" The man behind Wyman cleared his throat. "Should we…should we go ahead and inject Flynn Haddox before removal? His body *did* go through the preservation process."

Wyman smiled. "We are absolutely going to inject him." Elizabeth had done it. She'd brought back the dead. Talk about a fucking miracle.

And a perfect weapon.

Elizabeth didn't know that he'd altered her formula, just a bit. Landon had been only too happy to make the changes, per Wyman's instructions. He'd needed a soldier who came back with a strong desire to hunt. To destroy.

A soldier with no emotions.

Smoke began to fill lab five. Not smoke, though—gas. A very powerful gas that would knock out the newly risen Sawyer Cage.

The gun fell from Sawyer's fingers. He staggered forward, and then he sagged to his knees...right beside Dr. Elizabeth Parker.

Elizabeth's shirt was soaked with blood.

"I might need her," Wyman said, frowning. *Her mind would be a terrible thing to lose.* "Get medics in there."

Sawyer reached out to Elizabeth. His hand pressed to her chest. He shuddered.

Then he collapsed, his body falling on top of hers.

When the medics rushed into the lab, their faces covered by masks, they dragged Sawyer off Elizabeth. Surprisingly, he roused enough to fight them...

And to try and hold tight to Elizabeth Parker.

Wyman leaned toward his monitor, watching the feed avidly. "Now isn't that interesting..."

As far as Wyman was concerned, the experiment had been a full success, and things were truly just getting started.

CHAPTER SIX

Three Months Later…

"It's really quite phenomenal," Landon said, and there was admiration in his tone. "Your research and work were so ground-breaking, Elizabeth. The things that we've accomplished in a short amount of time — it's just, well, like I said, phenomenal, truly."

Elizabeth just stared at him. She didn't let her expression alter even the tiniest bit, but her heart raced frantically in her chest. The rhythm was so fast and hard that Elizabeth was surprised Landon couldn't hear the desperate beat. Her palms were wet with sweat, yet her back was ramrod-straight. She was afraid, and she was desperate, but she would *never* show those emotions to Landon.

The guy was on her shit-list, and he'd forever remain there. *Fool me once, shame on me. Fool me twice…and it will be your last mistake.*

Landon gave her a warm smile. The overhead light glinted off his glasses. "I'm so glad that you're back with us. I had faith in

Wright, of course. When he wants something…"
His smile faltered. "It's pretty hard to tell Wright
no."

And the great Wyman Wright had wanted
her back on his team. Well, he wanted her back at
the moment. But that hadn't been the case
originally. Not when Project Lazarus had
first…*been a damn go.*

After that nightmare day, she'd been
abandoned. When Elizabeth had gotten out of the
hospital, Wright had been nowhere to be found.
He'd emptied their labs and offices in D.C. and
shut down the facility there. All of the other
employees—everyone had vanished. Elizabeth
had been left alone, with a healing bullet wound
in her chest.

*And Sawyer was gone. They took him
away.* She'd tried desperately to find out where
Wright had relocated his group, but she'd gotten
stone-walled at every turn.

But then—two weeks ago—things had
changed. Wright had come back to D.C. The
conniving bastard had literally just appeared at
her door. He'd acted as if he were just dropping
by for a visit. A friendly little chat. As if she
hadn't spent months tearing D.C. apart as she
searched for Sawyer. *And as every door got
slammed in my face.*

"Wright needs me." Elizabeth was proud of
the fact that her voice came out calm and steady.

She and Landon were walking down a long, curving corridor. They were in the middle of Arizona, at Wright's *new* research facility. What he'd called the Lazarus Facility. *No wonder I couldn't find the place in D.C. He moved everyone across the country!*

Just getting inside the place had been one hell of a challenge. The outside entrance had been heavily guarded by armed men and women. Before she could get *inside,* she'd had to be thoroughly searched and show her ID at four different checkpoints. Then, and only then, had she gained access to the main facility…a facility that happened to be carved into the very side of a mountain. She figured the new Lazarus research location was only creepy by about—oh, *one hundred percent.* "Don't bother trying to sugarcoat things for me, Landon. I know exactly why Wright came to me. Something is wrong with the program, and he thinks I can fix the problems."

Landon was sweating, too. Only his sweat was more obvious than hers. She could see the trickles sliding down his temples. At her words, Landon stilled in the corridor and faced her. He swallowed, once, twice, then said, voice hushed, "I didn't want things to end…that way."

Her brows rose. "What way, exactly?"

His Adam's apple bobbed.

Elizabeth moved closer to him. Her shoes slid over the stone floor. "You mean…with you stealing *my* project? Or with me getting a bullet to the chest?"

Silence.

"Perhaps you mean that you didn't want things to end with me being abandoned in a hospital as I fought to live? With me waking up and discovering you and Wright had shut me out completely and *left* me? That you had stolen *all* of my research — both from the facility in D.C. *and* my home?"

Landon licked his lips. "Pretty much all of that." He cast a frantic look around them, and his gaze lingered on the security camera perched high on the wall to the left of them. "I didn't have a choice. Wright called the shots." Landon barely seemed to breathe the words. "He still does. When the guy says jump, I do."

But I don't. She had her own agenda. She wasn't jumping for Wright, no matter what the sonofabitch might think.

"I know he offered you a whole lot of money to come back on board…" Landon began.

Right. Like money was the reason she'd come back. Money might matter to Landon and to Wright, but she had other priorities.

"We need you," he added grimly. "There are things — "

A door opened down the hallway. A guard appeared. Elizabeth knew he was a guard because this guy was dressed just as the others had been — all in black from his neck to his boots, and he had an earpiece tucked into his right ear. A gun was holstered on his hip.

The guard nodded to her and Landon as he passed by them in the corridor. Landon didn't speak again, not until they were alone once more in that narrow hallway.

"Our test subjects are perfect weapons." He nodded briskly. "Their heart-rates are steady, their adrenaline levels stay within our new parameters when stressed, but more importantly, their senses are enhanced. It's pretty unbelievable what they can do. Their hearing, their sight...hell, they perform ten times better than normal soldiers. They're *super* soldiers, I guess you could say."

No, she wasn't going to say that.

"They're stronger than normal humans. They move faster. They have reflexes that will blow a typical human's off the charts." He turned and began walking down the corridor. "Because your test rats showed increased strength and enhanced reflexes, we were hoping to replicate those results with the Lazarus subjects. We had no idea just how significant the changes would truly be for them, though. Developments we didn't expect, but are certainly thrilled to see."

She followed him, slowly. She was wearing a white lab coat, and it fluttered behind her.

"They sound perfect." Her voice drifted around them. "But if they are so perfect, why do you need me?"

They slid around the curve in the corridor. Up ahead, another guard waited. When they approached him, both Landon and Elizabeth had to show their ID. *Five times now.* After he verified their identities, the guard typed in four digits on the key-pad that waited near the heavy, metal door. A loud beep sounded, and then the door opened. She started to step forward —

"Sorry, doctor," the guard told her, immediately moving into Elizabeth's path. "I know you're new here, so you don't know the drill yet. But *no one* gets past this check-point without a pat-down."

Her brows lifted. "I've already been searched."

The guard — a big, red-headed guy with dark green eyes — exhaled on a heavy breath. "Sorry, ma'am, but you're going to be patted-down again right now. It's procedure. Everyone must follow procedure, or I can't let you into the tombs."

The tombs.

Goosebumps rose onto her arms. Was the place called the tombs because all of Landon's "super soldiers" had once been dead?

Since she had nothing to hide — not then, anyway — Elizabeth lifted her arms. The pat-down was fast but thorough, and Landon was searched as soon as she was done.

Then they went inside. They crept down three flights of stairs and Elizabeth saw — "The tombs."

Only they weren't tombs. Not really. They were more like cells. Small rooms that she estimated to be about fifteen feet long by ten feet wide. A bed was in each room, a small table and a chair. A toilet.

It's like prison.

Only there were no bars on the cells. The walls were big, clear chunks of glass.

"We can see them, but they can't see us," Landon said as his shoulder brushed against hers. "One-way mirrors for walls. Kind of like what cops use in their interrogation rooms. Only from inside, the material doesn't look like a mirror. It looks like a plain, white wall—a wall that happens to be very, very strong."

Her legs were shaking as she stepped forward. "You have…there are a lot of rooms here." She didn't see anyone in those rooms, not then. *Where are all the test subjects?*

"Wright wanted us to increase our research pool." A new tension had entered his voice. "And that's where the trouble began."

She'd been gazing down at all of the rooms, desperately looking for one test subject in particular, but at Landon's words, her gaze swung back to him.

"That increased aggression that you were so worried about…" Landon licked his lips. "It's showing itself."

Her heart stopped beating. "You don't think that when Sawyer woke up and immediately attacked everyone around him that he wasn't exhibiting *increased* aggression?"

"Uh, yes, about that…" He hurried past the cells. "Sawyer Cage was pre-programmed, if you will."

She lunged forward and grabbed Landon's arm. *"What?"*

He was sweating even more now. "I guess Wright didn't tell you that part, huh? Didn't mention it when he came to see you?"

She gave a hard, negative shake of her head.

"Um, well, our additional research has shown that when you administer too much of the Lazarus formula, the brain's functioning is altered. Emotional responses to situations can be amplified and primitive instinct takes over. Sawyer woke to find himself surrounded by unfamiliar, armed guards. His primitive response—it was to attack. To eliminate the threat. To kill."

"You gave him too much," she gritted out. "I was telling you that *then!* We could have all *died.*"

He sucked in a sharp breath. "And that's why you are here. So that no additional miscalculations will be made."

He opened a door to the right, and she saw a small office waiting inside.

"Some of the subjects are showing low serotonin levels. I think their pre-frontal cortexes have a harder time creating an appropriate response to anger — and that's where we're seeing the surge in aggression." He walked around the paper-filled desk and crashed in his chair. "We did expect the aggression, but we had no idea about the memory loss."

She stood in the doorway. "Memory loss?"

He glowered at her. "You didn't warn me about that part. It *wasn't* in your notes."

"That's because none of the *rats* I used exhibited memory loss. They could still perform all of the same functions that they'd completed before being dosed with the Lazarus formula. I tested them all to make certain their brain function was within normal parameters, but I didn't test on humans." *Because we were not ready for them. Not even close. You don't go from rats to humans, that was bullshit.* Wright had been working his own agenda, from day one. He'd wanted super soldiers, and he'd wanted them *immediately.*

Landon's fingers steepled beneath his chin. "Is it possible the rats only recalled procedural memories?"

"I don't know — my research wasn't completed," Elizabeth snapped out. Procedural memory…the memories that most people took for granted. Memories that allowed people to do simple things like tie their shoes or use a knife and fork when eating. The simple tasks that people completed over and over again became procedures for them to follow, and these memories were attached to the cerebellum, the motor cortex, the putamen, and the caudate nucleus. "Areas involved in instinctive action," she murmured as her mind puzzled out this new development. Dammit, yes, it *was* possible that the rats had been displaying procedural memories when they ran through the mazes. They'd gone through her mazes over and over again. She'd assumed memories were intact for them, but that had been a huge mistake on her part. The aggression displayed by some of her test subjects had captured her attention, and she hadn't even stopped to consider—

"The memory loss isn't necessarily a bad thing."

What?

"If the subjects had remembered their pasts, then they might have wanted to reconnect with loved ones. Not really a possibility. The memory loss allowed the subjects to start with a clean slate, if you will."

Elizabeth glowered at Landon. She bit her lip, hard, so she didn't scream at him. *Sawyer doesn't remember me? At all? None of the subjects remember?* "Anything else?" Elizabeth asked carefully. "Things I need to be told about now?"

His gaze darted away from hers. "The subjects perform well in the field. Far better than regular soldiers—"

She flew across the room and slapped her hands down on his desk, sending papers flying to the floor. "They've already gone in the field?" Wright was a freaking lunatic. And she *would* be shutting his ass down. The sonofabitch thought that all he'd needed to do was throw money at her, and she'd been right back on his team.

Wrong. Elizabeth couldn't be bought. She was in that facility for one reason and one reason alone...to fix the nightmare that she'd helped to create.

"Yes." Landon spoke haltingly as he explained, "Wright wanted a full test. He wanted to see just what the subjects could do. We began with simulated missions."

"It's been *three months.*"

"Yes, I know, but the test subjects showed such aptitude that Wright insisted on sending them out right away, with proper supervision, of course."

She forced herself to take several long, deep breaths. Her temples were throbbing. "And there were no issues?"

His eyelashes flickered.

Shit. There were issues. Plenty of them, Elizabeth was betting. Wright had been desperate to get her back on his team, after all. There was always a reason for desperation.

Landon smiled at her, but it was a fake grin, she could tell. "You're here to smooth over any glitches."

That's what you think. "I want to see the test subjects. Immediately." She straightened away from his desk.

He nodded quickly. "Right. Absolutely. I'll get Subject Number—"

Her skin had iced. "You only speak of them by numbers, not names?"

Landon swallowed. She heard the faint click of his Adam's apple. "Y-yes."

"You're de-humanizing them. You can't do that. They are *people*."

Sweat trickled down his temple. "The men you knew before—Sawyer and Flynn—they're gone." His voice was careful. "You understand that, don't you? These subjects don't remember who they were before Lazarus. As far as they know, they *don't* have a past." He grimaced. "Using a name wouldn't have meaning for them. The people they were before Lazarus—well, those lives are over for them. The men truly died."

Like she needed that reminder. Elizabeth would never forget the sight of Sawyer's body spread out on that table. So still.

With a cough, Landon added. "So, um, yes, we give them numbers. Easier that way."

She turned away from him so he wouldn't see her rage. "You give them numbers and you keep them in cages and you think that's okay?"

"We monitor their mental health." His voice was sharp, as if she'd offended him.

Before she was finished, Elizabeth would do a lot more than *offend* the guy.

"And they aren't in cages. They have rooms, comfortable accommodations—"

"Accommodations that have walls you can see through! They have no privacy. No security!"

But Landon shook his head. "We need to be able to monitor them. For *our* safety. The men are able to come and go through the facility here, but they are always trailed by a guard. Until we can be certain of them—until we know that there won't be any dangerous surprises, the men *will* be watched."

He made zero sense. "But you send them out on missions. And I'm guessing guards *aren't* tailing them—"

"We have other ways of monitoring the subjects when they are sent on a mission. Believe me, we are never at risk of losing them." His lips thinned. "Should the worst-case scenario situation ever occur, safeguards are in place. The subjects would not get away."

Get away. They're prisoners. "Worst-case scenario?" Elizabeth asked softly.

He just stared back at her. "The guards here are armed with tranqs, not real guns. We value our test subjects. Despite what you may think, they are treated well here. Yes, we can see into their *rooms,* but the men don't mind that security measure. They understand that they have to prove themselves in order to be granted greater freedom."

Such BS.

"Wright even brought in the best psychiatrist available to counsel the men and help with any transition issues. Dr. Cecelia Gregory. She started seeing the subjects two months ago. Right after they began field missions. They each come in twice a week to talk with her, and she monitors them—"

"I'll need to speak with her," Elizabeth cut in, squaring her shoulders. She gave Landon her fiercest look. "But first, I want to see the subjects."

He nodded. "Okay, but I have to instruct you *not* to reveal the full details about Project Lazarus to Dr. Gregory."

"What? If she's the shrink for the subjects, then she has to know—"

"Dr. Gregory doesn't know that she's treating dead men." His lips tightened. "*Formerly* dead men. That is classified information. And it's information that isn't relevant to her. Dr. Gregory knows the men were given a serum that made them into super soldiers, and that's all. She understands the serum caused some unforeseen side-effects, like the memory loss, but she doesn't know that she's treating the dead."

Formerly dead men.

"Classified. You understand that, Elizabeth?"

She understood that Landon liked his secrets, but secrets could be very dangerous. "I heard you loud and clear." Now, to get down to business. Elizabeth could barely contain her emotions as she said, "I want to start with Test Subject Number One." Because she already knew who would have been given the number *one.* The guy Wright had wanted to lead his team of super soldiers.

Sawyer.

***

Elizabeth shut the exam room door behind her. Her fingers were trembling, and every breath that she took seemed to chill her lungs. Her gaze darted around the small room, checking out the instrument trays, the assorted machines, and the two security cameras positioned in two of the upper corners of the room.

Someone is watching. From what she'd been able to tell, someone was always watching in this facility. She'd spied plenty of cameras so far during her time at the —

"You're new."

She jerked at his voice. A voice that haunted her dreams. Rough and low. Dark. Elizabeth had deliberately kept her gaze away from the man who sat on the edge of the exam table.

But now her gaze slid toward him, helplessly, and the pain that hit Elizabeth seemed to stab into her heart with the force of a knife's blade.

Sawyer. *Her* Sawyer.

He wore a pair of jeans and a white t-shirt. His black hair was tousled, as if he'd run his fingers through it — and his hair was longer than it had been before. His dark blue eyes studied her. His handsome face was tense, and his head tilted as his stare swept over her.

Her knees gave way, and Elizabeth staggered.

Before she could fall face-first onto the tile, he was there. Sawyer vaulted off the exam table and grabbed her arms. His hands curled around her and heat surged through Elizabeth at his touch.

Sawyer.

Elizabeth blinked away tears as the pain in her heart just got worse. So much worse.

I found you, Sawyer. I found —

"Are you all right?" He frowned at her. "Maybe you're the one who should be on the exam table."

He stared at her with those familiar dark blue eyes. He stared at her...and there was zero recognition in his gaze.

No memory. No memory of his life before Lazarus.

No memory of...her. Elizabeth hadn't thought she could hurt more. She'd been wrong.

"Don't worry, I'll get some help," Sawyer assured her.

He isn't Sawyer. He's Test Subject Number One. I'm not supposed to call him by his name. I'm supposed to call him One. Those had been Landon's instructions to her. A requirement before he agreed to let her finally see the subjects. But...

Screw Landon.

"You stay here," Sawyer, said as he released her. "I'll be —"

"I-I don't need help." Her voice came out low and husky. Shaking.

He blinked at her. A faint furrow appeared between his brows.

"I'm fine." *Liar, liar.* "P-please...get back on the exam table."

But he didn't move. Was it her imagination, or had his shoulders stiffened? His body seemed tense. And he—

He leaned in close to her. He put his face right in the curve of her neck.

Elizabeth froze. Absolutely froze.

"Strawberries," he whispered.

Her body swayed toward him. Did he remember? Her scent, he'd—

Sawyer—Subject One—gave a little laugh as he pulled back from her. "You smell just like the strawberries we had for dessert last night."

Elizabeth licked her lips. "It's my lotion. Um, would you…would you please go back to the exam table?"

He lifted a brow at her. "Not gonna fall on me, are you?" And there it was. The faintest hint of his Texas accent. Hearing it *hurt* her.

"I won't fall." Another lie. She'd fallen hard for him, long ago. "I promise."

Sawyer went back to the exam table. He hopped up on it. His long legs dangled over the edge. He crossed his arms over his powerful chest and studied her. "You're new," he said again.

"I…I'm Elizabeth Parker."

A wry smile curved his lips. It was a smile that never reached his eyes. A smile Elizabeth recognized—his cold, pissed smile. His dimple didn't wink. "And I'm Subject Number One."

She flinched.

"But then, I guess you know that, don't you?" His eyes drifted over her. "Another doctor to poke and prod at me. Only I don't need prodding. I came back from the last mission just fine. Another exam is pointless."

"Don't be so sure of that." She forced herself to move closer to him. One halting step at a time. Her gaze darted around the room, and she saw a stethoscope on the exam tray. She grabbed it, sliding it around her neck. "I'd like to listen to your heart." *I'd like to make this nightmare go away. I'd like to make everything better for you. I'd like —*

"You're scared of me."

Her stare flew back to him.

His gaze was on her fingers, the fingers that were still curled around the stethoscope. "Your hands are trembling."

Yes, they were. Actually, every part of her body was trembling.

"That's why you stumbled when you came into the room, isn't it?" Sawyer — *Subject One!* — pressed, voice gruff. "Because you were afraid of being alone with me."

Once more, she forced herself to move forward. She stopped when she was right in front of him. His legs were spread, giving her the room to move even closer to him, if she wanted.

She didn't move closer to him. "Don't be silly," Elizabeth chided. "Why would I be scared of you?"

And then she remembered the sound of her own scream. The sight of Sawyer holding a gun.

Firing it at the guards. Then pointing the gun at her…as he stared at her with zero recognition in his eyes. Now she understood why he'd stared at her as if she was a stranger. To him, she *was*.

Dammit, yes, I am scared of him. I'm terrified. But fear wasn't going to stop her.

Elizabeth exhaled slowly. "I just need to listen to your heartbeat—"

"Yours is racing far too fast. A sure sign…that you're scared of me."

Her eyes widened. "You can hear my heartbeat?" Before coming into the exam room, she'd read the notes in his file. Landon had indicated all of the test subjects had elevated senses, but to be able to actually *hear* her heartbeat—

His right hand rose. His fingertips—slightly callused, just as she remembered—skated down the curve of her throat.

Elizabeth shivered as his gaze narrowed on her.

"I can *see* your pulse racing." His fingers caressed her skin. "Right…here." And his fingers were over her frantically racing pulse. "I scare you."

She forced a smile. *You terrify me.*

He blinked at her smile. "Wrong."

Her smile slipped. "Excuse me?"

But Sawyer shook his head, as if he were confused, and his hand slipped away from her throat. "I won't...hurt you." His words were halting, as if he had to force them out.

Elizabeth locked her knees. "I need to get started on the exam." Fumbling, she lifted the stethoscope—

Sawyer yanked off his shirt.

He had new scars. At least five of them. New scars that were white lines of raised flesh over his skin. Her lips parted as she stared at them.

"Thought that would make it easier for you."

Her stare rose to his face.

He shrugged one powerful shoulder. "Usually the male doc gets me to strip down to my underwear for the exam. You want the same thing?"

"Y-you've been injured."

Another shrug. As if injuries didn't matter. "Took a few slices from a knife on one of the earlier missions. Then had to get a bullet wound stitched up after a fire-fight. No big deal."

No big deal. "That hasn't changed." The words slipped from her, and Elizabeth immediately wished that she could pull them back. But for just an instant, she'd seen the man he'd been. Her confident soldier. The battle-ready warrior who never admitted to feeling pain.

The man who'd died.

His gaze was assessing as it focused on her face.

Get a grip, Elizabeth. If you screw up, the guards will drag you out of here, and all of your grand plans will go straight to hell.

"Want to say that again?" Sawyer muttered.

I can't think of him as Subject One.

"'Cause I don't think I heard you quite right."

Elizabeth sucked in some deep, steadying breaths. Her eyes flew to the nearest video camera. Someone was watching. Always. She *had* to remember that. "I need you to relax while I check your heart rate." She positioned the stethoscope right over his chest. She could hear the beat of his heart. But…faster than normal. Elevated. Her fingers pressed to his shoulder, and his skin's heat almost singed her.

Elevated body temperature. That bit had been in Landon's notes. The test subjects kept a slightly higher than average body temperature. Their heartbeats tended to stay faster than an average human's, too. Their reflexes were better. Their muscles stronger. Even their healing abilities had increased.

No wonder Wright was desperate to get you all in the field.

"So tell me the verdict, doc…"

Doc. She blinked fast, refusing to let any tears fall.

"Am I alive…or dead?"

His words were obviously meant to be flippant, but Elizabeth jerked away from him, pulling the stethoscope with her.

His hand flew out and curled around her wrist.

She stilled.

We've done this before.

So many times. Stood close in an exam room. Stared into each other's eyes. Felt the tension thicken the air. *Sawyer...*

Did he remember? At all? *Anything?*

His hold tightened on her. He pulled her closer once more, and she found herself standing between his spread legs. His heat surrounded her. His rich, masculine scent—still so familiar— tormented her. She was staring right at the man she'd loved and lost, and there was no recognition on his face. No hint of emotion. Nothing at all.

"Am I alive?" he repeated, and his mouth hitched up into the half-smile that was painful to see. "Or dead?"

My Sawyer is dead. Subject One is staring at me. Had Landon been right? Were the test subjects truly so different? Not the men they'd been at all...but new people now.

"Alive, of course." She tugged her hand free of his hold. She had to get out of that little exam room, if only for a few moments because Elizabeth couldn't *breathe* right then. Being so close to him was wrecking her. "Excuse me, I-I need to check something outside." She practically ran for the door. Her hand curled around the knob and—

"Wrong answer." His voice was so soft that she almost didn't hear the words. "I'm dead."

Her head whipped back. She stared at him in horror. "Y-you…you…"

Sawyer smiled at her, flashing the dimple in his left cheek. "Obviously, I'm kidding, doc. You seem stressed. Thought a joke might lighten your mood."

No, just the opposite. Because he hadn't been kidding. Sawyer didn't even realize it, but he'd just spoken the truth. He *was* dead.

And her heart hurt even more.

CHAPTER SEVEN

Lust was new. The desire that twisted his guts and made his cock ache — it was new. Since waking up in hell, Subject One hadn't wanted anyone. Not the female guards or doctors. Not the male ones. Not even the pretty shrink who came in to talk to them all about how they were *feeling*.

Subject One — or, well, *One,* as he was called by the others — he knew what lust was. Just as he knew about love and hate and rage. He was familiar with all of the emotions and needs out there. He knew what things were called — he knew he was currently sitting in a ten-feet-wide cell, that he was leaning back on a cot, and that the cell room door was automatically locked behind him every single time that he stepped inside.

He knew what *things* were called. He knew emotions. He knew how to fight. Oh, hell, yes, One knew how to fight. How to kill.

But…

His mind was messed up. One knew that, too. Because when he tried to see his past, to recall what his life had been like before he'd woken up in hell, there was nothing.

He didn't remember growing up. He was an adult, he'd seen his own reflection in a mirror— One figured he was in his late twenties or early thirties—so he must have been a kid at some point but…

Don't remember that. Don't remember a family. Don't remember a lover. Don't remember anything before this place.

So One didn't remember feeling lust before.

But he'd sure felt it that day, with her. With the new doc. Elizabeth Parker.

The doctor with the long, dark hair. Hair that she'd pulled back into a bun at the base of her neck. He'd wanted to pull her hair free, to see it tumbling over her shoulders. Her hair and her eyes had been so dark. That warm, chocolate gaze of hers had seemed to peer right into his soul.

Only I don't have a soul.

Her face had been damn beautiful. But…delicate. Fragile. She'd seemed too delicate, with her pale skin and the shadows that drifted under her gorgeous eyes. He'd wondered if something might be wrong with her. She was so thin, and when he'd first seen her, for just a moment, he'd actually thought…

She's lost weight.

Which was a fucking stupid thought, because he didn't know the new doc. So he had no clue if she'd lost weight or not.

He didn't know anyone, not really…just the other members of his team. The men who risked their lives with him as they fought the enemy.

The men who were kept in cages, just like he was.

If we're the good guys, then why the hell are we locked up? The question raged inside of him, a question that he'd actually asked that fucker Landon more than a few times. Only One never got any other answer except—

"The cells are for your safety."

Screw that shit.

They were weapons. One knew *exactly* what they were. Weapons that were kept locked up because they were so dangerous.

Only they weren't going to stay caged forever.

Even a beast dreams of freedom.

He spread his body out on the narrow bed. *More of a damn cot than a bed.* The ache of desire was still there, thickening his cock. The doc's scent—strawberries—had been so sweet. He'd wanted to take a bite…of her. He'd wanted to put his mouth on her skin, right there on the curve of her neck as it met her shoulder, and see if she tasted as good as she smelled.

Lust. Figured it would hit now, just when he'd been making plans to escape. No matter. The sexy little doc with her dark eyes and husky voice wasn't going to slow him down. He'd be getting out of hell.

One closed his eyes. His breathing slid in and out, and he slipped into dreams. The same dark dreams of fucking *nothing* that he always had.

Only…that darkness didn't last. Not this time.

***

He pinned the dark-haired beauty between his body and the wooden door. The scent of strawberries teased his nose. "You kept me waiting." His words were a growl.

"I—"

"Gonna have to make you pay for that." His right hand moved down to grab the material of her dress. "Feels like fucking silk…" He wasn't talking about the dress. He was talking about her perfect skin. The dress was just in his way. He wanted it gone. He wanted to be flesh to flesh with her. He wanted to be *in* her. "Are you wearing panties?"

He didn't give her a chance to reply. Instead, he shoved the fabric of her dress out of the way, and his fingers pushed between her legs. Sweet, fucking hell…she *wasn't* wearing panties. His fingers touched her naked sex. He almost came right then and there. His body shuddered.

"Fuck, baby, what you do to me…" His fingers slid over her sex. Carefully at first, because she was so delicate, especially compared to him.

Her head tipped back against the door, and her lips pressed together. So sexy. That dark hair. That gorgeous skin. Those red lips…

"You're already wet." One finger caressed her clit and her whole body jerked. His mouth pressed to her throat, kissing, licking, and then he gave a little nip. "Did you miss me as fucking much as I missed you?" Because he'd been in hell without her. Desperate, every single moment, to get back to her. Being apart from her was a raw agony that ripped right through him.

Her eyes opened. So dark and deep and beautiful. "I need you, Sawyer. *Now.*"

Sawyer.

Her hand reached between their bodies. She stroked his cock through the fabric of his pants. "*Sawyer.*"

Again…she called that name.

My name?

But the haze of lust was too strong. He had to have her. He was fucking insane with dark need. His hands curled around her waist, and he lifted her up. Her back shoved into the wood of the door even as her legs wrapped around his hips.

The head of his cock pressed against the entrance to her body. And—

He sank deep. Her breath choked out, and then he kissed her. His tongue thrust into her mouth even as his cock drove into her body, again and again. He used his hold on her hips to lift her up and down, moving her quickly over the length of his cock. He could hear the faint moan rising in her throat.

"No sound, baby. Remember…"

She came, biting her lip, choking back her cry of release, and he was lost. Her sex squeezed around him, white-hot, so tight, and he erupted within her. His cock jerked, his body shuddered, and he held her with desperate hands. *Can't let her go. Not ever. Not fucking*—

***

His eyes flashed open. His heart thundered in his chest, sweat covered his body, and his dick was rock-hard and currently shoving straight toward the ceiling.

One didn't move. His breath heaved in and out, and the dream slowly faded. The visions—so hot and consuming—of the sexy lover with the dark eyes, the dark hair, the perfect skin…

Elizabeth Parker.

He'd been balls deep in her, and she'd come for him, in that dream. She'd come for him.

And she'd called his name.

Sawyer.

What in the hell was happening?

***

"Thanks for coming in today," Dr. Cecelia Gregory said with a faint smile as she settled behind her desk. Her red hair was pulled back into a sleek ponytail and her hazel eyes gleamed at him.

One sprawled back against her couch. The easy pose was at total odds with the tension inside of his body. Where was Elizabeth Parker? He hadn't seen her in over twenty-four hours. "Not like I have a choice."

Her eyelashes flickered. "Is something wrong today? You seem tense."

Plenty of things are wrong. "What's my name?"

Cecelia swallowed. "I...you know that all of the soldiers in this unit have code names, you have—"

"We don't have freaking code names." Anger sharpened each word. "We have numbers. I'm One. The bastard in the cell next to me is Two. There are six of us total, and we're just numbers to you people."

She was breathing faster. Her heart was drumming faster, too, and, no, he didn't know that because he could see her pulse. He could *hear* her heartbeat. He'd lied to the doc before. His senses were far more enhanced than he'd let on to Landon and the other lab-coat wearing jerks. All of his team members had senses that were far stronger than *any* of them had revealed. They were keeping secrets. Only fair because it seemed their doctors and handlers were keeping secrets, too.

"You are a soldier," Cecelia began carefully. Sure, he was probably supposed to think of her as *Dr. Gregory*, but he didn't. She was Cecelia to him. Mostly because that was what Two called her. Two talked about her, far too often.

Because that guy has a hard-on for the shrink.

"You—you volunteered for this experimental group." Her words tumbled out quickly and her heart continued to pound. "You knew the risks involved going in, and the memory loss you suffer—"

"What if my memories come back?"

Her jaw dropped.

Should have kept that to my damn self.

Too late. Like a spider who'd just caught a fly in her web, Cecelia leaned forward eagerly. "Have your memories returned? Is that what you're telling me? Did you have a flash of—"

I had a wet dream.

"—of something? Or…someone?"

"No," he lied. He did it without blinking, without even a flutter of his heartbeat. The truth of the matter was that he didn't fully trust the shrink — or any of the people in that facility. They'd told him that he was a soldier, that he'd offered up his life to protect his country.

That he'd been a volunteer for this program.

Only...he and the others were kept in cells. *Cages.* White rooms that had no windows. And when they left their cells, guards always followed them around the facility.

They had zero contact with the outside world unless they were hunting their prey, completing a mission. The set-up was wrong, and he knew it. "I had a name before," his voice was flat. "We all did. So why the hell do you people just call us by numbers?"

She swallowed. "I...I was told not to use your names because we didn't want to create any false memories."

Bullshit. He didn't buy that story. "Maybe it's just easier to treat us as numbers and not people." He surged to his feet and strode for the door. "I think we're done for today."

Cecelia hurried after him. "But, One, wait—"

He whirled toward her. "I have a name." And in his mind, he could see Elizabeth, could hear her say...

Sawyer.

The shrink didn't respond, but her gaze *did* swing toward the video camera that was positioned in the nearby corner, right next to the ceiling. Their sessions weren't private, he knew that. Noting was private in the Lazarus facility. Someone was always watching. Yet another thing that made the place wrong. *Being under constant surveillance isn't normal.* He yanked open the door and stormed into the hallway.

And he almost ran straight into Elizabeth.

His hands flew out as he prepared to steady her. He could see two of the facility's guards rushing forward—

"We're fine," Elizabeth called out to them. "Stay back."

Instantly, they heeded her command. The new doc obviously had a whole lot of authority.

His fingers curled around her shoulders as he steered her to the side, moving them away from Cecelia's office. He lowered his head, bringing his face close to hers. "I have a name."

She licked her lips. "You seem stressed today."

Stressed? She had no clue. Driven to push her, driven to find out just how many lies were being told, he whispered, "You know my name."

And he saw it. The flicker of her lashes. The stutter of her breath. He could lie well, but the new doc couldn't. His hold tightened on her. "Say my name."

The guards were inching closer. Probably because he had his hands on the doc and was holding her too tightly. The subjects weren't supposed to touch the doctors. That was a rule. No physical contact, only that necessary for exams. But his hands were tight on Dr. Elizabeth Parker.

"*Say it.*" A snarled order that burst from him.

One of the guards shot forward and grabbed him. "You need to back away," the guy blasted.

But...

"Sawyer," Elizabeth said, the word barely more than a breath, but he heard it. *His* name. His heart pounded wildly in his chest as he let out a guttural growl. The guard was pulling him away from Elizabeth, but One — *Sawyer, my name is fucking Sawyer!* — shoved the bastard back. He grabbed for Elizabeth, yanking her against him, and she *felt* familiar.

An alarm began blaring overhead. The second guard grabbed Sawyer's shoulders, but Sawyer just ignored the guy. Sawyer's hands were on Elizabeth, and he wasn't letting her go. "What else do you know about me?"

Fear flashed in her dark eyes, and something...something deep inside of him broke loose.

"Get your hands off her, One!" the guard pressed his gun to Sawyer's back.

Regular bullets weren't in that gun. Sawyer knew the gun was just loaded with tranqs. The guards wouldn't actually risk killing him or any of the other subjects there. They were too valuable. The prisoners – *the weapons* – were too valuable.

"What else do you know?" Sawyer demanded of the doc. "Tell me. Fucking *tell me.*"

The alarm kept blaring. More guards were coming. They were going to take him away from her. Rage twisted inside of him. Growing stronger. *I'm not a caged animal.* They weren't going to keep treating him like one.

The rage grew, as did a thick darkness that swept through his mind. *Attack. Destroy.*

He whirled, fast, and he yanked the gun right out of the hand of the bastard who'd been digging the muzzle into Sawyer's back. He fired without hesitation, and the bullet—the tranq— shoved into the chest of the guard. The guy went down.

Elizabeth screamed.

Sawyer whirled back at the sound and saw that horror was on her face. Horror on her face and terror in her eyes.

I've seen that look before.

Every muscle in his body locked down. "Elizabeth—"

"*Get away from the woman, now!*" The other guards were closing in, and one had just shouted that order at him.

Sawyer didn't hesitate. He grabbed Elizabeth, shoved her behind him so she'd be safe, and he fired. He aimed with cold accuracy and squeezed the trigger. *One down, two down, three…*

His shots flew right into his targets. The men fell in the hallway.

"Stop it!" Elizabeth screamed. *"Stop! This isn't you! Stop attacking them!"*

He turned back to her. "Tranqs. They aren't…dead."

Tears slid down her cheeks. It was wrong for her to be crying. Wrong for her to be afraid. Everything that was happening…it was just *wrong*.

His left hand lifted—the hand that didn't grip the gun. His fingers brushed over her cheek, wiping away a tear. "Don't cry, doc," Sawyer told her. "Don't—"

The tranq slammed into his back. Sawyer grunted and twisted his body, turning his head so that he could see the shooter. His gaze fell on the open doorway to the left, the doorway that led to Cecelia Gregory's office. Cecelia stood in that doorway, her hand gripping a gun. Her face was stark white, and her body was shaking.

The tranq was in his system, Sawyer could feel it snaking through his bloodstream—an icy cold that would soon overwhelm him. But, unlike the guards who littered the floor, Sawyer didn't collapse immediately. His body was different, and it took longer for the tranq to take him out.

He was building an immunity to the damn thing. *Soon, it won't impact me.* Soon.

His weapon was trained on the shrink. He could pull the trigger and knock her out with the hit but…

But I won't.

"Don't," Elizabeth said, her fingers sliding over his and, just like that, she was in front of him. The gun was at her chest.

Wrong. Wrong. Wrong.

Because he had a terrible vision filling his head right then. Of Elizabeth rushing in front of him. Of him holding a gun, of Elizabeth…falling. Being shot. He could see her blood — Elizabeth's blood soaked her shirt.

The gun dropped from his hand, and he wrapped his arms around her, pulling her against him. "Sorry!" The cry burst from him. *Elizabeth, bleeding, shot…* "Can't hurt…*you*…" Talking was hard. The tranq had iced his whole body. He could feel it move through his veins. It had already made his tongue turn thick in his mouth. "*Never…hurt…you…*"

His knees gave way. They fell to the floor, but he twisted, making sure his body hit and cushioned hers. He held her close, locking her against him. He couldn't let her go. Not Elizabeth. *His* Elizabeth.

Their mouths were close. He could see the tear tracks on her face. He could see —

"I'm going to help you," Elizabeth whispered. "I swear."

The words were only for him.

And they were the last thing he heard before the heavy darkness surrounded him completely.

Fucking tranq.

When he woke up, there was going to be hell to pay.

CHAPTER EIGHT

"Are you okay?"

Elizabeth exhaled slowly and tried to school her features. Sawyer's slack body was being dragged away, and she wanted to rush after him.

Don't. Stay in control.

"Uh, Dr. Parker? I…I'm Cecelia Gregory. I'm the psychiatrist here at the facility. I was told you were coming here—only I certainly didn't expect to meet you under these circumstances."

Elizabeth turned and found Cecelia Gregory staring at her with a wide, nervous stare. She knew Cecelia was the shrink who was supposed to be monitoring all of the Lazarus subjects. Sawyer had been in the room with Cecelia before he'd come rushing out into the hallway, his body tight with tension.

What happened in that room?

Elizabeth nodded to the other woman. "I'm fine. Thank you."

Cecelia looked down at the weapon she still held in her hand. "Landon told me to keep this, just in case. I always feared the moment when I'd have to use it—" She turned and went back into her office, and Elizabeth followed her. Cecelia put the weapon on her desk. "Just a tranq." Cecelia's shoulders were stiff. "I was assured all weapons in the facility were only loaded with tranqs. Subjects aren't to be killed, just contained."

Elizabeth's stare swept over the office. There was no missing the video camera and its little green light. *Always watching.* Elizabeth glanced over her shoulder. The unconscious guards were being moved—a new team had swept into the area as soon as Sawyer went down. She had no doubt that Landon would be rushing to intercept her at any moment. So she'd better ask her questions, fast. "Has, um, has One ever exhibited aggression like this before? Has he attacked the guards?" *Please say no, please—*

"I think they're all becoming a bit more...aggressive." Cecelia exhaled as she faced Elizabeth. Cecelia propped her hip against the side of her desk. "It's only to be expected, really, given the way we treat them here. We can't tell them that they're free men, but treat them like prisoners. We can't keep them in cages and send them out just to hunt and expect them to be perfectly behaved when they return. We can't give them *numbers* and strip them of their identities and expect—" She broke off, clamping her lips together. "Sorry. I—it's been a rough morning."

Elizabeth sidled closer to her. The shrink didn't like what was happening at Lazarus, that was obvious. Good. Maybe the woman could be an ally. Elizabeth made sure to position her body between Cecelia and the video camera. She made her voice as quiet as possible as she asked, "How much do you know about Lazarus?"

A furrow appeared between Cecelia's brows. "What?"

"I—"

"*Elizabeth!*" Landon's voice boomed from the doorway, making her jerk in surprise. "Dear God, I saw the security feed!"

Why couldn't the guy have waited a few more moments before appearing? She schooled her features and glanced his way. "I'm okay."

Landon rushed into the room. He put his hands on her shoulders and pulled her toward him. "I thought he was going to attack you!" His cheeks were stained red. "It was just like before! I knew it could be dangerous if you were put in his path—"

Cecelia cleared her throat. "Um, excuse me? Does anyone want to tell me *exactly* what's happening here? *Before*? Before what? I thought Dr. Parker was new—"

Landon's gaze flew to the video camera. His lips clamped together. In an instant, he yanked his hands away from Elizabeth and straightened to his full height. "Dr. Gregory." He glowered at the shrink. "You were supposed to report any aggressive instances *immediately.* Your sole job here is to monitor the test subjects. For us to have an incident right after a subject left your office for a session...that's inexcusable."

Cecelia jumped away from her desk. "Hold up. You're blaming this on me? *Me?* I'm operating in the dark here! You and the other jerk in charge have barely given me enough information to work with my patients. I keep telling you that they need to be given normal rooms, not cells. That they should have access to the outside world, and not just on their missions! They are all like ticking time bombs because of this unnatural lifestyle."

"Subject One was a bomb who exploded today." Landon was grim. "This *cannot* happen again. If it happens again..." His gaze darted to the camera, then back to Elizabeth. "We certainly don't want to have to end this research project."

End it? Was he saying — was the guy threatening to *kill* the test subjects?

Landon pointed his index finger at Cecelia. "I want a full report on my desk immediately — and be ready to come in and brief Wright via teleconference within the hour. You know after this situation, he will want to talk directly with you. We can't afford these mistakes, not if we want this facility to succeed." His hand dropped.

Once more, he looked back at Elizabeth. "You're…you're sure he didn't hurt you?"

"I'm fine."

Landon leaned in close to her. "See, Elizabeth, it's just like I told you. He's nothing but a weapon now. Aim and fire. The man you knew is *gone*."

She flinched.

Landon backed away. "I need to go and check in on One. Subject One *and* the guards who were taken out." He marched out of the office, his lab coat flapping behind him.

Elizabeth pulled out her phone. No service, of course, not in this place, but she didn't really want service. She typed out a quick text, and then, instead of trying to send it, she just lifted her phone toward Cecelia. She didn't know how sensitive the audio surveillance might be in that room, so she figured she'd better play things safe.

Is there a place we can go and not be watched?

Cecelia's head inclined in the briefest of nods. Without saying a word, Cecelia hurried from the office, and Elizabeth followed right on the psychiatrist's heels.

***

"That didn't last long."

Sawyer opened his eyes and found the asshat, Dr. Landon Meyer, glowering at him.

Landon's brows were pulled low over his eyes. The glasses were slightly tilted on his nose. "The tranq isn't keeping you under for as long now. Not as long as it *should* be keeping you sedated."

Sawyer lunged up toward him—only to be jerked back by the chains around his wrists.

No…not chains. Handcuffs are around my wrists. But those cuffs are connected to the wall by a chain. Fuck. He was back in his cell, and he'd been *secured*. That was the term the bastards at the facility used whenever anyone got out of line. The subjects were put back in their cells and locked down with the cuffs.

"Definite high aggression," Landon muttered. His gaze raked over Sawyer. "I hope this is just a fluke, One."

I have a name.

"You took out quite a few guards today. You attacked men who are here just to keep you and the others safe." He opened the black bag at his feet and pulled out a stethoscope. "How can we possibly trust you to keep leading missions, if you are attacking those on your own side?"

They aren't on my side. "Tired of being a prisoner." Each word was guttural. "You said I was a fucking volunteer…then why am I caged?" He jerked up his hands, and the handcuffs gleamed under the light. "Why am I in these?"

"For your protection." Landon's hold on the stethoscope tightened. "And for the protection of the employees who work in this facility. Do you even remember how out of control you were before Dr. Gregory administered the tranq? I mean, you were terrifying Elizabeth Parker. She's new here, and she certainly never expected to face your fury—"

"I didn't attack Elizabeth."

Landon blinked.

"I would *never* hurt her."

Landon's lips twisted, as if he'd just been told some joke. "Really? Are you quite sure about that?"

What in the hell?

Then Landon's body straightened. "Sit back on the bed. I need to perform an exam on you—check your heart rate, get a blood sample, find out why you're responding so differently now to the tranq—"

"Good luck with that shit," Sawyer cut in. "I'm not in the mood to be poked or prodded."

A guard stood just behind Landon. A guard who already had his weapon pointed right at Sawyer. Sawyer gave the guy a go-to-hell grin. "You gonna shoot? I bet you won't." He turned his grin on Landon. "If I'm unconscious, those test results just won't be the same, will they? The tranq will slow down my heart rate, it'll—"

"I don't want you unconscious." Frustration boiled in Landon's voice. "I'm on your side. We are all working together here at the Lazarus facility."

He didn't buy that shit, and Sawyer decided to push the guy. "Really? If we're all on the same team, then get Dr. Parker in here to perform my exam."

Landon's eyes widened. "The woman you just attacked?"

I didn't attack her!

"You actually think she wants to be anywhere near you now?"

Sawyer's muscles tensed. "I *won't* hurt her. And you can keep a guard with us every second." That guy with the gun didn't have to leave. "Dr. Parker can exam me, and I can make sure she understands that she was never in any danger from me."

"No danger…" Landon laughed. "If you're not dangerous, then what about those guards you shot? Want to tell me why you went so wild?"

Because I wanted my name.

"No? No answer? See, that's part of the problem, One. I feel like you're holding back on me. I feel like *all* of the subjects have been holding back, and that just can't happen." He squared his shoulders. "As far as Dr. Parker is concerned, you don't give the orders. You don't get to dictate to me and say that she has to be brought to you.

That isn't the way things work here. You might lead in the field, but inside the Lazarus walls," he stepped closer to Sawyer. "*I'm* in charge."

A dull ache pounded inside Sawyer's head. Rage ate at him, the dark fury that seemed to be growing stronger lately, but he didn't let the emotion show. He kept his control in place. Sawyer's gaze swept over Landon. Even with the cuffs binding him, Sawyer could knock that guy out in two seconds flat. The fool had gotten too close to Sawyer. It would be so easy to take him down.

But I can't reach the guard. He's too far away. He'll shoot me, and I'll be out until the tranq pushes from my system again. He was so tired of this shit. There had to be a way to end the nightmare. To get answers.

Elizabeth. Elizabeth is my key.

Landon smirked at him. "Ready for your exam?"

Are you ready for an ass kicking?

No, dammit, wrong response. He had to play this scene right. He had to think, and he had to plan. Sawyer lifted his bound hands. "Go the fuck ahead." *For now. But your time is coming, Landon. Sooner than you think.*

***

Cold air filled the women's locker room. Cecelia glanced around, her body tense, as if she were double-checking to be certain that she and Elizabeth were truly alone in that area.

They were.

"No cameras," Cecelia said quietly. "Can't be, you know. Since women are changing in here. It's um, a workout space that Wright put in for us. I don't know if you've had a chance to fully explore the facility yet, but the exercise area is—"

"I don't care about that," Elizabeth cut in. She didn't give a damn about the Lazarus exercise program. "Tell me about Subject One. What happened to him in your office? Why did he go tearing out like that?"

Cecelia hesitated. "How do I know I can trust you?"

You can't.

"I mean, all I know is that your name is Dr. Elizabeth Parker, and you were handpicked by Wright, just as I was." She gave a bitter laugh. "Let me guess, he gave you an offer you couldn't pass up, right?"

"Right." No way would she have walked away from the chance to get in that facility.

"His offers sound good on the surface." Cecelia's lashes swept down to cover her gaze. "Then you realize that you're in deep, and there is no going back."

Elizabeth shifted her stance. "You want to help the test subjects." Elizabeth sure hoped she was reading the other woman correctly.

Cecelia nodded. "They're all here voluntarily, I get that, but surely they should be treated better—"

Don't be too sure about them being here voluntarily.

"The confinement, the missions, the solitary life that has been created for them—it isn't healthy. I keep being told to monitor them for aggressive behavior, and I am seeing more and more of that aggression. They need outlets. They need relief before the situation gets out of control."

Elizabeth was pretty sure things were already at the out-of-control point. "How long have you been monitoring the subjects?"

"Two months. And they've become tenser during that time. A few of them…during our sessions…" Her hand rose to the base of her throat. "They've started to make me uncomfortable."

That wasn't good. "What do you mean?"

Cecelia held her gaze. "It's in the way they look at me. Too focused. Too intense. And I…I feel like they may be lying to me when I question them."

Elizabeth's stomach was in knots. "If this is happening, why in the hell are they even sent out on missions? That doesn't make sense to me! Why send them—"

"They're suicide missions."

Those knots in her stomach got worse.

Cecelia gave a rough laugh. "Surely you realize that? The men here are the ones who volunteered to handle the worst of the worst. They are given the missions that have a low hope of survival. That's why the men here are the only ones who can handle those cases. Because they are the ones who agreed their lives were expendable."

They never made that agreement. Their lives ended. She forced out a slow breath. "If the men don't want to stay here, why do they come back from the missions? Why not run—"

"Because they are monitored. Every single step of the way. A tracker is put on their ankles, one that only Landon can remove. He keeps a lock on their locations for the entire time they are gone, and then the crew is picked up once their mission is complete."

Another piece of the puzzle slid into place. She'd wondered exactly what Landon had meant before and now she knew.

"The men are enhanced," Cecelia continued flatly. "And I guess...maybe giving up their freedom was the price they paid for increased strength and speed. For a healing ability that blows my mind. But I don't like this situation. I don't like it at all."

Join the club. "Tell me about what happened today with Subject One." She needed to know what had sent Sawyer running from Cecelia's office.

But the shrink shook her head. "I've already said too much. I know the nature of this job means I can't give those patients the confidentiality they deserve, that I have to share my analysis with Landon, but I don't know *you* — I don't know whose side you are on here."

Sawyer's side, dammit!

"Maybe you're just like Wright. After the bottom line. I can't be like that. I need to try and help these men. This experiment — it changed their lives. No, it *obliterated* their lives. They were like robots when I first met them. Following the commands they were given, no emotions impacting them, but…that's changing."

"Changing how?"

"They lost their memories. The personal memories that made them into the men they were. They woke as blank slates, and I think that is the way Wright thought they would stay."

Excitement had her pushing up onto the balls of her feet. "They're not staying blank. That's what you're saying? They're remembering their old lives?"

Cecelia's lips pressed together.

"Don't stop now!" Elizabeth was practically begging. "I want to help them, I swear, I do. I want to make a difference with these men. I am not the enemy. I truly want to make things right!"

And she'd just misspoke. Elizabeth could tell that Cecelia had caught what she'd said because the woman's eyes narrowed to slits.

"Want to make things *right*?" Cecelia repeated as she backed up a step. "That would mean…just what did you do wrong?"

Elizabeth didn't reply.

Cecelia's expression shut down. "I have another appointment waiting."

Dammit. "Dr. Gregory—"

"I think we've both said enough for the time being." Cecelia turned on her heel and began to walk away.

"No, we haven't," Elizabeth called out. Cecelia kept walking. "I didn't say thank you!"

Cecelia stilled.

"You thought Saw—you thought Subject One was going to hurt me, so you stopped him. You were trying to save me, and I won't forget that." Cecelia had helped her. And Cecelia legitimately seemed interested in helping the subjects at the facility.

Now Cecelia glanced back at her. Her brows had risen. "You weren't afraid."

Elizabeth wasn't sure what the woman meant. She'd pretty much been living in a state of fear ever since this nightmare began. *A nightmare I helped to create.*

"When Subject One had you in that hallway, you didn't try to run from him or fight him."

Cecelia spoke consideringly now. "Why? Running would have been a natural response. So would fighting. And you didn't *freeze*. I saw you. You were staying at his side willingly."

The psychiatrist apparently saw far too much. Elizabeth would have to be more careful. She lifted her chin as she strode toward the other woman. "Everyone responds to fear differently. Surely you, of all people, realize that." She brushed past Cecelia. It was definitely time for this little chat to end. The shrink was too insightful with her observations.

But Cecelia's hand flew out and curved around Elizabeth's arm. "You're not afraid of One."

She remembered the thunder of a gunfire. The sight of a lab littered with the dead. "Trust me, I am. But fear can't stop us, can it?"

Cecelia let her go. Elizabeth kept her spine straight and her steps slow as she headed for the exit. Elizabeth's fingers had just closed around the door handle when she heard the shrink's soft voice say, "It's okay…I'm afraid of them, too."

CHAPTER NINE

She shouldn't be there. She should *not* be standing in front of Sawyer's cell. Elizabeth knew she was running a risk, but she hadn't been able to stop herself. She'd waited until everyone else had turned in for bed. The Lazarus facility was freaking huge — cut into the side of the mountain, the place just stretched and stretched as it tunneled underground. She had quarters there now, a studio apartment right next to Cecelia. Moving *into* the facility had been one of Wright's conditions. He'd wanted her back, but he'd said that in order for her to work at Lazarus, she had to stay inside the base.

So now she was as trapped as the others. *But only for the time being.*

She'd needed to see Sawyer again. Elizabeth had desperately wanted to speak with him, so she'd waited until just before midnight, waited until she thought it would be the perfect time to slip out of her quarters...

And then she'd gone running to Sawyer.

She'd been careful, though. That day, she'd learned all about the placement of the security cameras. She'd learned the schedules for the guards. She'd learned how to stay in the shadows. Elizabeth had always been a very fast learner. And *maybe* she'd even paid a visit to the guards in the main security room after dinner. *Maybe* she'd chatted them up, distracted them, and uploaded a tiny little virus into their computer system while they weren't looking. A virus that would temporarily take down their video feeds just before midnight.

An undetectable virus, of course. Because she wasn't an amateur. Her expertise didn't just focus on genetics and neurobiology. She'd picked up quite a few tricks over the years. Hacking and computer programming — she'd learned quite a bit about both from an ex-lover. Jennings Maverick — or Jay as he preferred to be called — was a master when it came to computers. He'd taught her plenty, and, when she'd realized that she was getting a chance to head back into Lazarus, Jay had helped her out again. He'd been the one to give her the timed virus to take out the security cameras.

She'd owe him now. Jay always collected on debts that were owed to him.

Elizabeth glanced at her watch, then she eased out a slow breath. It was time. The feeds were down, and she had to get inside the cell with Sawyer. She crept toward his cell door. The trick was going to be getting *in* that cell. She had managed to grab a set of keys from the guards but—

The cell door opened. It opened from the inside. Just when she was about to start trying every single key that she had, Sawyer's door simply swung open. Her mouth dropped in surprise, but then a big, strong hand shot out from the darkness. Callused fingertips curled around her wrist, and she was yanked inside of Sawyer's cell. The door shut behind her, not even making a whisper of sound, and she found herself caged with the door at her back—and Sawyer pressed to her front. He was a big, hulking shadow, dark and dangerous, and it took her a minute to actually *breathe*. When she did manage to suck in a deep breath, she immediately expelled it with a cry of, "*You're not locked inside! You can get out anytime you—*"

His hand covered her mouth.

Fear spiked inside of her.

He moved even closer to her, and Sawyer's mouth feathered over her ear as he rasped, "I'm going to need you to keep that sexy voice of yours at whisper level, doc. Wouldn't want the wrong people knowing that you just slipped into my room."

Her heart nearly burst right out of her chest.

"Stop." More than a hint of anger was in his growled word. "I won't hurt you." His hand slid away from her mouth. His fingers trailed down her body, going to curve around her hip as he held her against him.

It wasn't exactly easy to turn off fear. And his touch only made things worse. "H-how…" That was all she could manage and the word definitely came out as a whisper. Or more like a weak breath.

"How did I pick the lock on my cell? Easy. Took about three seconds. I've been able to come and go as I please since pretty much day one." Again, the words were whispered against her, but she felt the edge of his lips on the shell of her ear, and Elizabeth shivered.

His body pressed even closer to hers.

"The lock isn't a challenge. The tricky part is timing my exits so that the video cameras don't see me."

"But…the guards…" She knew they patrolled, too. She'd been worried about making sure they didn't see her during her little visit. If they looked through that one-way glass…

He gave a faint laugh and this time, she thought his *tongue* swept against her ear.

Elizabeth stopped breathing.

"I can always tell *exactly* where the guards are. Let's just say that I can truly hear them coming from a mile off. Just as I heard you coming to me."

Her breath expelled in a startled rush. So the guy had just been waltzing around Lazarus at night, doing whatever he wanted—for weeks?

Sawyer Cage isn't the man you knew before. Be very, very careful. Jay had told her that when she'd spilled the whole dark story to him and begged for his help. He'd been hesitant, to say the least. He'd told her she was walking straight into a minefield.

And he hadn't wanted to see her explode.

"Are the others...do they get out, too?" Her whisper was weak.

"Like I'd tell you that, doc."

Was that a yes? A no? A fuck off?

"What I want to know..." That was *definitely* his tongue sliding against her ear, and Elizabeth could not control a shiver in the dark. "I want to know why you were sneaking into my room."

"I-I was worried...wanted to check on—"

"*Lie.*"

Her lips parted.

"Your heart sped up too much when you lied." Again, she heard anger in his voice. "Don't lie to me, doc. Not ever again. I can tell when you lie. I will always be able to tell."

Was that true? No, surely not. He wasn't some kind of human lie detector. He wasn't—

I don't know what he is, not anymore. Because of me and Landon, because we messed with the laws of nature, I don't know what we have now.

She wasn't even sure *what* Sawyer was any longer.

"You know me." His fingers tightened on her hip.

"Y-yes…You're Subject One here at Lazarus, you—"

He nipped her ear lobe. She was so surprised that she started to give a little cry, but—

His hand flew back up to cover her mouth. So fast. Way too fast.

"Don't lie, doc. You know me. I know you." His rasp was dark and dangerous, and her shivers just got worse. "Intimately."

What?

His hand was still over her mouth, and she was nervous and scared and completely freaking out, and she *accidentally* licked his palm.

When she did…

Elizabeth felt his body stiffen. He'd already been aroused, there had been no missing the length of his cock shoving against her, but his erection stiffened even more. Longer, thicker, harder. And the very air around her changed. It heated. Seemed to thicken.

Slowly, his hand lifted from her mouth once more. Only this time, his fingers brushed carefully over her lips.

She had to fight the urge to open her mouth. To lick his index finger, to take it inside her mouth—

He's not the man you remember. You are all messed up! Stop it, Elizabeth!

She'd always had a weak spot for Sawyer. He touched her, and her body erupted. Their physical attraction had surprised her, at first. And the fact that it had only gotten stronger after they became lovers...

His fingers slid down her throat. "No more lies."

She couldn't make that promise. She didn't know if she could trust him, but she desperately wanted to help him. He'd never volunteered for this life. She knew that truth, even if the others at Lazarus—others like Cecelia—had bought Landon's lies.

"You know me." His fingers were at the base of her throat. She knew he had to feel the frantic beat of her pulse. "You know my name."

Her eyes widened. Her vision had adjusted a bit to the darkness in his cell. She could just make out the hard lines and edges of his face. They were positioned in such a way that she knew the video camera in his room couldn't see them. Even if her little virus hadn't done its job, Sawyer was making sure no one saw them. "I—"

"Sawyer," he growled. "You know my name. *Don't lie.*"

She wouldn't, couldn't. "Yes." Hope was there, bursting inside of her. Was he remembering? Could the man she'd known be trapped deep inside, desperately trying to break free to the surface? "You're…*Sawyer.*" Once, he'd been *her* Sawyer.

And then she'd turned him into a nightmare. *I'm so sorry. I never wanted this for you.*

One of his legs slid between hers. A powerful, muscled thigh brushed against her. "I know what you look like…" Such low, growled words. "When you climax for me. I know what it sounds like…when you call my name as you come."

He remembers! "Sawyer—"

He jerked against her. "And I know…what you taste like."

She licked her lips. Landon had been wrong. Sawyer's memory was there, it was—

"How the hell do I know any of that?"

Before she could answer, his mouth was on hers. He was kissing her, hard and deep and wildly. No tentative touch of a new lover. He was taking. He was claiming. Kissing her with passion and familiarity. Kissing her the way she loved to be kissed by him. As if she were the only woman who'd ever mattered to him. As if he couldn't get through another single second without her, as if—

"Just like in my dream..." His voice was gruff. "*Just like in my damn —* "

An alarm blared. The shriek was high and echoing, and Sawyer jerked back from her. "Lockdown," he gritted out. "Fuck." Then he was wrenching her back from the door — opening it, and shoving her *out* of his cell as the alarm kept blaring. "Sixty seconds until all the doors are sealed. Get your ass moving, doc."

What?

"*Get moving!*"

She stumbled away from his cell, keeping to the shadows she'd memorized. She ran toward her quarters, moving as fast as she could. And as she rushed away, Elizabeth was counting down in her head.

Forty, thirty-nine...

She wasn't sure she'd make it to her room.

Twenty, nineteen...

She slipped around a corner in the hallway. Dammit, she was too far away from her quarters, but the main lab was right there —

Six, five...

Elizabeth shoved open the door to the lab. She had the key code for that place, and her breath burst out of her as —

Two, one —

The blaring stopped. Behind her, the door she'd just opened — she heard a long, loud *clang* as it closed and sealed shut.

Elizabeth spun around. She twisted the handle on that door, but it didn't open. She tried using her code, but the lock wouldn't disengage. *"Lockdown."* Sawyer's whisper played in her head, and she realized exactly what had just happened. The alarm had been sounded by someone—and every room in the facility had been sealed shut. The scene was like a very, very extreme prison lockdown. Sweat covered her body as she backed away from the door. Had this happened because of her? Had the virus she uploaded been detected? So much for Jay and his perfect plans. Crap. She had to *think, think* and—

"The facility is secured." The announcement seemed to echo around her as it blasted from the intercom system. "Guards will be conducting a room by room sweep for everyone's safety."

Her eyes squeezed closed. She'd screwed up. Barely in the place, and now she'd be sent away. Time crept by in painful silence as she stood, trapped, in the lab. There had to be a way out of this mess. A way to help Sawyer. A way to help—

The clang sounded again. *The clang of the lock.* Only this time, the clang wasn't because the door was locking—it was being unsealed. Opened. Her eyes flew open, and she found herself staring into Landon's wide eyes. He wasn't wearing his glasses, and his hair was disheveled. He entered the lab first, followed quickly by an armed guard. "Thank God," he exclaimed, relief evident on his face. "After Cecelia sounded the alarm, I was worried something might have happened to you."

Cecelia had sounded the alarm?

"I-I was just coming to do some research." The lie fell from her lips. The guy wasn't Sawyer, so she didn't worry about any human lie detecting tricks coming from him. "You know me, I can never sleep well. Since I was here, I thought I'd come to the lab and do some work—"

Landon caught her wrist and pulled her close. "How long have you been in here?"

His hold was too tight.

"I, uh, don't know. I lose track of time when I'm working."

He grunted. Landon would buy that excuse because it was true. She *did* lose track of time when she worked. She'd gone twelve hours once without any food, and he'd been the one to force her to take a break.

"Did you see anyone?" Landon demanded as his gaze darted around the lab. "Hear anything strange while you were in here?"

"I...what do you mean?" What exactly was happening?

"Security cameras have been down since eleven."

What? Wait, that wasn't due to her virus. It had been timed to take the system down right before midnight.

"And Cecelia swears she woke up to find someone in her room." He was pulling her toward the door and then out into the corridor. "I think she scared him off with the alarm, but we have got to figure out what is happening here." He was walking so fast that she stumbled to keep up with him. "If someone is trying to steal our secrets—"

She dug in her heels. There were guards running all around, and she knew they were checking every room, looking for an intruder. "You think someone broke in? This place is like Fort Knox! It took *forever* just for me to get inside. I passed so many check-ins that I lost count." No, she hadn't. "How would anyone get past your guards?"

He stopped and leaned in close to her. "You know how valuable the Lazarus formula is. It's literally something people would *kill* to possess. It wouldn't be the first time we had an attempted break-in." He started walking—more like nearly running—as he practically dragged Elizabeth down the corridor with him. "We'll need to heighten our security even more."

They rushed through the hallways, and Landon barked out orders to the guards they passed. Her thundering heartbeat filled

Elizabeth's ears. Her feet rushed over the tiled floor, and, a few minutes later, they were back in front of her quarters. Nearby, Cecelia stood in her doorway, wearing a white robe, her hair trailing over her shoulders. Her eyes were big and stark, and she appeared far too pale.

"No one will steal the Lazarus technology," Landon swore. "We'll find the bastard." Then he nodded grimly toward a guard who stood poised and ready just a few feet away from Cecelia. "Stay here, Hugh, and keep a watch on them while I finish helping to search the facility."

After giving that order, Landon vanished. Didn't even say anything else before he rushed off — looking for his intruder.

As directed, the guard stayed close by. "You'll be safe, doctors." He gave them a nod. "I'll be right here if you need me."

If they needed —

Elizabeth hurried toward Cecelia. "What happened?"

Cecelia jerked her head toward Elizabeth's door. "You...you weren't there. I screamed for you, but you weren't there." Her voice was husky.

Elizabeth winced. "I was in the lab, working."

Cecelia just stared at her. *What? Can she tell when I'm lying, too?*

Elizabeth looped her arm with Cecelia's. "Come on. Let's go in my quarters. No sense in us staying in the corridor all night." They went into Elizabeth's room, and she felt the watchful eyes of the guard on them.

"I can't go back into my space," Cecelia said. "Not until the guards have searched for fingerprints and DNA—"

Shit, but that was intense. "You can stay with me tonight. I've got plenty of room." So maybe *plenty* was a small stretch, but they could easily make do. "Um, why don't you take the bed? I can sleep on the sofa." She shut the door behind them, blocking the guard's gaze.

Cecelia stood at her side, not advancing toward the bed. "Were you really in the lab?"

No, I wasn't. Elizabeth strode away from the door. "What happened tonight? The alarm started blaring, and the next thing I knew, the lab was sealed. I couldn't get out." That part, at least, was true.

"*All* of the doors seal during a lockdown. It's a secondary locking mechanism, part of our security system here. When I realized someone was in my room, I ran—and I hit the lockdown code in the hallway. The rooms remain locked until they have been cleared, one by one." She wrapped her arms around her stomach. "He was standing right over me when I woke up. The room was so dark, but I could *feel* him."

Elizabeth blinked. "Slow down, Cecelia. Start over for me."

Cecelia shook her head. "They aren't going to find him. It will be just like before."

Elizabeth got a very, very bad feeling in the pit of her stomach. "I don't understand."

Cecelia glanced at her. "This is the second time he's come into my room. Sneaks right in. I-I think he watches me."

That bad feeling got worse. "Landon believes someone is trying to steal the Lazarus technology." But...why be in Cecelia's room if that was the case? Cecelia didn't know much about the design of the Lazarus serum. She knew that it made stronger, faster, better warriors, but she didn't know how the compound was created. *She doesn't even know we've brought these men back from the dead.*

"Landon is looking for someone who broke *into* the facility." Cecelia's gaze darted back to the closed door. "I'm worried he should be focused on someone who is already here, already inside." She wrapped her arms around her stomach. "I think the test subjects are deceiving us. I think they can get out of their rooms."

They can.

Cecelia's worried stare came back to Elizabeth. "And I think—for the second time— one of them broke into my room."

The breath that Elizabeth drew in chilled her lungs.

"Increased aggression," Cecelia murmured. "That's what I was originally brought on to watch out for, but I'm worried that's just the tip of the iceberg."

Goosebumps covered Elizabeth's arms.

"The government made stronger, *better* soldiers, but the side effects I'm seeing aren't just faster healing abilities or quicker reflexes." Cecelia shook her head. "I think they all grew smarter, I think…I think the darkness inside of them—the very thing that made them such good soldiers in the first place—I think that darkness got worse, too."

"Have you told this to Landon?"

Cecelia nodded.

"And what has he done? What did he say?"

"He said their darkness isn't a weakness. It's a strength." Cecelia gave a grim shake of her head. "But he's wrong."

***

When his door swung open, Sawyer opened his eyes. Landon and two guards rushed in, sweeping flashlights into every corner of the space. Yawning, Sawyer stretched. "There a problem?"

"We may have a facility breach," Landon said, his voice clipped. "Have you seen or heard anything unusual tonight?"

Sawyer sat up on his bed. "Not a thing. I was sleeping, until the alarm started blaring. After it stopped, I figured everything was all right, so I laid back down." He shrugged, as if to say…*but that's when you guys burst inside.*

"It's clear," the heavy-set guard announced.

Sawyer raised a brow. "Of course, it is. Don't you think I'd notice if someone were in the room with me?"

Landon just growled.

"And wouldn't *you* notice?" Sawyer added dryly. "Not like it's a secret that you guys have special one-way glass in our cells. And you watch our every move with your cameras."

Landon didn't respond. The guy spun and marched out. The guards immediately followed. When the door closed behind them, Sawyer exhaled slowly.

Doc, I sure as hell hope you got clear in time.

He spread his body out over the narrow bed, staring up at the ceiling above him. A faint tremble shook his fingers, so he balled his hands into fists.

Elizabeth Parker knew him, and he knew her.

Sawyer. My name is Sawyer. He'd had a life before he woke in hell. A life that was connected to the doctor's. The image of him with the doc—

that hadn't just been a dream. It had been a memory. He knew what the sexy doctor looked like when she was naked. He knew the way she sounded when she came. He knew the way she felt against him.

They'd been lovers, no doubt about it. But…

What had happened? How had he wound up with no memory, trapped in hell? And how — how in the fuck had his lover become one of his jailers?

His eyes closed again as he focused on regulating his breathing. In and out. In and…

Hey, One, why are the guards freaking the hell out? The question slipped into his mind, rough, rasping.

He turned toward the wall that separated him from the man known as Subject Two. Keeping his eyes closed, Sawyer sent back the fast, mental message. *They're looking for someone.* The telepathic communication was another secret. One that Sawyer and the test subjects hadn't shared with the people at Lazarus. The soldiers had enhanced strength, enhanced speed, fast healing abilities, and they could communicate with each other, telepathically. It was a communication method that took one hell of a lot of energy, so Sawyer didn't do it often. But being able to communicate this way could sure come in handy.

On the battlefield, in enemy territory, and…in hell.

Someone was in your room earlier, Two told him.

Sawyer hesitated.

Don't lie to me, man. I heard her.

Shit. *Keep it quiet. She's mine.* He'd meant to say…*She's my problem.* But the hard and possessive, *She's mine* had slipped out instead.

What's going on? Something wrong with her? There a problem? Two demanded via their link

No. Yes. *She knew me…before.*

He had the impression of rough laughter from Two. *They're the scientists. We're the guinea pigs. Of course, they all knew us before we got the Lazarus serum.*

Two didn't get it. *No. We were lovers.*

Silence. The thick, dangerous kind. Then, again… *There a problem?*

My name…it's Sawyer. He was remembering, and he didn't see that as a problem. He saw it as the best thing that had happened to him in months.

Who is she? Two asked.

A headache built behind Sawyer's temples. Whenever he communicated telepathically for more than a few moments, the headache came. *Dr. Elizabeth Parker.*

Don't remember seeing her around here.

She's new here. As soon as I saw her… But he didn't continue. He didn't really know what to say. As soon as he'd seen her, Elizabeth had seemed familiar, on a deep, primitive level? As soon as he'd seen her, his whole body had stiffened and his heart rate had doubled? As soon as he'd seen her, he'd wanted to grab her and pull her close, and never, ever let go?

As soon as he'd seen her, he'd heard the echo of a woman's scream in his ears?

I want to meet Elizabeth Parker. Two was determined.

And suddenly, the tension was back in Sawyer's body. *She's mine.* He sent out that thought again, but this time, it was a hard warning.

Two didn't respond.

But Sawyer knew the guy had gotten the message, loud and clear.

CHAPTER TEN

"We didn't find any sign of an intruder last night," Landon announced as he stood in the observation room, glowering at the screen to his right. It was a screen that showed Cecelia's office and the man who reclined on her couch.

Subject Number Five.

He was a tall man, with bright, blond hair and glittering, green eyes. Like Sawyer, he was tall and fit, built along the rough and ready battle lines of a soldier. His posture was relaxed, easy, and he stared at Cecelia with a faint smile curving his full lips.

Elizabeth tucked a lock of her hair behind her ear as she watched Cecelia and her patient. She'd been surprised when Landon had brought her into the observation room. The room was filled with different monitors, but, right then, the only monitor working was the one that showed Five's session. "The shrink thinks the guy in her room wasn't an outsider. She thinks it's possible he was one of the test subjects." *Tread carefully, Elizabeth.*

"Highly unlikely. Actually, I'm starting to think the whole thing was a false alarm." Impatience hummed in his voice. "Wright said she was the best psychiatrist out there, that she'd be able to perfectly monitor the subjects, but this is the second time she's jumped at shadows."

Not just any shadow. A man who was watching her.

"I looked into her past."

Her head turned toward Landon in surprise. Now he was spying on the shrink who worked for him?

His gaze was on the screen—on Cecelia. "You know, there's often a reason why people enter their particular fields." Now he glanced at Elizabeth. "Take you, for example. We both know you created Lazarus because of your parents. You became obsessed with death, and your obsession changed the whole course of your life."

She felt heat sting her cheeks. He was right on target with her.

His left hand waved vaguely toward her. "In many ways, Cecelia is like you. So colored by her past. By the things that happened to her. There is plenty of darkness in her personal history. And that darkness came back for her. I think it's plagued her since she was a teenager, and it makes her jump at shadows."

"I don't understand." Actually, she did, but she didn't like the coy *share-a-few-details-*

only game that the guy was playing. If he knew something specific about Cecelia, Elizabeth needed Landon to spill the information.

"When she was fifteen, Cecelia was kidnapped. She was taken right off the street. Held for twenty-four hours and then she escaped."

"How?"

"She shoved a knife into her abductor's throat. That's the *how* part."

Surprise rocked through Elizabeth. Cecelia appeared so delicate—

"And then she dedicated her life to understanding the darkness of the human mind." He paused. "I'm not a shrink, but I figure a woman with her past would have a certain amount of bad dreams or flashbacks."

Her brows lifted. "You're saying she had a flashback last night?"

"I'm saying we found zero evidence to suggest that anyone was in her quarters." His voice hardened. "And if this behavior continues, I'll have no choice but to recommend that Wright replace her. We can't afford distractions like this." He gave her a nod and then headed from the room.

Elizabeth exhaled slowly. Cecelia's fear had been real, she knew it. She also knew that if Sawyer could get out of his cell, then some of the other subjects could, too.

And that scared her.

I came here to help these men but…

What if some of them were too dangerous to help? She *had* to tell Cecelia the truth about Lazarus. Every twisted part of the truth.

***

"You have shadows under your eyes," Five said as his gaze swept over her face. It was a stare that often seemed a bit cold to Cecelia. He lifted one blond brow at her. "Rough night?"

She was sitting behind her desk. Her back was ramrod straight. And her palms were damp with sweat. "We're not here to talk about me."

Five gave a little laugh. It was a deep, rumbling laugh. One that she was sure—in another life and another time—plenty of women had found sexy. Five *was* sexy. He was handsome and fit, and when he smiled, deep slashes appeared in his cheeks. He always said the right thing when she questioned him, always acted perfectly in control but…

There was something about him that set off alarm bells within her. Maybe because he always seemed *too* in control.

"Sorry. Didn't mean to step out of line." His laughter ended, but the faint grin still curled his lips. "Forgot this was all about me and my mental health." His body still appeared relaxed. "Any news on our next mission?"

"I'm not usually briefed on the missions." She learned about them after the fact. Landon had told her the mission intel came on a need-to-know basis. And, apparently, he thought that she didn't need to know about them. Landon was wrong. Then again, she figured he was wrong about plenty of things. "But the missions…" Cecelia cleared her throat. "You enjoy them, don't you?"

His smile stretched. "I was made for them." Again, laughter spilled from him. "I mean, that's why we are all here, right? Why we *volunteered* for the program?" There was just the faintest emphasis on *volunteered*, and her eyes narrowed. "We wanted to be the baddest of the bad, and in return for that, we had to give up our freedom." The smile didn't reach his eyes. She didn't think that it ever did. "That was the price, wasn't it? But I don't expect to pay that price forever." He straightened. "One day, the guy in charge will see what a total success this project has been. We'll pass all of his tests, jump through all of his hoops, and then we'll all be able to walk away. Free and clear. There won't be any more checks-in with shrinks." His gaze hardened, just the faintest bit. "Or nights spent in rooms that resemble prison cells."

He's planning for his freedom. That should have been a good sign. He was looking forward to the next step in his life. He was—

His bright stare slid over her once more. "I'll miss you." His voice dropped. He rose and stalked toward her desk.

Cecelia stiffened. She started to rise but—he was there. Already. So fast. Standing on the opposite side of her desk, but still seeming to tower over her.

"Maybe I'll just have to plan for more visits with you."

This time, she could have sworn that his grin held a cruel edge.

More visits.

She shot to her feet. "What do you—"

The alarm on her desk beeped, signaling the end of her session. The quick, fast beep made her flinch.

He didn't look away from her. "Time's up." Five gave her a little salute. "Thanks for a great chat, Dr. Gregory. Always a pleasure." Then he turned and sauntered toward the door. "I'll send in the next patient."

The door clicked closed behind him. Cecelia realized that her heart was racing too fast. She was on her feet, and her hands were gripping the edge of her desk. Her gaze jerked to the security camera perched in her office. Five's comments had been so careful. *He's always so careful.* There was never any wrong word spoken from him. Was she being too sensitive? Or was there something she was missing? Was—

Her door opened, and her next patient walked inside.

"Hi, there, Cece."

Subject Number Two. Two's brown hair was tousled, as if he'd run his fingers through it time and time again. He probably had. She knew he didn't like coming to the meetings with her. His eyes—an unusual shade of pure gold—swept the room before coming back to her, and then—

He was across her office in an instant. "What's wrong?" When he'd first entered the room, his voice had been light, teasing. That was Two—always putting on the front. And she *knew* it was a front. But for the first time, she could see a crack in his armor. She could see the warrior that she knew him to be. His face had gone iron-hard, and his golden gaze blazed. "What the hell happened?"

She was still gripping the edge of her desk too hard. Cecelia forced herself to let it go. "Nothing, nothing happened." She sucked in a deep breath. "We should get started." Cecelia motioned toward her couch. "You know the drill. Why don't you sit down and we can talk about—"

He didn't sit down. Instead, he walked around the edge of her desk and came right beside her. Far closer than any of the subjects had ever been before. Close enough for her to smell his crisp, masculine scent, close enough for her to feel the heat from his body.

Close enough…to make her afraid. Her hand flew up and pressed to his chest. "Stop!" The command came out sharp and scared.

Two looked down at her hand, and then back up at her face. "You don't need to be afraid of me."

I think I do. Because while Landon might believe that she'd imagined her late night visitor—yes, Cecelia had seen the doubt in the guy's eyes—she knew the truth.

Someone at Lazarus was hunting her. She'd been hunted before, and the terror was familiar to her.

***

Flynn. Elizabeth's hand lifted and pressed to the screen. She'd known Flynn Haddox was at Lazarus, but this was the first time she'd actually seen him since…

Since the day everything turned to ashes around me.

Flynn Haddox. He'd been Sawyer's best friend. His right hand man. Flynn had always worn a ready smile on his face, and he'd quipped jokes constantly.

He wasn't quipping jokes any longer. In fact, he was far too close to Cecelia, and if Elizabeth read the shrink's body language right…

She's afraid of him.

Oh, hell. *Enough.* Cecelia couldn't keep dealing with the subjects without knowing the truth—and without knowing the true danger that she faced. "I need to get in there," Elizabeth said. A guard stood a few feet away, a man who'd been silently watching the entire session with her. Apparently, Landon always made sure a guard watched Cecelia's sessions. Elizabeth had learned that fact this morning.

"Sorry, ma'am, but we don't go in unless there's a damn good reason. Landon's orders."

What? Two was *scaring* Cecelia—that was reason enough for Elizabeth.

"Physical confrontation," the guard said gruffly, as his shoulders squared. "That's when I go inside. I have my orders, ma'am."

Screw his orders. She'd just take matters into her own hands. Elizabeth hurried out of that damn room without another word. She headed straight for Cecelia's office. When she got there, Elizabeth immediately threw open the door. "*Get away from her!*"

Only…

Two—Flynn—wasn't anywhere near Cecelia. The shrink was behind her desk, sitting in her chair, appearing completely poised, while Flynn was lounging on the couch.

But at Elizabeth's very loud interruption, Flynn jumped to his feet. His hands fisted at his sides, and he immediately moved his body…*between* Elizabeth and Cecelia. As if he'd protect the psychiatrist.

"Who in the hell are you?" Flynn demanded roughly.

"I—"

His eyes widened as he stepped closer to her. Elizabeth saw his nostrils flare and then his lips curved the faintest bit. "I know you…" His voice dropped.

He did? He remembered her?

"You're…his."

Flynn's voice had been so low, she wasn't sure she'd even heard that last word.

"Dr. Parker!" Cecelia hurried across the office. "What is going on? You can't burst into a session this way!"

Right. This looked bad. She'd overreacted, but, jeez, better safe than sorry, right? "I thought you were in trouble." Flynn's hands had unfisted, but his body was still tight with tension. She studied him carefully, seeing no sign of the quipping, laid-back guy he'd been before Lazarus. His face seemed harder, his gaze sharper.

"Cecelia is in no danger from me." Flynn rolled back his shoulders. "Haven't you heard? Uh, what was your name? *Dr. Parker?* We're the good guys here at Lazarus. We go out and we save the day. We do the dirty jobs that the government doesn't want anyone else to ever know about." He smiled, but it wasn't a smile she remembered. Far too cold. *He's changed.* "And in return, we get to live in this glorious facility. A true hole in the ground."

"I think we should end our session for today," Cecelia announced quickly. "Two, you have a workout scheduled for ten a.m., anyway—"

He glanced back at her. "Been memorizing my schedule again, have you? See, I knew you were into me."

And there it was—in the light tone of his voice—for just a moment, Elizabeth glimpsed the man he'd been.

But then his golden gaze swept back to Elizabeth, and she saw the light tone was a total lie. His expression was flat and cold. He stared at her as if—as if she were the enemy.

"I'm sorry," Elizabeth's words blurted from her before she could stop them. But she was sorry—sorry for all of this and she just wanted to make things *better*. Was that even possible? Could it be possible?

Flynn closed the distance between them. He wasn't quite as tall as Sawyer, but he was very close, and she had to tip back her head to stare into his eyes. "Now just what would you be apologizing for, Dr. Parker?"

"I—"

"Back the fuck away."

The cold, snarling words came from right behind Elizabeth. Her shoulders stiffened because she recognized the angry voice—she was pretty sure she'd know Sawyer's voice anywhere. Anytime.

Flynn immediately lifted his hands and displayed them—palms out—toward her. *No, toward the man behind me.* "There's no problem here, One. Just a little curiosity." More than a *little* curiosity glinted in Flynn's eyes.

He walked past Elizabeth, taking his time, and she turned as he passed. Sawyer was in the doorway, and a guard waited just a few feet behind him. Odd, though, that Sawyer had been the one to shout the order. *Not* the nervous-looking guard.

And Flynn had immediately obeyed. The hierarchy was clear to Elizabeth.

Sawyer stepped closer to her. His fingers brushed down her arm. "You okay, doc?"

She nodded. "Of course."

He shook his head, and she knew he was calling her on the lie. "I'm going to run training exercises with the team. You should come. You might find them…enlightening."

She'd watched him train before, back in D.C., and she'd found the sight frightening even back then, but he was trying to give her a message, she knew it. He wanted her at the training, so, fine, she'd be there. "I'll be sure to check in."

His gaze held hers for a few moments longer, and she could *feel* the tension between them like a physical presence. Even before he'd spoken, ordering Flynn to stand down, her body had tensed. She'd known he was behind her, without a word. Instinctively. That was crazy but—

The connection between them hadn't ended when he'd died or when he'd come back from the grave. It was as strong and terrifying as ever.

Sawyer inclined his head to her, and then he turned away.

Sawyer and Flynn strode down the hallway. The guard stayed close behind them. Elizabeth hurriedly shut the door to Cecelia's office, and her gaze shot to the video camera. The video camera. Shit, *shit*. She and Cecelia needed to talk, but not there. Elizabeth couldn't risk someone witnessing their conversation. And she knew there was a guard still positioned in the control room.

We have to go somewhere else. I have to tell her the truth.

***

When Sawyer and Two entered the training room, the others were already there, stretching, warming up. Getting ready for the workout that could be so brutal.

They were supposed to push their limits in these workouts. To see exactly what they could do. Normally, the men held back, on Sawyer's order. *Keep some secrets from the doctors and our handlers. Just until we figure out what is happening.*

Because Sawyer knew the folks in charge at Lazarus were keeping secrets from him and his team. So it only seemed fair that he and his team held onto their secrets, too.

Two headed toward the locker room. The guards who'd been tailing them finally stood the hell down. About time. But none of the guards were allowed past the entrance room in the training area. The guards on surveillance duty were told to line the walls and observe. Landon's rules. The guards never interrupted. Not in that space.

Sawyer followed Two toward the locker room, and as soon as they were inside, he shoved the guy against the nearest wall. "I warned you."

Two grinned at him. "Dr. Parker's pretty, but not really my type. You know that I have a thing for the shrink. I think it's the red hair—"

He wasn't buying the grin and the easy voice. Two wore a mask all the time, Sawyer had figured that shit out early. "You scared her."

Two's grin faded.

"You're gonna pay for that today." It was a grim promise.

***

"I had the scene under control," Cecelia said as she lifted her chin. "Didn't need you rushing in."

They were back in the women's locker room, the only place that Elizabeth thought was safe for a one-on-one chat. Safe, for the time being.

"You didn't need to interrupt, Dr. Parker, because despite what happened last night, I am *not* prone to panic and—"

"That's good," Elizabeth cut in swiftly. "Because I'm panicky enough for us both."

Cecelia's eyes widened. "What?"

"You need to know the truth about Lazarus." She didn't see any video cameras. Just like last time, the place seemed clear. "The program is not what you think. Those men—they didn't *volunteer.*"

But Cecelia shook her head. "You're wrong. I wouldn't be here if this wasn't a voluntary program. Yes, the men are housed in rooms that are closely monitored but—"

"The dead can't volunteer." The words fell heavily from Elizabeth.

Cecelia blinked. "Um, what?"

"You heard me." Elizabeth paced closer to her. "The dead can't volunteer. These men — they *didn't* volunteer. They didn't ask for this. They didn't —"

Cecelia's expression had turned considering. "Have you been feeling stressed, doctor?"

Elizabeth locked her back teeth. "Hell, yes," she snapped. "I have been because *I* made Lazarus."

The shrink didn't speak, but her expression still clearly said she thought Elizabeth might be in need of a session with her — a session or twenty.

"The Lazarus formula brings back the dead." Elizabeth spoke quickly, because there was no time to waste or mince words. "I had success in the lab, with rats, and Wyman Wright wanted to test on humans."

Cecelia shook her head. "No, that's not even possible —"

"It's very possible, but I'm not going to run through the formula and the regeneration process right now — we don't have time." They'd be missed by Landon soon enough. "*If* the test subject is preserved properly and *if* the Lazarus formula is injected correctly, reanimation occurs with the subject. But I only tested on rats. And there were side effects—"

The shrink's face darkened. "What kind of side effects?" She gave a short, brittle laugh. "Wait. Just, hold up. Say I believe this story— I'm *not* saying that, but, hypothetically—what exactly, were the side effects?"

"Increased aggression. It wasn't present in all of the lab rats, but it did manifest in some. Those rats—they attacked the others. They killed some of them. I warned both Landon and Wright about this side effect, I told them that we were far, far away from any human testing, but they didn't listen to me."

Cecelia bit her lower lip. "Were the human test subjects made aware of the risks?"

"They weren't aware of anything! That's what I'm trying to explain. They didn't volunteer. They *died.* Sawyer Cage and Flynn Haddox— Subject One and Subject Two—they were killed while on a covert mission. They were never informed about the Lazarus formula. Wright made the decision to bring them into the program without their consent. They never—"

"You're lying," Cecelia's voice was flat. Spots of red stained her cheeks. "I don't know why you're lying. Why you're coming to me and spinning this story, but it isn't true."

Elizabeth had to make the other woman believe her. "I get that the idea of bringing the dead back sounds crazy, but it can be done. It *has* been done. The test subjects you see were killed in action, and they were brought into the program by Wright. They never agreed to any of this!"

Cecelia's delicate jaw hardened. "Yes, they did. I've seen the videos." She shook her head. "Do you think I'd be here, watching the men be kept in these particular living conditions, if I didn't have proof they'd volunteered for this experiment?"

"Videos?" Elizabeth repeated blankly. "What videos?"

"The videos that show the test subjects agreeing to take part in Project Lazarus." Cecelia huffed out a breath. "I don't appreciate being lied to, Dr. Parker. I'm not sure what your agenda is here, but I want no part of it." She straightened her shoulders. "And I will be informing Landon about this conversation."

What?

Cecelia marched away. She yanked open the locker room door and didn't look back as she exited.

The videos that show the test subjects agreeing to take part in Project Lazarus.

But, no, that wasn't possible. Sawyer hadn't volunteered. He hadn't even known about Project Lazarus when they'd been together in D.C.

Had he?

CHAPTER ELEVEN

Elizabeth slipped into the training room. Her gaze slid to the left, and she saw a line of guards stationed near the entrance. The guards were standing near the wall—all armed. Their attention was in front of them, on the test subjects.

The subjects were separated into pairs, grappling in hand-to-hand combat. Six subjects, three pairs. They moved so quickly. They attacked viciously. The air filled with the thud of flesh hitting flesh. The men moved so fast that their bodies seemed to blur.

"Damn impressive, aren't they?"

Elizabeth glanced to her right. A man stood at attention there, his hands behind his back, his chest up, his chin out. She recognized the strict pose and would be willing to bet he was a life-time soldier. Spots of gray were visible in his hair, and lines slid away from his eyes and mouth. He wasn't dressed like a guard. Instead, he wore blue jogging pants and a white t-shirt.

Casual clothes, but there was nothing casual about *him.*

"You're Dr. Elizabeth Parker." He kept his eyes on the men, but she had the feeling his real attention was on her. "I'm General Andrew Jamison."

The name was familiar to her. General Jamison was close to Wright—he'd even come to their old facility a few times, but Elizabeth's path had never crossed with his. She'd just heard the whispers about him from other staff members.

"General," she spoke quietly, "I didn't realize you were training the Lazarus men."

"They're the best of the best, so it only stands to reason the best should train them." There was no boast in his voice, just flat fact. She knew the guy had a trunk load of medals at home. Everyone knew Jamison's reputation. "These men—they *are* the future for us."

She glanced at the subjects. Unerringly, her gaze went to Sawyer. He was fighting with Five, she instantly recognized the blond. For every hit that was thrown by one man, it was blocked perfectly by the other.

"It's like they know what's coming. They can anticipate every attack." Pride came through from Jamison now. "There is nothing like these men in the world. Our enemies won't be able to compete."

"General—"

His gaze swung to her. A dark gaze, intense. Measuring. "You did this."

She wouldn't flinch.

"I wasn't sure how I felt about Project Lazarus, not at first, but I've seen the men in the field. I go with them on the missions. I'm their main handler, and I watch everything they do." He nodded. "They are perfect. No hesitations. No mistakes. They will change the world."

No mistakes. She wasn't so sure about that part. "You haven't noticed any issues with the men?" Because surely, as their handler, Jamison would be the one to witness any cracks.

"None."

She wasn't about to let this drop. "No increased aggression? No—"

His short bark of laughter cut her off. "They're hunters. Weapons. If they weren't aggressive, *then* I'd consider that a problem." His gaze narrowed on her. "We have another mission at 0600 tomorrow. A domestic terrorist cell has been located in New Mexico. These men will go in, they'll eliminate the problem, and no civilians will ever even realize how close they were to danger." Before she could speak, he pulled out a whistle and blew it, hard. "Time for firing practice."

The men on the mats stilled.

Sweat coated their bodies, but they barely seemed to be breathing hard. Sawyer's head swung toward her, and she could have sworn that his gaze heated. He even took a step toward her.

Elizabeth tensed.

Five said something to him, something that was low, too low for her to hear, but Sawyer swung back to him. Sawyer moved with that fast, blurring motion, and suddenly, Five was on the mat, he was pinned beneath Sawyer, and Sawyer's fist had slammed into the side of the other man's face.

"Hot damn." Jamison blew his whistle again.

He was going to berate Sawyer for his attack. *Increased aggression.* Jamison would—

"Fantastic job, One! See, men, that's what I'm talking about. You're good—too good—but there is always room for improvement. One saw the perfect opportunity for a surprise attack, and he went in for the kill. Excellent. That's why he's the leader!"

Sawyer's back was stiff. His hand was in a fist, and it had frozen mere inches from Five's face, as if he'd love to pound the guy again. Elizabeth's own hands had clenched into fists, too, but not due to anger. Fear filled her. Jamison might like what he was seeing, but she didn't. In fact, it scared the hell out of her.

Sawyer leaned toward Five. He didn't say a word, Elizabeth was staring at Sawyer and she never saw his mouth move, but…Five nodded.

"All right, man," Five said gruffly. "I get it. My bad. Hands the fuck off."

Sawyer rose and spared Elizabeth one hard, glittering glance.

The subjects filed into the connecting room. She hurried after them and saw that targets were already set up. The subjects grabbed for their guns.

"You give them real bullets?" Elizabeth blurted to Jamison. He was right at her side. "I thought all of the guns in the facility were loaded with tranqs."

"The facility guards carry tranqs because our subjects are so valuable. We would never want a guard to mistakenly kill a man on the Lazarus team." Jamison gave a faint laugh. "And relax. The guns that my team uses here are loaded with rubber bullets, Dr. Parker. The Lazarus team only gets the real deal when we're on our missions."

Rubber bullets would still knock the guards on their asses. "You aren't worried that they'll turn on you? When you have them out on a mission, you never become afraid one of the subjects might attack you?"

She was watching Sawyer. He'd picked up a handgun. He pointed at the target. He squeezed the trigger. Again, again, again.

The bullets hit straight into the dead center of the target. All perfect shots.

"I'm not at all worried about that possibility."

Her head jerked toward Jamison. He was watching her.

"These men know there was a price for their new abilities. They realize that a certain testing period is required. Once we are sure that the men have adjusted well, we'll begin to integrate them back into society."

She didn't speak. The guns kept firing.

"They'll be monitored, of course, but they'll have a more normal lifestyle. They'll be activated when missions call for their services. The men understand all of this. And they are willing to wait and follow orders until they are cleared."

"Cleared." Her body was so tense that her muscles ached. "And you don't think these men might be a-a threat to the public? You don't think that one day releasing them—releasing men with superhuman strength and speed—might be dangerous?"

Jamison's face could have been carved from stone. "This is about the situation with One and the guards, isn't it? I heard about what happened yesterday." His voice was low, barely above a whisper. Just for her. "And I hold you responsible for that situation, Dr. Parker. Subject One would never have responded that way if you hadn't been present."

He was not saying that shit to her.

"If you weren't the creator of Lazarus, I would never have given my approval for you to come into this facility. Your history with One is too intimate."

She felt her cheeks burn. *Jamison knows I was Sawyer's lover. How does he know?*

"And while Subject One may no longer be the same man he once was, I think there is a part of him, a part deep inside, that has a primitive memory of you. It was that primitive memory that led to his actions with the guards. Though it should be noted that *they* attacked first. He was just responding to their aggression."

Her mouth had dried up completely.

"Those particular guards have been removed from our facility, and the men who have replaced them will not make a similar mistake."

She had the feeling Jamison viewed *her* as the mistake.

The men aren't firing.

It took a moment for that knowledge to sink in for Elizabeth. Her stare flew toward the Lazarus subjects. They were all still holding their weapons, all still aiming at the targets, but they'd stilled. As if…as if…

Oh, my God…can they hear us? Jamison had barely been whispering to her, but the goosebumps on Elizabeth's body had her fearing that these men — with their enhanced senses — *could* hear their conversation. Maybe…maybe their enhancements were far more profound than she'd realized.

Maybe the test subjects had been keeping secrets of their own.

They volunteered. Cecelia's words echoed in Elizabeth's mind.

The men all began shooting at once. Aiming with absolutely perfect accuracy.

"Amazing," Jamison praised, his voice loud again. "They never miss."

Her heart was racing too fast in her chest.

He put his hand on her shoulder and leaned toward her. "I can't afford any distractions for my Lazarus team. They have to be in top form. We want them to keep progressing. As I said, our goal is to integrate them back into society and to call them up when their services are needed. I think we are close to that point now." He moved even closer to her. Once more, his voice lowered and he said, "Provided no one disturbs their progress."

Her spine stiffened. "You think I'm a disturbance?"

The men were firing.

"I think you're the creator of Lazarus. I think you're the reason we've had the best breakthrough of the century, but I think if Subject One loses his focus, then it *will* be because of you. You need to stay away from him. Do your research on the others, but don't get close to One again."

There was something about his voice, about the way he looked at her. "Are you threatening me, General Jamison?"

He laughed and his hand slid away from her shoulder. "Of course not. You're needed, Dr. Parker. Your mind would be a terrible thing to lose."

The sonofabitch *was* threatening her. And—

"Looks like we have company." His gaze was fixed over her shoulder. "And someone sure looks pissed."

Her head whipped around. Landon marched toward her, and, oh, yes, he definitely looked pissed. His face was twisted in anger.

"Elizabeth," Landon bit off her name. "We need to talk. *Now.*"

***

It would be so easy to shoot the asshole. Sawyer's fingers tightened around his weapon. Landon was rushing away with Elizabeth, and she was afraid. He could *feel* her fear. He didn't like it. His hold tightened on the gun. Sure, it was loaded with rubber bullets, but those bullets would hurt like a bitch—

Don't do it. Sawyer recognized the push in his mind as coming from Two. Two was distinct. His thoughts *sounded* like his voice—that was the way it was for them all. Sawyer heard the voices in his mind, muted, but recognizable, when the team used telepathic communication.

His emotions must have been rawer than he realized, especially if Two had just picked up on his urge to attack.

Nah, I say go for it. Five's mocking laughter seemed to echo in Sawyer's ears. But Five didn't look his way. He just kept firing at his target. Head shots. Over and over. *Landon is a prick,* Five told him. *At least shoot him in the ass and give him a scare. Not like we have real bullets anyway.*

Sawyer locked his jaw and put down his weapon. He'd never listen to advice from Five. That bastard had already driven him to the edge — and over it — that day. All because the jerk had said the wrong fucking thing about Elizabeth.

But…Elizabeth…

They'd all just heard what the general had said to her. Elizabeth *was* Lazarus. They'd all been wanting a key to unlock their pasts. Elizabeth was that key.

She was the tool they needed to truly be free.

Fuck. He hated what was going to come next for her, but there wasn't an option. He'd have to use her, he'd have to scare her, and he might even have to kidnap her. He didn't have a choice. The plans for escape had been put in motion for too long.

***

"You broke confidentiality!" Landon blasted as he threw open the door to his office. "You went to Cecelia and told her information about Project Lazarus that she did not have the clearance to hear and you—"

"I don't know what you're talking about," Elizabeth lied. "Who told you this?"

"Um, I did." Cecelia stepped from the corner of Landon's office. She gave a little wince. "I told him."

Elizabeth glared at her. *Sell-out.* So much for getting an ally in that place. "Right. Makes sense. Landon thinks you're having a breakdown, so to get some of the pressure off yourself, you toss me under the bus. Nice play, *Dr.* Gregory."

"I—you *lied* to me," Cecelia threw back as her hands went to her hips. "These men volunteered!" Her attention flew to Landon. "Prove it to her, Dr. Meyer. Show her the videos."

Elizabeth's heart thudded hard in her chest. "Yes," she immediately agreed. "Show me the videos. Right now."

A muscle jerked in Landon's jaw. She'd just called his bluff. There *were* no videos. Sawyer hadn't volunteered, none of those men had.

Landon marched around his desk. He opened his laptop. He paused just a moment, to put his index finger down on the sensor pad, and she knew he was unlocking the system. *Worried someone will steal your files, Landon?* He stabbed his fingers over a few of the keys, then he flipped the laptop around to face Elizabeth. "See for yourself."

She took a step forward. A video was already playing on the screen, and she recognized Subject Five.

He flashed a broad smile.

"*State your name.*" Landon's voice came from off-camera.

"Bryce King." He lifted a blond brow. "What? You want my rank and serial number, too?"

"No, I want you to state that you are willingly offering yourself as a participant in Project Lazarus."

"Hell, yes, I'm in. I've seen the results, and I want that power boost myself." His eyes gleamed. "I willingly volunteer."

Chill bumps rose on her arms. "It's not that easy," Elizabeth murmured as she stared at the screen. "He has to die first. He can't be injected while he's living. The formula doesn't work that way."

Landon snapped shut the laptop, closing it in an instant. "Bryce King was aware that the formula could only be administered to the dead. But considering his very high risk job, Bryce also knew that he might meet his end at any time. He wanted to go on record as being a volunteer for the program."

Why had Landon stopped the video? She'd been able to see that at least two more minutes remained of that filming, she'd noted the little line at the bottom that showed the video had barely begun to play.

"See, Dr. Parker?" Cecelia approached her quickly. "These men volunteered for the project. I don't know about the death that you keep mentioning—"

Elizabeth turned and locked gazes with the shrink. "Lazarus only works on the dead. Every man in this program *died* before being given the Lazarus formula. They were brought back from the dead. That is the truth."

Cecelia swallowed. Her attention immediately shifted to Landon.

"Tell her," Elizabeth barked as the silence stretched too long in that room. "If you want her to treat the patients, to truly monitor them, then you should have told her everything from the beginning."

"It wasn't my call," he snapped back. "Her clearance isn't—"

"Screw her clearance."

But Landon shook his head. "Wright dictates what we share, you *know* that. I told you the rules—"

"Then tell Wright it's on me." Her shoulders squared. "Say I'm the one who told her. Blame me, and keep your hands clean."

"*Is it true?*" Cecelia pushed.

"She needs to know what she's dealing with! You realize that, Landon, I know you do, and—"

He gave a jerky nod. "It's, fuck, yes, it's true." Silence.

Then Cecelia staggered back. "Oh. My. God." Her eyes had doubled in size. "They're *dead?*"

"Actually, they *were* dead," Landon explained quickly as he rolled back his shoulders. "Now they're part of Lazarus."

The shrink was having a moment. That was obvious. Her breath was coming faster and her body swayed as she tried to wrap her head around the fact that she'd been treating dead men for weeks. Elizabeth let the woman have her moment, and she focused on Landon. "I want to see the other videos."

He sighed. "Why? They're all the same. The men volunteering, agreeing to participate in Lazarus—"

"Sawyer never volunteered." She slapped her hands down on his desk. "He didn't know about Lazarus. He didn't know what I was doing. He was *leaving,* getting out, planning for a civilian life. Not planning for this."

Landon's lips twisted. "You never once considered that you weren't the only one keeping secrets, did you?" He turned the laptop back around to face him. He opened it once more and activated the system. She could barely hear the taps of his fingertips over the frantic beating of her heart. "Here you go." He presented the screen to her once more. "Just click the arrow to make it play."

"I know how to make it fucking play." She clicked the arrow.

Sawyer's face filled the screen. "Why the hell do you need to record this?"

"For the record," came Landon's fast response.

Sawyer rolled his eyes. "This is such bullshit. Fine. Okay. I, Sawyer Cage, volunteer to be part of Project Lazarus."

That was it. All of thirteen seconds. Her stare rose to Landon's face. "That's bullshit. He didn't know that you were talking about bringing the dead back to life! He just thought you were talking about the work we were already doing. *He didn't know.*"

"Keep telling yourself that," Landon muttered.

"If he'd volunteered, *you* would have told me when I tried to stop you from administering the formula to him!"

He rocked back on his heels. "There wasn't time then. You knew we were working against the clock with the injections. The preservation process only lasted so long before deterioration began! Was I really supposed to stop and show you a damn video? Sawyer Cage *volunteered.* He wanted to keep working for Wright. He had no intention of leaving. If Sawyer told you anything different, then he was lying to you."

She almost punched him in the face. *Almost.*

"You want all the cards on the table? Is that what this is all about?" Landon's hands flew into the air. "Fine. *You* were fucking Sawyer Cage."

She couldn't move. Cecelia was dead silent.

"I knew about it. Wyman Wright knew about it. You thought you were keeping the affair secret? You weren't."

She should say something. Do something.

"Sawyer knew you two were breaking the rules by getting involved," Landon continued doggedly. "So he told you that lie to make you feel better. The guy was a ladies' man, you had to see that. And you aren't the first woman he misled."

No, *no.*

"They *all* volunteered," Landon said. "Every single test subject. No one is a prisoner—each man is here willingly. They wanted the power we could give to them. And now they have it. They are the best fighting machines in the world, and each day, I swear, they just get better and better."

Her cheeks were burning hot, but her body felt ice cold. Was it possible that Sawyer had lied to her all that time? She didn't want to believe it. But she'd been keeping secrets from him. Maybe he *had* kept secrets from her, too.

"You're not at Lazarus to hook up with your ex." Landon's words battered her. "You're here to do more research, but if you can't do the job, even *you* can be replaced, Dr. Parker."

She gave him a hard smile as she tried to keep her shit together. "If I could be replaced, Wright would never have come crawling back to me." She pushed away from his desk. "Wright needs me. *You* need me. But if you piss me off again, I'll walk the hell out without any hesitation."

He laughed. *Laughed.* "Now who is lying? We both know that you won't leave Sawyer." He leaned toward her. "Wright knew you'd be tied to the program through Sawyer, and he was right."

Her heart just—stopped. Was it possible...no, surely they hadn't used Sawyer as the first subject *because* of her. Had they? The horror must have shown on her face.

Landon blinked. His expression immediately closed down. He shoved his laptop into his desk drawer. "I hope this has reassured you—"

Not even close.

"We have a lot of work to do, and it's time we get busy." He nodded briskly. "The men have a mission at 0600 tomorrow. We have to make

certain they are in top form before they leave."
His gaze slid back to Elizabeth. "Can you handle
this?"

I can handle anything you throw at me.

But before she could respond, she saw that
his stare had dropped to her chest. He wasn't
staring at her in some kind of ogling way.
Actually, pity flashed in his eyes.

And she realized that her hand had risen.
She'd been pressing her fingers over the scar
hidden just beneath her shirt. The scar from the
gunshot wound she'd gotten in D.C. when she
stepped between a guard and Sawyer.

Her hand fell. "I can handle this."

CHAPTER TWELVE

He waited until night fell, until the facility was locked down and silence reigned. The folks in charge had tried to ramp up security, but their efforts were pretty much useless. Sawyer still easily opened the lock of his cell, and he crept down the hallway, going straight for his target. He didn't make a sound, and he stayed in the shadows. He knew the placement of every security camera, and he knew exactly how to avoid being seen by those cameras. He also had the guards' schedule memorized. But even if he hadn't, Sawyer would have heard the guards approaching from a mile away.

He made his way to the staff quarters— specifically, to *her* room. Sawyer followed Elizabeth's scent straight to her door. When he reached for the knob, he wasn't surprised to find it locked. Not after last night's activities. Dr. Cecelia Gregory's room was right next door, so he made sure to not even let a whisper of sound escape as he picked Elizabeth's lock.

Then he was inside. The room was pitch black, but he could see well—very well—in the dark. Another Lazarus bonus. He locked the door behind him, and he headed for the bed. Elizabeth was in that bed, turned on her side away from him. She was beneath the covers, her shoulders hunched a bit. He didn't want to scare her with his approach, but it wasn't like he'd be able to wake her up gently.

Before he left on the morning's mission, they needed to clear the air. And *after* the mission…

Everything will explode.

He bent over her, his hand reaching out to curl around her shoulder, but before he could touch her skin, Elizabeth erupted. She lunged up, and he saw the gleam of a knife's blade.

She wasn't asleep. She knew I was in her room. She was waiting for her chance to attack. The knife was going straight for his throat.

Impressive.

But not quite good enough. He tore the blade from her hand and threw it right at the wall. It sank in deep even as he grabbed her hands, yanking them above her head and pinning them to the pillows. "Now, doc, is that really a polite way to greet a visitor?"

She'd been twisting and struggling for her freedom, but at his words, she went statue still.

Sawyer didn't make the mistake of letting her go. She was far too much of an unknown for him.

"How about you promise not to attack me again? And we'll see if we can have a nice, civilized talk."

"Talk?" Her voice was husky and sexy and it made his dick twitch far too eagerly. "Is that why you broke into my room? To *talk*?"

One of the reasons, yes. He'd also come in because he'd needed to see her. No, it went far past need. More like he'd been obsessed with seeing her. The hours had ticked away after Landon had taken her from the training area, and Sawyer hadn't seen her again all fucking day. He'd *had* to go to her room. Had to find her. Touch her.

I'm touching her now.

"You kept secrets from me," he accused.

She yanked against his hold, and he just tightened his grip on her wrists. His body covered hers, holding her easily in place, but the position also meant that he was between her legs. The bedcovers separated their bodies, yet he could still feel every inch of her beneath him. He was pretty sure she felt all of him, too, including the erection that had to be impossible to miss.

The doc turned him on — with a wild, dangerous hunger.

"You kept secrets, too," she whispered back. Then she said, "Asshole. I *trusted* you."

What? He had no clue what she was talking about. "I'm the one without the memories, so if I did something to piss you off, well, sorry, doc, but I don't know what it was."

"You just broke into my room! You're holding me down!" Her voice started to rise. "*That* pisses me off, that—"

He kissed her. Sure, there were plenty of other ways that Sawyer could have gotten her to quiet down, but kissing her was the most pleasurable way. His lips took hers, and it was just like before. He tasted her, and desire exploded within him. She was sweet but rich, and her lips were soft as silk beneath his mouth. He licked her, then nipped that plump, lower lip. His tongue thrust into her mouth, and she kissed him back. Kissed him with the same hunger.

They'd been lovers, no doubt about it. And he would bet his life the sex between them had been absolutely phenomenal. He wanted to take her, to feel the pleasure that he'd experienced in his dream. Would it be as good in reality? Even better?

Not fucking now.

Sawyer made himself pull back. Rather, he pulled back, but then he kissed her again. *I missed her.* The thought slipped through his mind, and it chilled him. If he'd missed her...

She mattered.

And that was about to make things very, very complicated.

With one hand, he secured her arms above her head. Sawyer locked his fingers around her delicate wrists. His legs stayed between hers, pushing her thighs wide and his body trapped her against the mattress.

"Stop this." Her voice was thready, scared. She wanted him, there was no missing her physical response, but she was also scared to death of him. "Let me go."

"I could have said you were in my cell last night. Could have let Landon and the guards find you with me. I saved your sweet ass." He wanted that reminder. Wanted her to know he'd protected her. So she should stop fearing him.

"And I saved *your* ass," she whispered right back. "I didn't tell anyone that you could get out of your cell, even though I damn well think that one of your men broke into Cecelia's room last night."

Yeah, he thought so, too. Though every man had denied it.

"You made Lazarus." The words broke from him. They were angry and rough and his muscles were rock-hard with fury. "*You* did this to me."

He waited for her denial. Waited for her lies. Waited for—

"I'm sorry."

Her pain?

Because pain was in her voice, he was sure of it. She trembled beneath him. Elizabeth didn't fight. She just stared up at him in the darkness. He could see every detail of her perfect face. And her expression was filled with true sorrow.

"This isn't what I wanted. I never meant..." She bit her lower lip, stopping the words.

"No, doc, you don't stop now. You tell me every single thing that I want to know." He was sick of being blind. Sick of being a test rat.

"Did you volunteer?" Elizabeth barely breathed the words.

"Volunteer? How the hell should I know? I remember *nothing* about my life before this place." His hold was too hard on her wrists. He didn't want to bruise her. He eased up and said, "No, that's a lie."

Beneath him, Elizabeth flinched.

"I remember *you*. Fucking you. Holding you between my body and some wooden door. You were wearing a black dress that was as soft as silk — but not as soft as your skin. I shoved that dress up — "

A tear leaked from the corner of her eye.

"And I put my hand on your sex. I had you coming for me. I remember you didn't cry out, but I wanted to hear you. I wanted to hear you when you came because I love the sounds you make for me." He leaned forward and kissed away her tear drop. His mouth lingered on her skin. "I remember that you were *mine*."

"You died!"

His heart jolted in his chest.

"You said you'd always come back, but you died!" She struggled against him, twisting her body with a sudden fury. He didn't let her go, though.

I won't let go.

"You died on that mission! You were on the exam table and you were so still, and I was telling Landon that he couldn't do it. Not to you. He couldn't give you the Lazarus formula. The guard pulled me out. I was screaming and you were *dead*."

The sound of her ragged breathing hurt him. But…

Dead? No, that had to be a lie. "I'm breathing. I'm talking to you right the hell now." Anger churned inside of him, deepening with every word that he spoke. Why was she deceiving him? "Cut the bull and tell—"

"Lazarus brought you back. Why do you think this place is called the Lazarus facility? You were given the Lazarus formula—my formula, a formula that *wasn't* ready—and just like the story in the bible, you came back from the dead. Lazarus rose."

He shook his head. No, there was no way—

"The formula has side effects. That's why you're stronger, and your senses are sharper. That's why you heal faster. It's also why you don't have memories of your past. Because we're dealing with life and death, and the human body — God, there are still mysteries out there. I shouldn't have been freaking Frankenstein, I shouldn't have been — "

Frankenstein. The name had a flash appearing in his eyes.

He was suddenly in a bedroom. Elizabeth was there, standing in front of a large window. A glittering city waited beyond the glass, shrouded in the dark.

I think I'm Frankenstein.

For an instant, he could hear her words so clearly.

And then...

Then the image was gone. He was back in the bed with her, holding her tight. He tried to think. Tried to push through the fury that was crowding in his thoughts. "I've been here for *months.*"

She shivered beneath him.

"Where in the hell have you been, doc?"

"I've been looking for you."

His eyes raked over her.

"Wyman Wright is the man in charge of this program. He's Landon's boss. When we were all back in D.C., he was my boss, too. But after they gave you the formula, there was...something happened, okay? You were taken away, and no one told me where you went. You were gone. Landon was gone. Wright was gone. I tried to find you, I swear I did, but it was as if you'd never been there at all."

He let her go. Jumped from the bed. Sawyer had to put some space between them because the rage he felt was too strong. He could feel his control shredding.

I died? I fucking died?

The bedsheets rustled as Elizabeth climbed from the bed. His gaze shot to her as she stood, her body stiff and nervous, a few feet from him. She wore a faded, blue t-shirt. One with the world NAVY across the top. It was too big for her, falling to her thighs and covering her body. A man's shirt.

His hands clenched into fists. "Who the fuck does that shirt belong to?"

His thoughts were twisting, becoming too chaotic. Too enraged.

My life…gone. Dead.

Elizabeth.

Lying…

Everyone had been lying to him. He was a prisoner. A weapon.

Attack. The sinister thought slipped through his mind as a wave of darkness seemed to overwhelm his thoughts. *Destroy…*

"It was your shirt," Elizabeth said.

Sawyer shook his head, trying to clear the darkness as he took a step toward her.

"You were in the Navy. You were a SEAL. The shirt was one of the only things I had left that belonged to you."

You fucking belong to me. The knowledge was burning inside of him. He found himself lunging toward her, grabbing her arms and yanking her toward him.

"*Three months. I've been in this hell for three months.*" He sounded like a man possessed. Maybe he was.

"I came to help you. Wright approached me recently. He wanted me back in the program, and I just came to help *you.*"

He wanted to believe her, but her heart was racing like mad. Fear had turned her pupils into pinpricks. Her breathing hitched. She was giving every single sign that she was deceiving him—or that she was utterly terrified of him.

The only time she didn't seem afraid was when he kissed her. When he made her want him as desperately as he wanted her. Despite everything, he craved her. His dick was still fully erect and straining against the front of his jeans. Her soft body called to him.

Too long. I've been without her too long. Need her. Want her.

Take her.

He pulled her flush against him. Sawyer's mouth crashed down on hers. *Can't be dead. Can't be dead when she makes me feel this alive.* His tongue drove into her mouth. She gave a little moan in the back of her throat, and it was a sound he remembered. His hands were sliding along her body, moving over her back, down to the curve of her sweet ass, and he remembered how she felt beneath him.

I remember how she feels. I remember what she likes.

If he remembered that…

Have to see if it's true. Have to see.

He lifted her into his arms. She was kissing him back with a hungry desire that matched his own. A wildness that he hadn't expected, but he wanted. He wanted her desire for him so badly.

Have to make her want me. Have to make her need me. Have to make her mine.

Something deep inside was driving him. Something dark and dangerous. He should let her go. He should get the hell out of there, but he couldn't.

He dropped her onto the bed. She had a real bed, not a damn cot like he had in his space. Her legs sprawled in front of her. Long, perfect legs. He wanted her legs wrapped around him. But first…

Make sure it's real. Make sure it's all real.

He yanked back his savage hunger. His fingers trailed up her legs, moving slowly, sliding up her skin. His fingers were big and callused, and she was like silk.

Softer.

He shoved the too big t-shirt up, and his gaze fell on the slip of black lace she wore. "Panties, this time," he growled. His fingers caught the lace. "In the way." He yanked, and the lace tore beneath his hand.

Elizabeth gave a sharp gasp.

He should be using more care. He should be—

His fingers touched her sex. Stroked her, remembered her. The way she liked for him to rub her clit, the way—

Her head tipped back on the bed as she gave a soft moan.

"Careful, baby," he warned. "No one can hear."

Her head immediately whipped back up. She stared at him, the desire momentarily clearing from her gaze. Her eyes widened and—

He pushed her legs farther apart, then he pulled her hips to the edge of the bed. He worked her with his fingers, sliding them in and out, watching her face, watching her body, loving the way she tensed and jerked and bit her lip to hold back her cries. When he stroked her just this way, moving his fingers fast and deep...

Her hips surge up toward my touch. That gets her to climax faster.

The past and present merged in his mind. Memories of how to touch her.

When I slow down, when I glide my thumb over her clit…

Her hands fisted around the bed covers. "Sawyer!" A low hiss of demand.

I draw out her pleasure. I get her body bow tight. Then…

His fingers pressed harder. He stroked her faster.

She came. Her body stiffened, and she whispered his name.

His control shattered. He clawed at the top of his jeans. Yanked out his cock, and he had the head of his dick pressed to her sex. She was still trembling, still quivering with her release, and he had to take her. He drove into her, and it was like coming home. Her sex was wet and hot and so damn tight. Holding him so close, driving him insane.

Her legs locked around his hips. Sawyer stood poised over her, leaning over that bed, bracing his hands on the mattress as he drove in and out of her. Every move had her twisting against him, had her breath choking out. He could make her come again. She always came fast the first time, but she came *harder* the second. He could get her there.

He withdrew, then positioned his hips down in a hard thrust, one that would take his cock right over her sensitive core. Her hands locked around him, her nails raked over his back. He still wore his damn shirt—and she still had on the Navy t-shirt. He wanted them both completely naked. Wanted her skin to skin.

But…

No time.

His climax was bearing down on him. He was about to erupt, and she had to find her pleasure first. He always made her come first because he needed Elizabeth to know pleasure with him, to know he took care of her.

His hand slid between their bodies. He stroked her. Demanding, rough, because she liked that, she'd come for—

Her sex squeezed him hard with the contractions of her climax, and then he was pounding into her. Control gone, lust driving him. He thrust deep and hard and he came, exploding into her. His breath sawed from his lungs as he emptied out into her.

Elizabeth.

His heart thundered in his chest. His cock— shit, the damn thing was still erect. He wanted to go again. Wanted to take her endlessly. Wanted—

Footsteps.

He heard them, the soft pad was approaching. Could be someone just walking by. Could be someone…

Coming to Elizabeth?

Growling, he withdrew from her and whirled for the door. *Who the fuck is coming to her room at this hour?*

She grabbed his arm. "Sawyer? What is it? What are you doing?"

"Someone's coming." He hauled his jeans back up and took a step toward the door.

"What?" She rushed around him and put her body between him and the door.

Oh, the hell, *no.*

"You can't go running outside!" Her voice was barely a breath. A very angry breath. Her cheeks were flushed, her lips were red and swollen, and her tight nipples thrust against the shirt-front. "You're supposed to be in your room, remember? *Locked* in your room!"

"And no asshole is supposed to be headed to *your* room." Not after midnight. No way in hell.

Her lashes flickered. "Someone was in Cecelia's room last night…"

His shoulders tensed. The footsteps were getting closer. Was the late-night stranger coming to Elizabeth? Or heading for Cecelia?

"Could be a guard patrolling." She swept a nervous glance at the door. "And if you go rushing out there, what will happen?"

He'd get tranqed. Maybe the tranq would work on him. Maybe this time, it wouldn't.

Maybe all of his plans would accelerate, and the facility would get ripped to the ground.

She shook her head. "Wait, okay? I don't want you hurt." She licked her lower lip. "I never wanted anyone hurt."

The footsteps were coming closer. And they were coming right to her door.

His hands were clenched into fists. He was going to—

A knock sounded at her door. "Elizabeth?"

Landon's voice. That motherfuck—

"Stop." She put her hand on Sawyer's chest and stared into his eyes. "We have to think." Her words were whispered. "Think, and not attack." Her gaze searched his. "Let me see what he wants."

Sawyer thought he knew exactly what the bastard wanted.

He wants you, Elizabeth.

She carried Sawyer's scent on her body. He'd marked her.

But he felt like she'd marked him.

It was real. Not just a dream. I know her body. I know her.

"Just hide, okay?"

What the fuck had she just said? Hide?

"I came here to save you, not to watch you crash and burn in front of me." She blinked quickly, as if—as if she were trying not to cry. He stiffened. Oh, hell, no, Elizabeth couldn't cry. Not on his watch.

She put her hand on his chest and pushed him back. "Get in the closet. Let me deal with Landon. We have to—"

"*Elizabeth!*" Landon's voice was even louder. "I need you, *now!*"

The guy needed a long overdue ass-whooping. That was what he needed.

"Please," Elizabeth begged softly. "I can't watch while everything goes to hell in front of me again."

Shit. He had his own plans that couldn't be screwed. Hating it, he gave a grim nod as he retreated. Sawyer yanked the knife from the wall before he slid into the closet. But he didn't shut the door completely. He left a small slit so that he could peer out and watch Elizabeth.

My Elizabeth.

She yanked on a pair of jeans even as a fist pounded into her door. She was just jerking on her shoes when that door burst open.

Landon and a guard stood in her doorway. Landon's face was flushed, and Sawyer tensed when the guy lunged forward and grabbed her arm. "You didn't open your door!"

She shoved him away. "I was getting dressed, Landon. Give a woman some time, would you?" Elizabeth put her hands on her hips. "And I don't like this bursting in crap. I'm not a prisoner here, I'm a co-worker, and you don't get to just—"

"There's been an incident." Landon's voice was off, stilted. The guy had turned his body, and his gaze seemed to be sweeping all over Elizabeth's quarters. In the closet, Sawyer tensed. He hadn't left any of his clothing behind, but Elizabeth's bed was damn well wrecked. And her lips were red and swollen. Her hair tousled.

"What kind of incident?" Elizabeth had moved a bit, subtly positioning her body between the closet and Landon. *She's protecting me.* That was…unexpected.

But then, everything about Elizabeth was unexpected.

Dead. She said I was dead.

There was a faint commotion near the doorway. Sawyer shifted a bit to get a better view, and he saw Cecelia appear. The shrink was wrapped in a thick robe, and her hair trailed over her shoulders. "What's happening?" Cecelia's question was sharp. A guard stood just behind her.

"An incident," Elizabeth repeated what Landon had just said. "Only Landon won't tell me what—"

"Because you need to see for yourselves. Follow me, ladies, now."

They headed for the door. Elizabeth was moving with fast, jerky motions, obviously wanting to get out of there. *No, she wants to get him away from me.*

Hiding in that closet didn't sit well with Sawyer. He wanted to leaped out of there, wanted to grab Elizabeth and hold tight. But his team was counting on him. Plans were in place.

He couldn't jeopardize them.

Not even for the woman who held the key to his past.

CHAPTER THIRTEEN

Elizabeth swore that she could still feel Sawyer's touch on her skin. That she could feel him *in* her.

It had been just like before—so many times before. They'd touched and the rest of the world had fallen away. Her response to Sawyer had always been off the charts. He'd been the only man to make her lose control. The only man who could drive her absolutely wild.

When he'd kissed her, she'd been lost.

Now she hurried away from her quarters, trying to smooth her hair back and wishing that her frantic heartbeat would calm down. A guard was behind her. Cecelia was in front of her. And then Landon—and another guard—they led their little party through the narrow corridors. Elizabeth wanted to look back, she wanted to make sure Sawyer was safe, but she didn't dare risk a glance over her shoulder. She had to protect him.

"Down here." Landon had stopped in front of a big, metal door. The thin, dark-haired guard yanked it open and the loud screech of grating metal had Elizabeth tensing. She peered forward and saw a dark stairwell waiting.

And the knot in her stomach got worse. "What is this place?" she whispered to Cecelia.

"I think it's some kind of storage area. I've...never been here before." There had been the faintest of hesitations in Cecelia's voice. Landon and the guard near him were shining flashlights into the stairwell and motioning them forward.

Cecelia went first, but Elizabeth didn't advance. She stared at Landon, narrowing her eyes against the glare from his flashlight. "Why are we here?"

"Go down the stairs and you'll find out." His voice was clipped, but she could see the faint tremble in his fingers. He was nervous. So was she.

She walked forward, but didn't head down the stairs. Instead, she stopped right in front of him. "This area is deserted." Deserted, dark. Creepy. But then, the whole facility was creepy.

His head cocked.

"Why aren't there lights in the stairwell?" Elizabeth asked. *Bad sign. Very bad.*

"Glitch with the power grid. This whole section is without power."

Wonderful. "Can't help but think..." She motioned toward the stairwell. Elizabeth could hear Cecelia and the dark-haired guard as they headed down the steps. "This would sure be a great place to eliminate someone."

Landon stepped toward her. "Yes, it would be, wouldn't it?"

Her lips parted.

And from down in that stairwell, she heard Cecelia scream.

***

Sawyer had just entered his cell when he heard the scream. It was faint, coming from too far away, but *definitely* in the facility. He whirled back around and lunged for the door.

What in the hell is happening? That was Two's sharp voice, rolling through his head.

The scream had died away. A woman's scream. Had that been Elizabeth? He grabbed for the door. He was about to rush right out when—

The door opened. A guard stood there, frowning at him. The guard's tranq gun was in his hand. "Why are you out of bed?"

Better question, how had the guard gotten there without Sawyer hearing his approach? Shit, he'd been distracted. Focusing and thinking too much about Elizabeth. He hadn't paid enough attention to his surroundings.

Sawyer could rip that gun away from the guard. He could knock that bastard out. He could be free of the cell and looking for—

Footsteps. Close.

Sawyer kept his hands loose at his sides. He breathed in and out, slowly, finally using his enhanced hearing as he should. He'd been obsessing about Elizabeth and he'd almost screwed up. He couldn't afford those kinds of mistakes.

A second guard appeared in the doorway. For just a moment, Sawyer was tempted to attack. He could take them both.

"Why are you out of bed?" the first guard repeated. He was a short guy, wide in the shoulders, with small eyes.

"I thought I heard a scream." And that was the truth. Sawyer's brows lowered. "Is everything okay at the facility? I could have sworn I heard a woman—"

"Everything's fine. The facility is secure."

"Then why are you in my room?" Sawyer fired back.

"Because we're doing a sweep. Orders from up top. We're to make sure everyone is accounted for."

Fuck. Extra security. Just what he didn't need.

The guards backed away. Sealed his door shut.

Sawyer didn't move.

What in the hell is happening? Two was practically shouting in his head. *That scream – it was Cecelia!*

Shock slid through Sawyer. *How do you know that?*

He had a fast impression of fury…and fear. *I know her. What's going on?*

Sawyer stared at the sealed door. *Landon came and got Elizabeth and Cecelia. Said he had something to show them.*

And what, Sawyer wondered, had they seen? What had made Cecelia scream?

***

Landon went down the stairs before Elizabeth. She hurried after him, even though Cecelia's scream had died away. Landon's flashlight hit the figures at the bottom of the steps.

The young, dark-haired guard.

Cecelia.

The dead man.

The dead man.

Behind her, Elizabeth heard the other guard release a rush of air, it sounded as if he'd been punched in the gut. She felt the same way. Elizabeth staggered to a stop on the stairs. Her hand gripped the metal handrail, holding too tight. And then she became aware of the stench. Thick, cloying. Death.

"I-I found him half an hour ago." It was the young guard who spoke. The man who'd led Cecelia down the stairwell. He ran a shaking hand over his hair — hair, Elizabeth finally noted, that was disheveled. "I was just patrolling. Never expected to see..."

Slowly, Elizabeth crept down the stairs. Her gaze was on the dead man.

"I didn't touch him. Didn't move him at all," the guard said quickly. "Went straight to get Dr. Meyer."

"An accident?" Cecelia questioned. She was standing a few feet from the body. "He's...he's a guard. You can tell by his uniform. He must have slipped on the stairs and fallen. Broken his neck."

The poor man's head was twisted, so that certainly fit but...

"He has more wounds," the words slipped from Elizabeth. The guy wore the customary black attire that all of the Lazarus guards were given, so at first glance, she hadn't noticed the blood soaking him. But the longer she looked, unable to glance away...*Oh, my God.* Elizabeth snatched the flashlight from Landon and rushed forward, moving to get a better view. She crouched right beside the body, but didn't touch him. "No accident." Not by a long shot. There were *stab* wounds in the guy's chest. She could see the cuts in the black fabric now. The deep slices into his skin. Not just one or two. She counted at least… "Thirteen," she whispered. That was an awful lot of rage.

She looked up and found Landon staring at her. She could see the fear in his eyes.

"How long has he been dead?" Landon blurted.

Her eyes widened. "You want *me* to tell you that?"

"You're a doctor, for Christ's sake!"

"So are you!" Elizabeth threw back. "And the last time I checked, neither one of us were medical examiners!"

He glared at her.

Shit. "Lividity has set it." That she knew. And the blood had…congealed on the stairs.

The two guards who'd accompanied them didn't speak.

Cecelia shuffled forward. "Was his neck broken before—or after—all of those stab wounds?" All of the flashlights were locked on the man's chest, the bright light showing the horror of his attack.

I don't know. "We need to get the body out of here," Elizabeth said, not answering her question. "We need the cops here and—"

Landon was already shaking his head. "*No cops.*"

She surged upright. "There's been a murder! We absolutely need the cops!"

"We'll take the body up to one of the labs. Examine him. Find out what's happening." Landon pointed at her. "You and Cecelia can examine him. You're both medical doctors."

She didn't point out—again—that so was he. "Do you know who this man is?" Her voice was low and flat as she tried to keep herself together. The guard's face looked familiar to her, but she couldn't quite place him.

"It's…Hugh. Hugh Cleston. He started here about a month ago." Landon's tone matched her own. "He didn't report for duty tonight, so that's why I had the guards patrolling. I wanted to make sure—" He broke off. "Let's get the body moved. We'll talk in the lab."

Hugh. "He was the guard who watched Cecelia and me last night." She remembered the name and the face now. After the lockdown, he'd been the one tasked with keeping them safe. Elizabeth remembered him watching them as they entered her quarters, but…*We didn't go out again until morning, and he was gone by then.*

"We need to move the body," Landon was adamant. "We have to get this situation contained."

Contained? Or covered up?

"You can't just move a body!" Cecelia burst out. "You'll destroy evidence! We can't—"

Landon snapped to attention. "I am in charge here, and I'm telling you that we're moving him to the lab. I don't know how long it will be before the power grid comes back on in this area—we need to examine him *now*."

"But—" Cecelia began.

"We *aren't* leaving him here." Landon's head bobbed decisively. "I'll have the guards transport the body. We're going to the lab. And that's an order."

***

After being in the darkened stairwell, the lab was too bright. Elizabeth didn't pace, she barely moved at all as she stared at Landon. Cecelia, though, seemed to be a bundle of energy. She was rocking back and forth, and the woman had waves of nervousness flowing from her.

"We have to be careful what we say in front of the others," Landon murmured. It was just the three of them in that lab. Landon had ordered the guards to transfer the body, and the guards hadn't arrived yet. He looked over his shoulder at the closed lab door. "I ordered a search when Hugh didn't report in for his shift—"

"Because you thought he might have been the man in my room?" Cecelia exclaimed.

Landon's expression was tense. "I thought he might be trying to steal Lazarus secrets. It fit. A new guard, sudden trouble...*if* you were telling the truth about someone being in your room—"

"*If*, you asshole?" Cecelia snarled. "There is no *if*."

He gave a grim nod. "No, I guess there *isn't* an 'if' any longer."

Elizabeth's temples were throbbing.

"Hugh was relieved of duty at 0400—that was when he stopped guarding your quarters. Another guard switched out with him at that time. I *know* that, but I don't know what happened to Hugh after that point. That's why I need his time of death. I need to know exactly *when* that man died."

Elizabeth drew in one long, deep breath. Then another. "You saw how many times he was stabbed."

Landon didn't speak.

Elizabeth had plenty to say. "You told me before that you worried someone was trying to steal secrets from Lazarus. So the way I figure it, we're looking at two options here." Her hands were wet with sweat, so she rubbed them over her jeans. "Option one is that someone does want the secrets here, and that person may have broken in and killed the guard. Hell, maybe the dead guard was even working with that individual, and the partnership went south."

Cecelia stopped pacing.

"Or option two…" The option that was already making Elizabeth shudder. "One of the Lazarus subjects killed that guard."

"But the subjects are supposed to be secured," Landon argued. "They were supposed to be locked in their cells."

They were *supposed* to be.

The lab doors burst open. The dead man's body was wheeled inside. He'd been zipped into a body bag. For a moment, she had a random, wild thought. *Why do they have body bags here?* Elizabeth didn't want to wonder too long about that—she was afraid of what the answer might be.

The body bag hit the edge of a cabinet as the men wheeled the gurney inside. The bag started to topple over, but one of the guards grabbed it, fast, holding the bag—and body—in place. So much for preserving any sort of crime scene. The guards weren't even wearing gloves.

Because Landon thinks this is the work of one of the test subjects. He doesn't believe option one at all.

She waited until it was just her and Landon and Cecelia in that room again. The guards practically ran out. She didn't blame them. But once they were gone, Elizabeth grabbed gloves and she slowly lowered the zipper of that bag. The dead guard's bloated face stared back at her. Hugh.

She began to examine the body, slowly and carefully. No, she wasn't a damn ME but she could help. She *had* to help. Hugh Cleston had been brutally murdered. Stabbed, again and again. Deep, hard thrusts. No shallow cuts at all.

"There was no hesitation." Cecelia stood beside her. "The killer struck hard each time. The wounds are so deep. They're...savage."

Elizabeth kept examining the body, and all she could hear in her head, over and over was...

Increased aggression. The subjects display increased aggression. "Have there..." She cleared her throat. "Have there been any other incidents at this facility?"

Last night, someone was in Cecelia's room. And now a man is dead.

Landon gave a jerky move of his head. "The subjects *are* secured."

God, she couldn't hold back the secret about the subjects being able to slip out of their cells. She couldn't. Not when a man was *dead.* But if she revealed what she knew, wasn't that a betrayal of Sawyer? *Is there a choice?* "There's...there's something you need to know —"

The alarm blared. The same wild sound that had startled her the night before.

Lockdown.

Her eyes flew to the lab door.

"Oh, shit," Landon muttered.

She could hear the thud of footsteps running toward her. Fast, hard, wild. She staggered back, wondering who was racing toward the lab. *Someone is coming for us.*

Landon rushed across the room and jerked open a drawer. He pulled out a gun, lifted it up and the barrel shook in his grip.

"They're out," Cecelia said, wide-eyed. "It's the test subjects. I think they've been getting out all along."

They were screwed. That was what they were. *Screwed.*

"Only takes sixty seconds and then the doors lock," Landon threw back. "We just need to make it—"

There was a guttural cry from beyond the lab. The guards that had gone back outside moments before—had one of them just made that cry? Were the guards being attacked? She lunged forward, determined to help them, but Landon grabbed her and pushed her back. "You're too damn valuable. You *can't* be risked."

Those thundering footsteps raced toward the lab. She could hear them closing in, even over the shriek of the lockdown alarm.

"About thirty more seconds," Landon said.

The lab doors burst open. Sawyer was there, breathing hard, his face was twisted into tight, angry lines. He had a gun gripped in one hand.

How did he get a gun?

Only Sawyer wasn't alone. Flynn was right beside him. Unarmed, but his hands were fisted, as if he couldn't wait to tear into someone.

Flynn's furious gaze—and Sawyer's—were both directed right at Landon.

The seconds ticked by…everything seemed to slow down.

The alarm stopped blaring. *Clang.* The door had sealed shut, locking them all inside the lab.

"Get the fuck away from them," Sawyer snarled at Landon.

Landon lifted his gun. "*Guards!*"

"They can't help you," Sawyer snapped as he took a step forward. "They're on the *other* side of that door, and they're taking a little nap right now."

Flynn was staring at Cecelia. "You screamed." His hands flexed, then re-fisted. "I heard you scream."

Cecelia backed up a step.

The tension in that lab was electric.

"Stand down!" Landon yelled at the Lazarus men. "Stand down or I fire—"

No, that wasn't happening. Elizabeth moved in front of him. This move hadn't worked out well for her before, and her knees were knocking. "Lower the gun, Landon," Elizabeth told him as she fought to keep her voice even. "We have to calm down, we have to talk—"

"They're out of their cells," Landon yelled back as spittle flew from his mouth. "And Hugh is *dead!* This is what you feared, isn't it? They've gone too far, they have to be —"

Sawyer lunged forward. He shoved Elizabeth out of the way, and she crashed onto the floor.

Landon fired.

"No!" Elizabeth screamed.

But Sawyer had dodged the tranq. He'd moved so incredibly fast. Landon tried to fire again, but it was too late. Sawyer ripped the gun right out of Landon's hand. He aimed it at the doctor. "Let's see how you like this shit." He fired.

The tranq hit Landon in his gut, and Landon dropped, sinking like a stone as he fell on the floor, landing in an unconscious heap.

The sound of Elizabeth's thundering heartbeat filled her ears. She was sealed in that lab. Trapped with Sawyer and Flynn, and Sawyer had a weapon. A weapon he was…putting down?

"Easy, doc. Got to say, I don't like it when you stare at me that way." A muscle flexed in his jaw as he placed the gun down on the tiled floor. He lifted his hands toward her, in one of those gestures people did to show they weren't a threat. "Makes me feel like a fucking monster."

Flynn gave a rusty laugh. "Maybe because that's what we are."

Sawyer ignored him. "I'm not here to hurt you."

She was still on the floor.

"I'm sorry about pushing you, doc. I was just afraid Landon was going to shoot, and I didn't want the tranq to hit you."

She made a mental note to stop jumping in front of guys. It never worked for her.

Sawyer offered his hand to her. "Let me help you up."

She could get up on her own just fine, but her fingers closed around his. He pulled her up, and their bodies brushed.

"I had to get to you," he said. So soft. "Had to make sure you were okay."

Flynn advanced toward Cecelia. "We heard the scream and we needed to fucking make sure you were both all right."

The two men had broken out of their cells to help them? She pulled away from Sawyer, trying to think clearly. Trying to figure out what to do next.

"Doc?" Sawyer called, but he wasn't looking at her. His gaze had fallen on the exam table. A hard edge entered his voice as he demanded, "Tell me about the damn dead man on the table."

She cast a quick, worried glance at Cecelia. Flynn was close to the shrink, but he wasn't touching her. And Cecelia—she looked both afraid and furious.

"How long have you been able to get out of your rooms?" Cecelia asked. "How long?"

"Rooms? Don't you mean our cages?" Flynn fired right back. "Since day one."

Cecelia flinched.

"The dead man," Sawyer gritted. "What the hell happened?"

"He's a guard. Hugh Cleston." Elizabeth's words came too fast. "He was killed...broken neck and thirteen stab wounds."

"Who killed him?" Sawyer had moved closer to the exam table, and he'd pulled her with him. One of his hands curled around her wrist, holding her tight. His skin seemed to burn against hers.

Landon was still sprawled on the floor, out cold.

"We're trying to figure that out." Elizabeth said but there must have been something in her voice...

Sawyer's head cocked toward her. He blinked, and then his dark blue gaze hardened. "You think I did it?"

The man she'd known before would have never attacked an innocent person. But...when he'd first woken up in D.C., she'd watched as he'd taken out the guards around him. "Did you?"

His face turned angry and dark. He pulled her flush against him as his head tilted over hers.

"I came to save you." Each word was bitten off. "I gave up one of my secrets, *for you*."

One of his secrets? How many did he have?

Then his head jerked toward the locked lab door. "I *know*," Sawyer snarled as if someone had just spoken to him. "I can hear their footsteps coming, too. Fuck, yes, there will be repercussions."

What? Was he talking to her? Or to someone else?

His hold on her tightened as he stared down at her once more. "I didn't do this."

"What about your men? Can you be so sure of the others?"

His jaw hardened.

"Sawyer? Can you be sure of them?"

And now she could hear pounding footsteps, too. Getting closer. Rushing toward the lab. The cavalry?

"Be sure of this." Sawyer was even closer to her now, leaning right over her, with his lips at her ear. "I wouldn't hurt you."

She wanted to be sure. But she still remembered what it was like to have him pointing a gun—at her. And the memory must have been in her eyes because he blinked quickly and instantly released her. He took a step back even as she heard the sound of the lab's lock disengaging. "Doc? Elizabeth?"

"Please don't fight the guards when they come in. You know they aren't a match for you."

His expression closed down. And the cavalry raced inside.

CHAPTER FOURTEEN

He was in chains again. Sawyer sat on his pitiful excuse for a bed, his body tense, and fury boiling inside of him. He could snap out of the chains. Do it in half a breath, but he was trying to play this scene right.

Landon was standing in front of him. What a prick. Asshole Landon. It had sure felt good to rip the gun out of the guy's hand and fire on him. *Your turn to get dosed.*

Landon still wasn't back to one hundred percent. The guy's left leg was dragging behind him. And Landon had half a dozen guards crammed into Sawyer's room. *Someone's scared.*

Sawyer didn't stop the small smile that spread over his face.

"You think this is funny?" Landon blasted at him. "A man is *dead.* You and your teammates have been breaking out of your cells. You've murdered—"

"I didn't kill that guard. And, for the record, I also didn't fight in the lab. When the doors opened, I let your men lead me right back here.

Like a good soldier." Because Elizabeth had asked him to stay in control. Because he needed to not screw things up more than he already had.

His head throbbed now because of the voices of his teammates. The others had been furious when he'd broke out of his cell to rush after Elizabeth.

What in the hell were you thinking? That was Three. Normally, he was the quiet one. Quiet, controlled, iced fury. He wasn't so quiet right then.

So what if it had been her screaming? She doesn't matter. Five had been raging the loudest and the longest, but he was dead wrong. Elizabeth did matter.

She mattered quite a bit to Sawyer.

"You were supposed to be leading the mission at 0600." Ah, not a voice in his head. Landon was snapping at him again. "Lives were depending on you! And you completely screwed —" The door opened behind Landon, surprising the guy and making him stop mid-yell. Landon whirled around. "No one else is supposed to be — *Wright?*"

Sawyer lost his smile. Because sure as shit, he was staring at Wyman Wright. He'd met the man twice before in the Lazarus facility. But they'd never been this close. *Close enough for me to grab the guy and snap his neck.*

Wright was the guy pulling the strings. The man in charge of this hell.

"Clear the room." Wright pointed at the guards. "You men—*out*. Landon and I are the only ones who need to be here."

Landon's mouth opened and closed, like a fish, but he didn't speak.

The guards got the hell out of there.

This is my chance. I can take them both out. I can kill them right—

The cell door closed behind the last retreating guard. Wright's heavy sigh seemed to fill the room. "I picked you to be the leader."

Sawyer lifted a brow. "I thought I had been leading."

"Six missions. Six successes." Wright shook his head. "This was to be mission seven. Lucky seven. After this one, I was going to give your team more freedom. You just had to get through this one final mission without an incident. But now I discover you've been breaking out—"

"I heard a woman screaming." He was sticking to that same story. Why not? It was the truth. "I went to help. What was I supposed to do? Let someone suffer?"

Wright took a step closer to him. "Did you think Dr. Parker was screaming?"

Tread carefully. That warning came from Two. Shit, he needed those assholes out of his head so Sawyer slammed the mental door on all of his teammates. As hard as he could. Then there was silence in his head. For the moment.

Wright kept staring at him. "Did you think it was her, One?"

"I wasn't sure. I just could tell by the pitch that it was a woman."

"And you broke out—rushing to save the day."

He shrugged and the chains rattled.

Landon gave a loud grunt. "Bullshit. He tranqed me, he—"

"When I arrived in the lab, I thought you were threatening Dr. Parker and Dr. Gregory." Had he always been so good at lying? "I asked you to lower your weapon. When you didn't, I took it away from you."

"You *fired* it at me—"

"I had to eliminate the threat to Dr. Parker." The words were calm, completely at odds with the tension in his body. "And to Dr. Gregory. You seemed highly…unstable to me at the time. I worried about what move you'd make next."

"He's lying." Spittle flew from Landon's mouth. "He's—"

"The video footage backs up One's account." Wright turned the force of his glare on Landon. "He never hurt the two women. After you were on the floor, he immediately lowered his weapon."

"But—"

"If he'd wanted to hurt Dr. Parker *or* Dr. Gregory, Subject One could have killed them in an instant.." Wright nodded briskly. "Instead, he made a moral choice—he broke out of his cell in order to help someone he thought was in danger. This is very, very good."

Landon stared at Wright in shock. "He tranqed me."

"Yes, but he didn't kill you. Now get the damn chains and cuffs off him. One has a mission to run."

What the sweet hell? Sawyer wasn't sure he'd just heard correctly but...

"What about the dead guard?" Landon made no move to free Sawyer. "If One and his men can get out of their cells anytime they want, then he may have killed that guard! Poor Hugh Cleston! The guy was stabbed *thirteen* times."

Wright crossed his arms over his chest as he studied Sawyer. "Did you kill that guard?"

"No."

Wright grunted. His eyes were slits on Sawyer. "Do you know who did?"

Sawyer let his gaze drift to Landon. "It could have been anyone."

Consideringly, Wright followed Sawyer's stare.

Landon flushed. "What? *What?* He's accusing me? *Me?*"

"You were the one going room to room, conducting the search, weren't you? You had access to the full facility." He shrugged once more, and the chains clinked. "I didn't."

Landon surged toward him. Sawyer let the bastard come at him. *Come closer. Come…*Sawyer lifted his foot up and slammed it into Landon's stomach. Landon's pain-filled grunt filled the air right before the doctor thudded onto the floor.

The guy didn't leap back to his feet.

Sawyer stared at Wright. "Am I heading out on the mission or not?"

Wright smiled at him. "You absolutely are. I count on you to lead these missions. There's a reason you were the first subject into the program. You are the best." He inclined his head. "But this time, you'll be going out without your wing man."

Sawyer didn't let his expression change.

"Gonna keep Subject Two here for this one. Gonna keep *half* the team. I don't think you need them. I want to see what you can do on your own."

Bullshit. You think if you have half my team here, you can control me. The damn thing was…the bastard was right. "Get the cuffs off," Sawyer gritted.

Landon was slowly rising.

"You heard the man," Wright said with a wave of his hand. "We don't have time to waste."

***

They were going on a mission. There was a dead body in the lab, a killer on the loose, and Wright was still sending out his team of super soldiers. The world had gone absolutely mad, and Elizabeth didn't know how to stop the insanity.

"You're the one he likes."

Her head shot up. She'd just entered the small exam room — under Wright's orders. He wanted her to examine the team of three men before they left on their mission.

Subject Five sat on the exam table. Bryce King. His blond hair was pushed back from his face, and a faint smile tugged at his lips.

"Our fearless leader," he added when she just stood there. "One. You're the lady he likes."

She gripped the clipboard tighter in her hand. "I think you're mistaken."

A guard was in the room with her. He stood to the side, silent, watchful, and armed. Her gaze darted to him.

Five laughed. "I'm not mistaken about anything. One didn't like the way I was looking at you in the training room, so he took my ass down." Another laugh, a warm rumble. "Marked you as his. Told me to keep my hands off."

She could feel heat staining her cheeks. "I'm his doctor. I'm a doctor for you all." She moved closer to the exam table. Elizabeth put down the clipboard and lifted her stethoscope.

He caught her wrist, curling his fingers around her and stilling the movement. "Is that true?" His gaze dipped over her. "Are you for us all?"

She didn't like his touch. Didn't like the way his voice had just turned cold. And she'd seen the flash of something ugly in his eyes.

But he smiled and his thumb stroked her skin. "I think there's a lot to learn from you."

Her shoulders locked. "Get your hand off me."

He immediately freed her. "Sorry, Dr. Parker."

The guard had stepped forward. Elizabeth gave a short, hard shake of her head. "We're fine."

"Better than fine," Five murmured. "As if I'd ever do anything to hurt what was *his*."

She checked his vitals. Touched him for only the barest of moments. Like Sawyer, his skin was warmer than normal, his heart-rate accelerated. She knew his senses were stronger, his reflexes sharper. And she wondered about his strength. Wondered about the secrets he might be keeping.

That Sawyer might be keeping.

"Are you afraid of us?"

Her gaze rose to meet his.

"The guards are. That fellow in the corner is about to shit himself because he hates to be in a room with me." Five flashed his smile. "When you're treated like a monster for so long, you start to feel like one."

She stared into his eyes, trying to see beneath his mask.

"But I guess you know all about monsters. After all, you made us, right?"

Elizabeth swallowed. "We're done with the exam. You checked out fine." Though she still couldn't believe they were heading on the mission. After last night, the murdered man...

"You didn't answer my question, Dr. Parker." Five tilted his head as he put his shirt on. "Are you afraid of us?"

A short rap sounded on her door.

"Ah, next patient." He jumped off the table and his body brushed against hers. Immediately, Elizabeth stepped back.

His eyes narrowed, just the tiniest bit.

The door opened. Her head turned, and she found Sawyer standing there. He filled the doorway with his broad shoulders. He was dressed in black, just like Five. Just like the guards. The clothes stretched over his muscled form. His face was expressionless, but his gaze was stormy. Filled with so many emotions.

NEVER LET GO   225

Five laughed. "Don't worry. I kept my hands off." He gave a little salute to Sawyer and headed for the door. "I'll wait for you at mission prep."

Another guard stood in the hallway, and when Five left, the guard followed him.

Elizabeth swallowed and motioned toward the table. "Just, um, take off your shirt, and I'll begin the exam."

Eyes on her, he yanked the shirt over his head and tossed it onto a nearby table. Then he stalked straight toward her, moving with a controlled, dangerous grace. Her stare jerked toward the guard who still waited in the corner of the room. He was there for her protection. Only…

"Three of us are going on the mission." A low hum of anger slid through Sawyer's words. "Fucking three. We need the whole team, but Wright is holding them back."

For once, she didn't blame Wright. They needed to find out what was happening in Lazarus. Letting the whole team of super soldiers out at the same time? Not such a good idea.

He sat on the table. She took his temperature, checked his pupil response, put the stethoscope over his heart…

And he watched her. Watched her with a stare that seemed to burn her skin. Watched her with a gaze that saw straight into her. Her fingers were trembling. Her knees wanted to shake.

There were a thousand things that she wanted to say to Sawyer, but Elizabeth didn't speak at all.

Her fingers lingered against his muscled chest as she listened to his heartbeat. They'd made love hours before.

Not love. It isn't love, Elizabeth. This man — he doesn't know you. He isn't the same. You had sex. Sex with a man you aren't sure if you can truly trust. Guilt and pain had driven her to find him. And now — now she didn't know what to do next.

"He's keeping the others as insurance. To make sure we don't step out of line."

She removed the stethoscope and stepped back.

Sawyer lifted the leg of his pants, revealing his right ankle, and the metal band that circled his skin. "Like we can just walk away when we have these on us. They track us, everywhere that we go. Only Landon can get them off us. He's got a program on his laptop — he has to type in a code to put these things on us and then to get them off. Even has to scan his right index fingerprint in order to get the program to open. Talk about freaking overkill."

She didn't know specific details about this mission. For a moment, it almost felt as if she were in the past. He was leaving on a mission. And she — she was trying to keep her emotions locked up.

Sawyer shoved away from the table. His body brushed against hers. But, unlike when Five had gotten too close, she didn't retreat. She stood right there because she was so desperate to be with the man she remembered.

"Don't be here when we come back." Sawyer's words were a bare breath of sound against her ear. A low whisper she couldn't even be certain that she'd heard.

Then he was nodding and striding away from her. Not glancing over his shoulder, not acknowledging her at all.

A shiver slid over Elizabeth's skin.

Don't be here when we come back. His words had felt like a threat.

Maybe because…they were.

***

Landon glared as the team loaded up. Sawyer gave the bastard a go-to-hell grin. General Jamison was already barking orders, telling the men to move out. A chopper waited for them on the helipad. They were on the very surface of the Lazarus facility—on top of a damn mountain—and the world stretched below them.

"Looks like someone will miss us while we're gone," Three said. Three—tall, lean, with eyes that were nearly black and always cold. Three was absolutely lethal in the field, a sniper who could take out anyone with no hesitation. The guy didn't joke as a rule, but his lips were curled as he stared at Landon.

"Not like we'll be gone long enough for him to miss us." Five checked his weapon. "We get the kill done, and then we'll be back to home, sweet home."

"Load up!" General Jamison shouted.

Sawyer jumped into the chopper with the others. As the bird rose into the air, the wind battered back on the helipad. Landon stood there, still glaring up at them, but he wasn't alone. Wright had joined him. Wright was smiling as the chopper lifted off.

Is the plan still a go? Three's voice slid through Sawyer's head.

The plan. Shit. Too late to turn back now. *Yes.*

He had the fast impression of satisfaction from Three. Three...the fellow wasn't much for conversation. More like the silent and deadly type.

The chopper flew fast away from the helipad. The whoop, whoop, whoop of the blades droned steadily overhead. Sawyer glanced down at the land below him. Red. The mountains and the rocks were so red there. They were close to Sedona. Not too close, though. Didn't want any tourists stumbling into their realm by mistake. Oh, no, couldn't have that.

Your doc is afraid of us. Five's voice filled Sawyer's head.

Sawyer's head turned until he was staring at Five's profile.

When she touched me, she was shaking.

Sawyer kept staring at the fellow.

Slowly, Five's head turned until their eyes met. *Do you like it when she's afraid?*

No, he fucking didn't like it.

Five's mouth hitched just the faintest bit. *Because I do.*

CHAPTER FIFTEEN

Don't be here when we come back.

Sawyer's words kept replaying in Elizabeth's head, and, yeah, they were freaking her the hell out. But then, the dead body was also freaking her out.

"I'll take care of the guard," Wright was saying. The body of Hugh Cleston had been zipped back up. "Despite what Dr. Meyer said before, there is no need for either of you to perform any sort of exam on the remains." His stare darted to Elizabeth and Cecelia. Wright had brought in a team, and they were currently wheeling Hugh out of the lab, and, presumably, away from Lazarus. "Don't you all worry."

"A little late for that," Cecelia retorted, her hands going to her hips. "A man has been *murdered.* Tell me that we're going to have justice for him, tell me that you aren't just going to leave us down here with a killer —"

Wright waved his team on, and they pushed the body out of the lab. Then Wright turned, a congenial mask on his face, as he peered at

Cecelia. "Dr. Gregory, you know I admire your work."

She stiffened. "Do you?"

"You like to explore the darkness in the human mind. You like to see what makes men into monsters."

"I try to *stop* men from becoming monsters. Men and women. That's what I do."

"You study killers. Actually, you made killers your life's work."

"I made *stopping* killers my life's work. You lied to me. You told me that I would be making a difference here, that I would be helping these men—"

"You are doing all of that."

Cecelia took a step toward him. "You neglected to give me all the necessary information on my subjects. You didn't tell me that they were *dead* men."

Wright's gaze slid to Elizabeth. Hardened. Then he focused once more on Cecelia. "They were only dead for a small amount of time. And they are obviously very much alive now." He rolled back his shoulders. "These men have far exceeded my expectations. The things they can do—absolutely outstanding. They will change the face of warfare. They will change the world." He nodded. "I am beyond satisfied with the progress here, and it's time we expanded our experimentation."

He had to be joking.

Or else he was just insane. "A man is dead." Elizabeth's voice shook but she didn't care. "And someone in this facility killed him. Stabbed him, thirteen times. Your test subjects have been coming and going as they please while they are here. One of them is quite possibly the killer and—"

"The test subjects didn't kill that guard. Someone else did."

He sounded so very certain. He was also very *wrong*. "You don't know that," Elizabeth argued. "You don't—"

"I know *exactly* where the subjects are, at every moment of every day." He crossed his arms over his chest. "Just as I know that, last night, Subject One was in *your* quarters, Dr. Parker. He was alone with you for fifteen minutes. And yet you told no one about that encounter."

She felt her face ice.

"Obviously, you didn't think One was a threat. You didn't think he was such a terrible killer, or you wouldn't have kept his secret."

How did he know? "Are you...do you have a camera in my room?" The bastard. He had cameras *everywhere*. Sweet hell, had he watched her and Sawyer together? The ice in her face gave way to heat.

"Of course, I don't have a camera in your room." He laughed. "However, I do have a tracking device implanted in all of the subjects."

Her jaw dropped. No, that didn't make any sense. If he had implanted tracking devices then why..."The ankle band—"

He put a finger to his lips. "Our little secret, ladies, but that band *isn't* for tracking. I tell the men it is, of course, but it's actually an explosive. While conducting these initial tests, I had to be certain the men would act...appropriately...in the outside world. If they step out of line, if I deem them a threat in any way, I can trigger the device. And the threat they pose would be eliminated." Now he snapped his fingers. "Just like that."

Elizabeth could only shake her head.

Cecelia had gone silent.

"The tracking device is implanted on each subject in a different location. Hidden under an old scar. Because of their lifestyles, the men all have scars, so concealment was easy enough. Through the trackers, I monitor the subjects, twenty-four seven. I've known for a while that they have been able to slip from their rooms and explore the Lazarus facility."

"You knew and you didn't stop them?" Cecelia blurted, breaking her silence.

"I thought *you* wanted them to have more freedom." He lifted a brow. "Isn't that what your reports have been saying, Dr. Gregory?"

Her jaw hardened. "That was before we found a dead body—"

"The subjects didn't kill that guard. I monitored their trackers. None of them were near that stairwell." He shrugged one shoulder. "So that means the guard was killed by someone else here, obviously. I don't think anyone snuck into the facility. I think the killer is here, an employee. A doctor. Another guard. An individual who works for Lazarus. I believe it was someone who wants the Lazarus secrets and was caught in the act of trying to steal intel. That individual turned on the guard. Now we have to clean up the killer's mess."

He spoke so easily. As if the murder of a man had been an inconvenience. And it wasn't about cleaning up after the killer. It was about stopping him.

"Don't worry," Wright assured them. "I will find the individual responsible. But in the meantime, Project Lazarus will proceed as planned."

"These men—they are dangerous!" Cecelia's voice rose. "You *know* one of them has been coming into my room, and you didn't say a thing—"

He turned toward her. "Ah, yes, sorry, that brings me to a bit of bad news. Lazarus will continue as planned, but I'm afraid you will not be the psychiatrist working with the subjects."

"What?"

"None of the subjects ever entered your room. Their trackers show that. I can't find any indication that *anyone* was there. I'm afraid that working down here isn't good for you, Dr. Gregory. Despite the esteem I hold for you, well, I'm afraid you just aren't the right fit for Lazarus. I think the facility and the people here…perhaps old memories are being stirred up too much for you."

"*Someone was in my room! He was watching me.*"

"None of our test subjects were in your room. And I'm sorry…" Wright sighed. "I just can't trust your judgment any longer."

Elizabeth moved to stand at Cecelia's side. "You just said someone was trying to steal intel. Maybe that person—the person who killed the guard—maybe he was the one in Cecelia's room. Maybe—"

"All of Dr. Gregory's notes and her files are kept in her office, not her private quarters. If someone wanted access to her files, the thief would go there. Not her bedroom." He shook his head. "No, all signs point to Dr. Gregory having…a bit of an episode." He tucked in his chin and stared at Cecelia a bit sadly. "And that's the story that will spread, Dr. Gregory, if you mention this facility to *anyone*. The world will know that you are suffering from a psychotic break. That you never quite got over your past. It will be unfortunate, but that's the way life works."

"You sonofabitch!" Cecelia lunged at him, but Elizabeth caught the other woman and pulled her back. "You're blackmailing me!"

"I'm telling you that your services are no longer needed. Your judgment is off when it comes to these men. You think they're psychologically unstable, but from where I stand, *you're* the one with the issues, doctor. You're jumping at shadows and at ghosts that aren't there."

"Someone *was* there!"

"Collect your belongings. You'll be leaving the facility this morning." Now he pointed at Elizabeth. "I should send you with her. After your...rendezvous with Subject One, I should make you leave the facility. You're endangering—"

"Cut the bullshit." She let go of Cecelia. If the other woman wanted to go after Wright, Elizabeth wasn't going to stop her any longer. In fact, she'd help Cecelia. "You came to me because your program needed help. *You* need help. But you're still dealing in secrets and half-truths. You want to go forward with Lazarus, but you don't even know what you've got yet, not fully."

"I do want to go forward, and you're the woman who will help me."

"You said there were problems—"

"I lied about those. My team is perfect."

The door opened. Guards marched inside.

"Perfect timing," Wright muttered. "Please escort Dr. Gregory to her quarters. Help her collect her belongings, and then we will be taking Dr. Gregory out of the facility."

Cecelia's body was bow tight. "You're making a mistake. The men give me only the answers they *want* me to have. They lie, just as easily as you do."

"Good-bye, Dr. Gregory." His voice was crisp. Final.

"This isn't over."

"For you, it is." He motioned to the guards. One took Cecelia's left elbow and led her from the lab. Elizabeth moved to follow her, but Wright stepped into her path. "I want you to stay."

Don't be here when we come back.

"I came to you in D.C. because I want you to help me." The lab door had closed. They were alone. "I need you to create a better formula."

"What?"

"The men…they shouldn't have to die first. I want a formula that will allow them to have enhanced healing and strength *before* death is necessary. You can do it, I know you can."

She wasn't making more formulas for him.

"Landon failed."

What the hell?

"He thought he could do it. But his formula *killed* the test subjects. And they couldn't reanimate, even with our preservation process in place. Landon just can't do what you can—his mind is limited, but yours isn't."

They were alone in that lab, and her skin was ice cold.

"The only way the Lazarus formula works is for the subjects to die, first. Landon can't find a way around that, but I know you can. You can fix that problem."

She wasn't doing anything for him.

His jaw hardened. "You owe me."

Now Elizabeth laughed. "How do you figure that?"

"Because I'm keeping you safe. I have been this whole time. Even when you were in D.C., I had a team watching you."

Shock rolled through her. "You were spying on me?"

"My dear Dr. Parker, surely you've realized the danger you are in by now?"

She was staring at danger.

"People want the Lazarus formula. I thought that by taking all of your research material and your notes, that I would be protecting you—"

A wild laugh erupted from her. "Oh, that's what you were doing? When you *stole* my life's work, you were protecting—"

"I believe that Hugh Cleston died because someone wants to steal the Lazarus intel. At your core, *you* are the Lazarus intel. If others have figured that out, then they'll just take you. They won't be as…kind…of an employer as I have been. They can force you to share the information in your amazing brain. They can torture you until you reveal everything that you know."

"Are you threatening me?" He'd blackmailed Cecelia, but with Elizabeth, he was taking a much darker course.

"No, I'm offering you my continued protection from those who *would* hurt you. That's one of the reasons I brought you into this facility. To assure that you'd be safe."

Bull. He'd just told her—not two minutes before—that he wanted a better formula. The guy was all about twisting truths and lies to get what he wanted.

"Stay here," Wright urged her. "Help me to make Lazarus even better. Even stronger. You can stay here, you'll be safe, *and* you'll be with Sawyer. You'll have him with you just like before—"

Her heart ached. General Jamison had known about her relationship with Sawyer. If Jamison knew…*Wright must have told him.* She'd put those puzzle pieces together. "Back in D.C., you knew Sawyer and I were lovers."

His smile was fast and sly. "I know everything about my employees."

"You knew…and you still put him into Project Lazarus."

Now he laughed. "My dear, that's the *main* reason I wanted him. I needed a subject you were linked with, someone that you couldn't turn away from."

Because he wants me tied to Lazarus. Always.

She fought to keep her emotions in check — a losing battle. "You weren't angry when you saw that he'd been in my quarters last night. You were thrilled, weren't you?"

Wright's expression didn't change. "I guess even without his memory, some things are the same."

Bastard. "Blackmail."

"Sorry, doctor, I don't think I heard —"

"You're blackmailing me, the same way you just blackmailed Cecelia. Only you're using Sawyer against me. You are dangling him as some kind of prize in front of me so that I'll do whatever you want, but I am *not* playing Frankenstein for you any longer." She rushed toward the door.

Don't be here when we get back.

"I'd hate for Subject One to be terminated."

Her hand stilled in mid-air. She'd been reaching for the door but now she whirled around.

"I mean…it would be unfortunate, wouldn't it? If we found out that Sawyer was responsible for the death of Hugh Cleston. Because if Sawyer was the killer, then we'd have to terminate him. He'd be too much of a danger for any other alternative."

"Y-you said Sawyer wasn't guilty. That none of the test subjects were near that stairwell —"

He advanced toward her with slow, gliding steps. "If you try to leave my program, if you don't give me exactly what I want, *Dr.* Parker, then I can make your precious Sawyer look guilty as fucking hell. And I'll let you watch while we terminate him."

She shook her head. "You *can't* do that to him."

"Of course, I can. And no one will do a thing about it. You see, Sawyer Cage is already a dead man. If he dies twice, well, who would care?"

I would.

"But that isn't necessary," he murmured as his cold eyes locked on her like a predator closing in for the kill. "Not necessary at all. You stay here, you continue your absolutely brilliant work, and you'll be able to see Sawyer whenever you want."

She searched his gaze. "You're never going to let those subjects go, are you?"

"No." He shook his head. "I'm absolutely not. They are far too valuable. But I like to dangle that reward before them, just to keep them motivated. If they found out that they were going to spend the rest of their lives in this place..." A low laugh rippled from him. "They wouldn't exactly cooperate with me, now, would they?"

She'd never wanted to kill anyone more than she did in that instant.

"But at least Sawyer will have time with you, Dr. Parker." He inclined his head toward her. "And if you'll just get me a better fucking formula, then I won't have to kill my soldiers again in order for this damn project to keep succeeding."

A dull ringing filled her ears.

I won't have to kill my soldiers again. Again. Again?

He—he hadn't...*no!* Her heart stopped. "You killed Sawyer?"

"You've gone quite pale, doctor. Perhaps you should go and rest before the men return from their mission." He tried to push her to the side so that he could leave the lab.

She wasn't in the mood to be pushed. Elizabeth grabbed him and held tight, nearly clawing into his arm. "*You* killed Sawyer?"

His eyes were so cold. "I needed the perfect subject. And, please, don't forget, he volunteered. I'm sure Landon has shown you the video by now. Sawyer wanted this program. And you wanted him." He jerked free of her hold. "Let's just say I gave you what you both wanted."

Numb, she watched him leave. The door clicked shut behind him.

Fury built in her. A deadly rage that wasn't going to be controlled. He'd killed Sawyer. It hadn't been a mission gone wrong. The sonofabitch had killed her lover.

And I am going to give you exactly what you deserve, you bastard.

***

The chopper touched down on the helipad. The blades spun slowly, and the men inside were quiet.

I won't go back to living in the dark.

Sawyer didn't move. Five's words rolled right through him. Five…he'd been particularly savage on this mission. Taking risks. Killing the targets…not quickly, but, slowly. Savoring.

The plan is in place. That was Three. He'd been like ice. Taking out his targets with no hesitation. Getting the job done. *We take over the facility. We get the others out. Then we vanish.*

A simple enough plan. One they'd formulated over the last few weeks when they'd grown tired of living in captivity. They'd needed this last mission, needed to get the chopper ready and positioned for their escape. It would stay on the helipad for a few more hours, until Wright left the facility. Wright was only at the Lazarus facility during the missions. He didn't always make contact with the subjects, but he was *there* at mission time. That was always the procedure. He came in the chopper, and he left in it, too.

Only that wouldn't be the case this time.

Sawyer and the others would be back for that chopper *before* it departed with Wright. And they'd never come back.

They were done being test rats. Worse, done being fucking attack dogs. They all had lives. Lives before Lazarus. They wanted those lives back.

Don't kill anyone in the facility. Sawyer sent his hard order to the others. *Do only what is necessary to escape. Subdue the guards. Haul ass.*

But they would also be taking data with them. Files. Intel. Any information that could help them unlock their pasts.

"Great job, men." General Jamison was pleased, as always. He beamed at them. "We'll be moving toward the next step in this program, you count on it. Soon you'll be freely moving in the outside world."

Did the man realize they could tell when he lied? That his breathing kicked up? His heartbeat accelerated? Sure, he was better at lying than most men, but Sawyer and the other subjects could still tell when he led them on.

Always leading us on. He kept giving them promises, but the general had no intention of keeping those promises. Jamison, Landon, and Wright were all fucking liars. And the time for captivity was over.

"You'll need to have a post-meeting check with the doctors," Jamison stated with an incline of his head. Standard procedure. No one needed patching. They hadn't been injured on the mission. They'd just been the killers. But they would still have to be checked by the doctors. "After that, we'll meet tonight to discuss future plans. Good things are coming, you can be sure of that."

No, very bad things were coming. The general could be sure of that.

They left the chopper. The sun was sinking low in the sky. Night swept down fast in the desert.

As they headed for the elevator that would take them down, down into the bowels of the facility once more, Jamison's hand clamped over Sawyer's shoulder. "Landon told me that Dr.

Parker should be leading the post-mission checks. Go see her first."

He didn't want her leading the checks. *I hope she's gone.* Because when he'd told her to leave, he'd meant those words. They'd been a warning. If Elizabeth was still there...

She was about to be dragged straight into hell.

They entered the elevator. Jamison had excited energy practically pouring off him. The smile on his face just kept getting bigger. "The enemy was no match for you," he praised. "No match at all! No one can fight your strength."

No, no one could.

"Sir..." Three's voice was mild. "What is the next step?"

"More men, ASAP. We need a bigger team. That's the next step. Increasing the Lazarus ranks. Can't handle the bigger missions without more manpower. But Dr. Parker can take care of that."

Sawyer's muscles tightened.

Jamison swiped his ID over the elevator's control screen, and then they were descending rapidly. If you didn't have the right ID, the elevator didn't move at all. Another part of their escape plan. *We need his ID.* Sawyer glanced at Three.

Three's head moved in the slightest of nods.

"Get your monitors removed after your checks with the doctor," Jamison advised, his voice jovial. "Then we'll hit the mess hall for dinner. I'd say you all more than deserve a good meal."

A good meal? In return for killing?

Sawyer stared straight ahead and watched as the lights on the elevator's screen flashed.

The plan is a go. He sent the message out, not just to Three and Five, but to every member of his team. As soon as the elevator doors opened, his team would act.

They weren't going to be prisoners any longer.

***

Elizabeth paused in front of the door to the first exam room. Sawyer was waiting in there. Sawyer, back from his mission.

He'd told her to leave, but that wasn't an option. Not now. Not with Wright threatening his life. She and Sawyer had to talk. They had to figure this thing out.

She opened the door. Her gaze swept inside, looking for the guard who should have been with Sawyer now that he was back in the facility but—

The guard was crumpled on the floor, his body twisted in a heap.

Elizabeth opened her mouth to scream.

Sawyer grabbed her. He yanked her forward, spun her around, then pinned her in front of his body. His hand covered her mouth, choking back the scream that had been trembling on her lips. His hold was too tight, too hard, too rough.

And terror clawed at her.

"I told you to leave, doc." His voice was a growl. *"Too late now."*

She struggled in his hold, twisting and kicking, but he just held her tighter. He held her tighter and then—

"I don't want to hurt you."

She wanted to yell, *"Then don't! Let me the hell go!"* But his hand was still over her mouth and he was dragging her farther away from the door. He shoved her against the wall, spinning her around and trapping her with his body. His hand stayed locked right over her mouth.

Elizabeth stared up at him in absolute horror. His face was blank, but his eyes blazed. And they blazed with a fury that froze her. This wasn't the same man she'd had sex with the night before. This wasn't the man she'd spent so many months with in D.C. This man, he was different.

He's Subject One.

"You should've left when you had the chance," he rasped. "Now, it's too late for you."

She stared at him, searching desperately for some glimpse of the man he'd been. Some small shred—

The door burst open. "The floor is clear!"

That was...Five.

Her gaze flew toward him.

He smiled at her, and Five lifted the gun he held in his hand. "Well, I guess we're almost clear." He stepped inside. She expected to hear shouts from the hallway or the shriek of an alarm. *Something.* But there was nothing. "You gonna take care of her?" Five demanded. "Or do you want me to do it?" And he came ever closer with his gun pointed straight at her.

CHAPTER SIXTEEN

"She is mine." Sawyer kept his hold on Elizabeth even as he turned his head to glare at Five. "You stand the fuck down."

Five only laughed. "I figured you had her in check. But it never hurts to ask." His smile slipped away. "I'll go make sure my favorite shrink isn't trying to sound an alarm." He backed away, making no sound at all, as he slipped from the room.

Elizabeth twisted in Sawyer's hold, trying to break free. Didn't she understand? It was too late now. But then, he knew, deep inside, it had been too late for her from the moment she'd stepped foot into the Lazarus facility. "You're coming with me."

Her eyes were wide and scared.

"Don't make a sound." He hated the way he spoke to her. But it wasn't just about him. There were others he had to consider. The team. "If you do, I'll have to knock you out." He'd knocked out the guard in that exam room and then taken the fellow's tranq gun. He'd hit the guard with a dose to keep him out of action for a while, but there were still plenty of tranqs left. "We're getting out of here, *now*. You move when I say move, and you don't hesitate." He stared at her a moment longer. "Nod, doc. Move your head and show me that you understand. Show me that you won't scream. Or else…" Shit, could he really tranq her? *Her?*

She nodded.

Good. His hand slid away from her, moving carefully from her mouth. As soon as his hand was clear, her little, pink tongue swept out to lick her lips. He tensed, thinking she'd cry out. Instead, she whispered, "Why?"

"Because Wright and Landon and Jamison—because everyone here is just lying to us. They aren't ever going to let us go, so we're taking our freedom. We're getting the hell out of here, and they won't *ever* find us again."

Her eyelids flickered. Her heart rate had also just jerked. He'd amped up his senses, the way he'd trained himself to do so that he could hear a freaking pin drop if need be, and he'd heard the lurch of her heart.

Fuck me. "How can they find us, doc?"

Her heart raced faster.

"Tell me, now!"

Then, before she could answer, he backed away. He bent low, and yanked up the edge of his pants. "This tracker? You think this is what will bring us down? Don't worry, Landon is going to take care of this for us. One way or another."

But...her eyes had gone even wider at the sight of the metal band on his ankle.

"You're fucking terrified." And it pissed him off. *Talk to me!*

She flinched. "It...it will kill you."

He grabbed her arms and yanked her toward him. *Too rough. Too hard. Keep your control.* But his control had been wearing away for weeks. All of the subjects had been slowly breaking apart on the inside. They'd held their masks in place, barely. That was why they had to escape. *If we don't escape, they'll find out.* And if those in charge found out how damaged the men really were, Sawyer thought Landon and Wright would terminate them all.

We're not their perfect soldiers. We're screwed.

"It's not a tracker. It's an explosive device." Her words were hollow. "And as soon as Wright and Landon realize what you're doing, they'll trigger them. You and your men—you won't get out of this facility. You're not going to escape. You'll die." A tear slid down her cheek. "And I don't want to stare at your dead body again. So stop this. Just—*stop!* Call off your men. There's another way. There has to be another—"

Her voice was rising. He clamped his hand over her mouth once more even as he sent a fast message to his men. *They lied to us a-fucking-gain. The metal bands on our ankles aren't tracking devices. They're bombs. The bastards will blow us up before they let us go.* Their advantage, though, only three of them still wore the bands. Sawyer, Three, and Five. *Get Landon. That bastard is going to take these off us.* Or he'd be the one dying.

Sawyer brought his face near Elizabeth's. "You're holding back more."

A tear leaked from her eye.

The sight of her tear made his head pound. A scene flashed in his mind.

Elizabeth…screaming. Elizabeth…falling. Blood on her chest. Blood pooling on the floor beneath her.

Then…then he'd been falling, too. Falling and reaching for her. Wanting to hold her, needing to get close to her one more time. They'd been in another fucking lab, in a sterile room, and gunfire had echoed around him.

He shook his head, hard, banishing the images. Then he stared down at her chest. She wore a white lab coat and a blue blouse under that coat. In his screwed-up visions, she'd been shot in the chest.

When he'd fucked her the night before, he hadn't taken off the Navy shirt she'd worn. He hadn't seen her chest.

His hand lifted from her mouth, and he grabbed her shirt-front. He yanked and the top two buttons on her blouse went flying. She gave a sharp gasp as she tried to shove his hands out of the way.

Too late.

He saw the scar—long, red, and raised—that slid under her bra. A scar that was too close to her heart. A scar…

"Sawyer!" She was screaming his name. Only the scream was in the past. In *his* past. In that sterile room, with the bodies on the floor. For one wild moment, Sawyer was back in that room, and as he looked down at himself, he realized he was holding a gun.

And Elizabeth—she'd just been shot.

Oh, my God…did I shoot her?

His knees hit the floor. In the past. In the present. He just fell.

And that was how the bullet missed him. A bullet thundered, the shot coming from the door, and it whipped by his head and it missed Elizabeth by inches – *damn inches* – as it sank into the wall of the exam room. Sawyer jumped to his feet and whirled to face the threat. And Landon Meyer was there, aiming a gun at him.

Only that wasn't a tranq he just fired. It had been a real bullet.

"Get away from her!" Landon yelled. "Get the hell away!"

Sawyer put his body firmly between that guy and Elizabeth.

"I knew, I *knew* you were hiding secrets!" Spittle flew from Landon's mouth. "Your men are running around this place like fucking ninjas, but you aren't taking control of the facility. I won't let you." Landon lifted the gun. "*I will stop you. I'll end you. There will be more to take your —* "

Sawyer charged at him. Landon fired, but Sawyer had anticipated the move. The bullet barely grazed his upper arm, and then Sawyer had the bastard. He hit Landon's wrist, he broke the bones with a snap, and the gun hit the floor. Sawyer shoved Landon back against the door frame. "Do *you* want to be ended?" In a blink, Sawyer grabbed the fallen weapon and aimed it at Landon.

Landon stared at him with fury and fear on his face.

"Take off the metal band, Dr. Meyer," Sawyer snarled. "Get that shit off me now."

Landon's gaze darted to Elizabeth.

"We're taking a trip," Sawyer put the gun to Landon's head. "To your office. You're going to use your computer and you're going to remove this band. You're going to disengage the lock on me and my two men."

Landon lifted his chin. "If I don't?"

"Then I *will* end you." Because Sawyer wasn't going to die.

"Elizabeth…" Landon's voice was choked. "You were right. They are monsters."

Sawyer's shoulders stiffened. He didn't take his eyes off Landon. If he did, he knew the guy would attack. But was Elizabeth about to attack him, too?

Shit. *No choice.*

"Elizabeth, come here," Sawyer ordered her flatly.

She didn't move.

His eyes stayed on Landon. "Do you want me to shoot him, Elizabeth?"

"No! I don't want you to shoot anyone."

"Then come to me." He held out his left hand to her. "Come here, doc."

Landon flinched. "Don't be fooled by him, Elizabeth. He's not the man you knew before. He's playing you. He's—"

"It doesn't matter." Elizabeth's quiet words seemed to fall heavily in the room as she shuffled closer. "I can't watch you die, Landon, even if I do think you're a prick."

She was close now. Sawyer reached out and grabbed her, pulling her against his chest, curling his body around hers. She felt so right against him, and some of the rage inside of Sawyer seemed to ease.

Never hurt her.

"We're going to your office, Landon. You're going to get this band off me." If he'd realized he was wearing a freaking explosive device, step one in their coup would have been to get the bands off and *then* to take over. But he hadn't known, and now he had to make the escape work, without getting anyone on his team blown to bits. "Move," Sawyer barked to Landon. "Get your ass in gear, now."

Swallowing, Landon followed orders.

Elizabeth was tense in Sawyer's arms. Tense and terrified. Sawyer bent his head. He had a role to play, men that were counting on him, but he couldn't stand her fear. It burned at what was left of his soul. His lips feathered over her ear as he whispered, "I swear, I will never hurt you."

***

Cecelia grabbed her bag and turned to face the guard who stood in her doorway. "I'm done, okay? Let's just get the hell out of—"

The guard fell. His body tumbled forward and crashed onto the floor. She stared at him, utterly horrified, stunned, and then...

"You're already packed?"

Her gaze flew back to her door—to the man standing there, smiling his fake smile. To the man holding a gun in his hand. To the man with the handsome face and the devil's eyes. Subject Five.

"How did you know it was time for us to make our getaway?" Five stepped over the unconscious guard, lowering the gun he'd used to slam into the back of the fellow's head. "I must say, I'm impressed."

"You shouldn't be here." He shouldn't be standing there, with a tranq gun in his hand. He shouldn't be smiling. He shouldn't be coming closer. He shouldn't—

"Why not?" He blinked. "I've been here plenty of times before. Not just the two occasions when you caught me." His head cocked. "I do love to watch you while you sleep."

What? She backed up, fear bursting past her shock. "*Help!*" Cecelia screamed.

"No one is going to help you now. No guard is coming in to save you." He aimed the weapon at her. "It's just you and me…finally."

***

Sawyer kept a tight hold on Elizabeth as they stood in Landon's office. She hadn't spoken, hadn't fought him, and he wanted to just get her the hell out of that place.

But I have to make sure that I don't explode on the way out. Shit. He should have realized that a contingency plan would be in place by the bosses of hell.

He used the gun and motioned toward Landon's laptop. "I've seen you disengage the bands plenty of times. Use your right index finger to access the program. Then key in your code and get the lock to open."

Landon reached for the laptop, no hesitation. "Fine, if that's what you—"

"If you trigger the band to explode, Elizabeth will be hurt, too."

Now Landon stopped.

Right, bastard. I knew what you planned. You were a little too eager when you grabbed the laptop.

Sawyer guided Elizabeth forward so that they were right next to Landon and his laptop. "We're going to watch you. Every single keystroke. Elizabeth is so close to me, if you trigger the explosion, you know she'll be taken out, too. And at this angle, you'll be hit, as well."

Landon's head turned as he glared at Sawyer. "You never cared about her, did you? Not back in D.C. Not here. Hell, you *can't* care about anyone or anything, can you? 'Cause you aren't human. Not anymore. You're just a weapon that's out of control." His gaze darted to Elizabeth. "You were right. I realized it back in D.C. But you don't say no to Wyman Wright. No one says no to him."

"You don't know a fucking thing about me," Sawyer's voice was low and lethal as the rage built inside of him again.

"No, you're the one who doesn't know anything. The woman you're holding—I think she loved you." Landon's face was sad. "That's why you came back to Lazarus, isn't it, Elizabeth?

Because you fell for him back when Sawyer was still human. Wright was thrilled as hell when I told him my suspicions about you two. I thought he'd kick Sawyer off the team, but no, not his bright, fucking leader. Wright had plans for him."

Elizabeth's body trembled. "What happened on that final mission, Landon?"

I think she loved you. Sawyer shook his head in hard denial. Elizabeth couldn't love him. She'd just come back to Lazarus. There was an insane desire between them, a primitive reaction, but there was no way she loved him.

Did she?

"He almost killed you before." Landon tapped on the keyboard. He scanned his index finger. "I think he'd do it right now, too, no hesitation."

No hesitation. The hell he would. But…

What the fuck am I doing? Sawyer tried to think past the red haze in his mind, the haze that had gotten worse with every test mission Jamison sent him out on. The rage was so strong it seemed to be choking him but…

This isn't me. This isn't who I am. "Get away from me," Sawyer gritted out.

The urge to kill. To hurt. To destroy—the darkness within him was stronger right then than it ever had been before, and it was *wrong*.

I wouldn't hurt Elizabeth. Never hurt her. So why the hell am I keeping her close when the band on my ankle could freaking explode?

He pushed Elizabeth away. "Get out of here." His temples were throbbing and everything around him seemed to be covered in a red haze.

Attack. Destroy. Won't be the prisoner any longer.

The feelings inside of him were getting worse. Bubbling up, consuming him and —

I'll start with her. The pretty doctor. Been watching her for so long now.

Sawyer's eyes closed. For just a moment, he could see…

Cecelia? Staring with terror on her face, holding up her hands as if she were fending off an attacker.

"He's unstable, Elizabeth! Run!" Landon shouted as the *tap, tap, tap* of his fingers flew over the keyboard, even faster now. "I'll terminate him, I'll —"

Sawyer's hand flew out and his fist slammed into the side of Landon's face. The guy fell back, his head banging into the nearby wall. Sawyer whirled and saw Elizabeth standing in the doorway. She stared at him with absolute horror on her face.

His hands flew to his temples. "It's not *me*." The words tore from him, but he finally, *finally* thought he understood what was happening.

The darkness swelling inside of him, the twisted fury that would come and go, eating away at him, screwing with his thoughts, messing with his mind. *"It's not me."*

"I know you aren't the same." She shook her head. "The Sawyer I knew would never—"

"It's one of the fucking others. It's *his* rage that's charging me, and I think he's attacking Cecelia!"

Her lips parted in shock. "What? That's— that's not possible!"

It was more than possible. It was happening. He had another flash. Cecelia, weak, helpless. "I have to get to her!" He still had the fucking band around his foot, and Landon was unconscious. No time. *No time.* The red haze was growing in his mind, building up. Fury had his muscles tightening, but the fury wasn't Sawyer's. It was someone else's.

The same way the team had been able to share their thoughts...shit, they were sharing emotions, too. Only someone's emotions had started to fuel Sawyer. To get in his head. *To control me.* Because he would never risk Elizabeth. Never put her in danger the way he had moments before. *This isn't me.*

"Run," he told her flatly as he tried to keep his mind from splintering. "Get the hell out of this place, and don't look back. Don't *ever* look back."

"Sawyer?"

"I'm going to save her. I swear, I will." And he didn't have time for anything else. Didn't have time to beg Elizabeth to forgive him. Didn't have time to tell her that he was wrong. That he was sorry he'd scared her. That he wished everything could have been different for him. That he wished—

Make her scream. Make her beg. Make her bleed.

The dark emotions were back, and Sawyer burst out of that room. He flew by Elizabeth, knowing that she had to get away from him. He was, quite literally, a ticking time bomb, and if he exploded, she couldn't be anywhere near him.

***

"Sawyer?" Elizabeth watched as he ran away from her. In those last few moments, his face had been absolutely savage. But his eyes had been full of pain and sorrow.

She took a step forward, hesitating. He'd said Cecelia was in danger.

He'd also said Elizabeth should run.

Cecelia saved me before. I can't leave her.

A groan came from behind Elizabeth. Landon. Damn, she'd almost forgotten him. She rushed to his side, and she shook him, trying to get him to wake up, but, despite the groan, the guy seemed to be out cold. Considering Sawyer had punched him with full strength—full enhanced strength—Elizabeth wasn't sure how long Landon would be unconscious. She didn't exactly expect him to wake back up anytime soon, though.

He hadn't released the band on Sawyer's ankle. But right before Sawyer's fist had collided with Landon's face, the guy had been typing frantically on the keyboard. The control screen was still on the laptop. He *had* opened the program, and she could see that in order to detonate Sawyer's band, all she had to do was click one button. *Landon scanned his finger already, he typed in the code.*

Elizabeth stared at the screen. There were two options right there for her.

Detonate.

Or disengage.

If she hit detonate, Sawyer would die. If she hit disengage, the lock would release. He'd be free.

He was going to risk your life! But…but he hadn't. Instead, he'd shoved her away. And he'd seemed so lost as he said, "*It's his rage that's charging me…*"

Her hand hovered over the keyboard as she replayed Sawyer's words.

"*Get out of here, and don't look back.*"

Was he the man she'd loved before? Or was he a monster now?

CHAPTER SEVENTEEN

Something is wrong. Subject Two slammed his shoulder into the door of his cell. The guards had changed things up on him, switched the access code to the cell, reinforced the damn door, and *trapped* him.

The team was supposed to be escaping, but he was trapped like a freaking rat. And something was wrong.

Fury twisted in him as Two rammed his shoulder into the door again and again.

I'll make her bleed. Make her beg.

He was tired of being a prisoner. Tired of not tasting freedom. He wasn't going to live this life any longer. The guards wouldn't keep him back.

The fury deepened, burned hotter. He hit the door again. It groaned. It—

I've been watching you, Cecelia.

Two froze. The rage was still inside of him, nearly choking him, but he had a flash of Cece. She looked terrified. She was holding up her hands, trying to fight—

Who is she fighting?

The rage grew inside of him. *I'll make her pay.*

No, wait, shit that wasn't *his* thought! Not his emotions, either.

But something dark and deadly had taken hold of Two. He wanted to attack and destroy, wanted to *kill* —

He broke that damn door. It flew off its hinges and hit the floor. He stood there a moment, chest heaving, hands fisted, and a guard came running toward him. A terrified looking fellow who'd pulled out his tranq gun. "Stand down!" the guard shouted.

"Make me," Two dared. He advanced.

The guard fired. He missed. Two easily dodged that tranq. The subjects were so much faster than the guards had realized. He grabbed the gun before the guard could fire again.

Attack. Destroy. The world seemed to be painted in shades of red. No, in shades of blood. *Kill.*

The guard tried to run away. Two shot him, and the fellow sank to the floor. Two walked toward him, glaring down at the guy as he held the gun gripped tightly in his hand. "I'm not going back into a cage again."

The guard was out cold. It would be so easy to finish the job with him. To reach down and to snap his neck. The guards had kept him locked up for so long. They'd thought they were the ones in charge.

Attack. Destroy. Kill. The darkness spread inside of Two.

The guards weren't in charge any longer.

***

Guards were slumped in the hallway. Sprawled on the floors. Sawyer rushed past them as he headed toward Cecelia Gregory's room. His heart was drumming in his chest, and he couldn't get to the shrink fast enough. Images of blood and pain were filling his mind, and Sawyer feared he'd be too late.

No innocents were supposed to be hurt. We were just going after our freedom.

He flew around the corner and caught sight of the guard who was lying spread-eagle in the middle of the hallway — a hallway that led straight to Cecelia's and Elizabeth's quarters. But as he approached that guard, Sawyer realized...

He's different. The guard wasn't breathing. Wasn't unconscious like the others. Sawyer's fingers went to the man's throat. *Dead.* The guy's neck had been broken, he could see it now. A vicious twist had ended the fellow's life in an instant.

Sawyer rose. The dark tendrils of emotion were trying to wrap around his mind, trying to pull him into a killing frenzy, but *that's not me.*

He stalked forward just as a woman's scream broke out. Cecelia's scream. Her door was shut, but Sawyer just kicked the thing inward.

Another body waited for him, just a few feet beyond the door. A guard who was on the ground. Unconscious this time, not dead. Sawyer could hear the faint rasp of his breath. Sawyer didn't waste time on that guard. He stared straight ahead instead.

Cecelia wasn't screaming any longer. He didn't see her...*I know she's here.* "Cecelia!" Sawyer bellowed. "Dr. Gregory!"

He heard a faint click, and automatically, Sawyer glanced down. The click had come from the band around his ankle. Sawyer tensed, knowing this could be it. He could explode right then and there. So much for escape. For freedom.

I'm sorry, Elizabeth.

But he didn't explode. Nothing happened.

"I've got her." Five's amused voice drifted to him, and Sawyer's head snapped back up as Five moved out of the small bathroom, holding Cecelia tight. "I'm taking good care of Dr. Gregory, don't worry."

She was trapped in his arms, pinned against him, and he had his gun to the side of her head.

Sawyer stared at Five a moment, then shook his head because the surge of fury had risen within him again. *Attack. Destroy. Kill.*

"She played with our minds."

A bruise slid across the top of Cecelia's cheek. Her hands had been bound together — looked like with some kind of torn bedding. And a gag was in her mouth. Again — a strip of bedding? A jagged piece of sheet?

"It's time for us to play with her," Five said. "I was going to leave the gag out, but, jeez, the woman's screams make my head hurt."

Attack. Destroy — "No!" Sawyer shouted, determined to block out the dark urges inside of himself and to stop Five. "This isn't the plan! We don't hurt her! We subdue the guards and we get out, that's all!"

Five leaned closer to Cecelia. He pressed a kiss to her temple. "It's my plan. It was always my plan."

Sawyer's head felt as if it was about to burst.

"You still don't get it, do you? What we are? What we can do?"

"I get that you're screwing things to hell and back — and that you're scaring the shrink!" He needed to get her away from Five. *Without* hurting her.

"You think she's scared?" Five laughed. "Good. I like it when they're scared."

"What the fuck is wrong with you?" Sawyer lunged closer, but Five immediately aimed the gun at him. "Stop that shit! You know I'll just dodge if you fire at me!"

"Because we're stronger, better, than the humans."

"We *are* humans," Sawyer reminded the bastard.

Five smirked at him. "We are fucking gods." Five kept the gun aimed at Sawyer. "Gods who were locked in hell. But we're breaking out, and the world is never going to be the same again."

"Let her go," Sawyer ordered fiercely.

"Why?" Now Five seemed legitimately confused. "You don't care about her. She's not the one you want. I left you with *your* doctor, didn't I? Pretty Elizabeth Parker. I let you keep her, and when I left you two…" His shoulders rolled in a shrug. "Weren't you holding her just as I'm holding Cecelia?"

No, fuck, *no.* "Mistake," Sawyer snarled. "My head…it's *wrong.*"

"No, it's right. We're right, but you can't see that yet. You're still limited and don't understand what we've become, but I do." And his smile lit his face. "It started with us being able to share thoughts, but our bodies adapted. Our brains changed. That's what we do, you see. We change. We adapt. We grow ever stronger. Once our brains started the telepathic communication, it was only a matter of time before we could do more."

Sawyer's head felt as if it were going to explode any second. He took another step closer to Five and Cecelia. He could grab the doctor and yank her to safety—

"It's not just thoughts we share. It's emotions, too. Only I've realized that when it comes to the emotions, you're not the Pack leader any longer." He laughed. "I am. I'm stronger than you are in that particular area. We all have different strengths, have you noticed that? Landon did, he let it slip to me one day, and since then, I've been working to perfect my area of strength. I can make the rest of the team feel what I do. I can get you to experience everything I do…"

Attack. Destroy. Kill. The red fucking haze… "It's you?"

"Feel it, don't you? The rush, the craving. We were made to kill, and there is nothing like the thrill of an attack."

Cecelia heaved in his hold, but Five just held her tighter. The gun was still pointed at Sawyer.

"I felt the rush of emotions on our missions, they gave me a dark taste when we'd take out the enemy. They made me remember things," Five's voice dropped. "And now, no one will stop us."

"*I'm* stopping you. Let her go."

Five blew out a hard breath. "Real bullets are in this gun. Not the tranqs. I can shoot you, but I don't want to do it. You're part of my team. My pack. Landon said we were a perfect pack, and we are, and pack members don't turn on each other. They protect each other."

"Let her go."

"We'll take her with us when we fly away. Cecelia and your Elizabeth. You can have as much fun as you want with your doc, and I'll play with mine. It will be the start. Just the beginning—"

No, it wasn't. "This isn't who we are. We're supposed to protect."

"But you don't want to protect, do you?" His eyes gleamed. "You want to kill, just as I do. And then you want to take. You want to take and take and take. And the thing you want to take the most? The thing you want to control the most? It's Elizabeth. *I* feel your emotions, too. She's an obsession, isn't she? Burrowing deep into you. You can take her now. No one can stop us. She'll be yours forever."

A quick gasp came from behind Sawyer, but he didn't look back. He knew who was behind him. He'd caught the scent of strawberries and he'd known she was creeping up the corridor. Elizabeth should have run away. *Why* hadn't she run away?

"Look, she wants to be with you. How sweet. She came to find her missing test subject." He laughed. "Step closer, Elizabeth. Come to Sawyer's side."

Elizabeth advanced. She clutched a laptop under one arm as she glared at Five, and she gripped a gun in her right hand. "Let her go, *now.*"

"But it took me so long to get her. So long to sneak into her room. I'd watch her. I'd think about touching her."

Cecelia slammed her head into Five's. He swore and jabbed the gun's barrel to her jaw.

"I'll make you want me, Dr. Gregory. I'll get in your head, too," Five promised.

The hell he would. Sawyer leapt toward the bastard. Cecelia's attack had given him just the opening he needed. He surged forward and he grabbed for the gun, but Five's attention had snapped back to him. Five swung the gun toward Sawyer and fired.

The bullet missed Sawyer. *Told you I'd freaking dodge it.* He drove his fist into Five's jaw, and the guy's hold on Cecelia loosened. The shrink jumped away from him and ran to the doorway. To Elizabeth? "Get to safety!" Sawyer yelled.

Five kicked him in the gut.

Bastard.

Five aimed his gun again, but before he could shoot, Five was being hit—hit by the tranqs in Elizabeth's gun as she took aim and fired. He jerked back at impact, but the guy just laughed. "Won't...stop me...*won't...*"

"I'll stop you," Sawyer promised. He drove his body into Five's. They fell back, and the weapon slipped from Five's fingers. They were pounding each other, hard, fast, brutal. But Five...*He isn't as strong as I am.* Sawyer had always held back with the guy during training, he'd held back with them all because he hadn't wanted Jamison to see the truth.

My strength is greater than anyone else's. Had Five been right? Did they each have an enhanced power that would —

"See?" Blood dripped from Five's mouth and nose. "You...like it, too..."

Like it? *Blood. Pain. Death.*

Sawyer heard the clatter of fleeing footsteps.

Five's eyes sagged shut. "They won't...get away."

"Yes, they will. Because your ass is done. You won't touch either one of them ever again."

You think the other test subjects are like you, One? Or do you think they're like me? Five's voice whispered through his head. *We fooled the general, we fooled Landon, we fooled...you.*

Sawyer froze with his fist still raised. The urge to keep punching was so strong. He wanted to hit and hit until Five was obliterated.

Attack. Destroy. Kill.

But those dark urges couldn't still be coming from Five. Could they? The guy was out cold now. Sawyer had *felt* it when Five passed out. So if those dark and insidious urges weren't coming from Five...

Then who the hell else is it? Who is sending that shit into my mind?

His head whipped toward the door. Elizabeth and Cecelia were gone. They were running wild because he'd told them to flee. But had he helped them? Or had he sent them running straight to death?

"*Elizabeth!*" Sawyer bellowed.

***

"*Elizabeth!*"

She jerked at the roar of her name, but Elizabeth didn't stop running. She and Cecelia were rushing down the hallway, flying away as quickly as they could. Elizabeth clutched the laptop to her chest. She'd dropped the tranq gun—she'd emptied it into Five's chest so the gun had been useless.

Cecelia had yanked the gag out of her mouth, but her hands were still bound. They were running down another twisting corridor and all Elizabeth could think was that there should be more guards there. Someone should appear. She'd had to go through so many check-points when she first arrived at the facility. They had to reach some kind of safety. They had to—

An alarm started blaring. The lockdown alarm.

Cecelia staggered to a stop. She looked back at Elizabeth. "They're locking us in."

Then that meant the guards on the surface—the guards *outside* – had found out about the chaos inside the place.

"They'll trap us in here," Cecelia said, voice shaking. "They'll trap us with the test subjects."

With Five? With others who might be like him?

"We need to get out of here before those doors seal up," Cecelia cried. "Hurry! This way!" She turned right and another corridor waited. But at the end of that corridor…

Someone was standing there. He was so far away she couldn't see him clearly. He was tall, muscled, wearing all black.

"This is the first check point to get up to the surface. That's got to be a guard. He'll help us. It's going to be—" Cecelia stopped. Went dead still. *"Three."*

Three?

Then Elizabeth got a better look at the man standing there. A man with his legs braced apart and a gun gripped in his hand. Not a tranq gun, but a rifle. One with a scope on the end. One that he was—*pointing at us.*

"Get down!" The shout came just as a big, hulking shadow appeared and hurtled at Cecelia.

Cecelia hit the floor, and Elizabeth jumped back—back, then *down* because Three had just fired his weapon. She felt the bullet whip right by her face. It had been that *close.*

She turned her stare on Cecelia and saw that Two—Flynn—had her secured beneath his body on the floor. "I've got them!" Flynn yelled.

No, no, he didn't have her.

"Drop the weapon, Three!" Flynn ordered. "We need to get out, now!"

But Three wasn't dropping his weapon. He was taking aim again. And the gun was pointed at Elizabeth. She sucked in a breath and tried to figure out how she was going to survive.

"Three!" Flynn yelled. "Drop it!"

"Attack," Three said quietly, but his voice seemed to echo. "Destroy." His voice slid over her body. "Kill—"

Sawyer jumped in front of her. She was crouched on the floor, holding that laptop, sure she was about to feel a bullet tear into her chest once again, but Sawyer stepped in front of her.

"If you want to hurt the doc, you'll need to shoot me first."

Three hadn't fired. Not yet.

"Drop that rifle, *now!*" Sawyer thundered.

She couldn't see around Sawyer's body. Elizabeth began to creep back. Flynn had risen, and he held Cecelia cradled in his arms.

"Run with her, Two," Sawyer urged. "Run hell fast and don't trust *anyone* but me."

Flynn rushed away without a word.

"Elizabeth!" Cecelia yelled.

Elizabeth flinched. She rose to her feet, but kept her body hidden behind Sawyer's form. She didn't know what the hell was going to happen next—

The alarm…stopped.

"That's it," Three called out. "Now we're locked inside. Just like we wanted."

Like they *wanted?*

"The guards from above won't be able to gain access to us, not with the modifications I made to this entrance. And we can haul ass out to the helipad. Free and clear." Three's footsteps shuffled forward.

Sawyer was tense and as still as a statue. "The guard behind you is dead."

"No, the *two* guards behind me are dead."

"Put down the rifle, Three."

"Not until the threats are eliminated."

Was she a threat? Elizabeth wanted to turn and run, but she was afraid any movement from her might set off Three.

"There was a flaw in your plan," Three announced. "I'm correcting the flaw."

"What flaw?" Sawyer demanded. There were no weapons in his hands, but…what was tucked into the back of his pants? Was that a knife?

"We can't leave anyone alive inside of Lazarus. If we do, they'll just come after us." Three's voice was calm. "We have to burn the place to the ground. Destroy everyone and everything here before we vanish. Attack," he said flatly. "Destroy. K—"

"Kill," Sawyer finished. He shook his head. "*No*. Those aren't my orders, dammit!"

His position had shifted just a bit—just enough for her to glimpse the terrifying image of Three lifting his weapon once more and aiming it at Sawyer.

"But you aren't the one in charge anymore," Three told him flatly. "You're not—"

He was going to shoot!

Sawyer's right hand flew up. The object that had been tucked into the back of his pants—the knife was now grasped in his fingers. He threw it, and it flew toward Three, flew fast and hit with deadly accuracy.

It hit Three in the throat and he fired the rifle, but the shot just blasted into the wall. Three dropped the gun and frantically clawed at his throat. Blood was pouring from his wound, and Elizabeth cried out in horror. Then she spun and she ran—ran as fast as she could to get away from Sawyer.

But he was running after her. She could hear the thud of his footsteps chasing her down. She shoved her hands against nearby doors, but they were locked. Everything was locked. The facility had shut down and she was trapped inside, trapped inside with killers. With men who'd become monsters.

With a lover she didn't know any longer. A man who terrified her.

And there was no way out.

CHAPTER EIGHTEEN

Sawyer grabbed Elizabeth's arm and spun her around, but when she whirled toward him, she brought up the laptop, and she slammed it against him. *Hard.*

"Shit! Doc, stop! I'm in control, okay? I'm not going to hurt you!"

"In control? You're out of control! You all are! You're killing each other — you're attacking — "

He blocked another hit from the laptop. "They're going to release the gas in five minutes."

She stopped hitting him. "What?"

His jaw locked. "It's shut down protocol. I planned for it." He just hadn't planned for the rest of the fucking madness. "They've sealed us inside. They think we can't get out. They're going to release the gas so that anyone here will be rendered unconscious, and then more guards will come back inside to take over. To lock up the test subjects."

Her eyes were wide. Her face was too pale. And she was staring at him as if he were a monster. *I am. I just killed one of my teammates.*

But what Elizabeth didn't know…Three had sent him a message. Right before he'd tossed the knife, Three had told him…*I'm going to put a bullet between the pretty doctor's eyes. Drive it right into her brain. She'll be dead before she hits the floor.*

Sawyer had stopped him. He'd stop *anyone* who came at Elizabeth.

"Maybe you need to be locked up, did you think of that?" Elizabeth shouted at him. He still held her left arm in his grasp, and Elizabeth tried to jerk away, but he wouldn't let her go. "You guys are insane, you are—"

"We're sharing thoughts and emotions. And someone is *poison* in our group. It's bleeding through to us all. It's been happening for a while, only I didn't realize how deep the darkness was spreading." Like a freaking virus.

Her lips parted. She blinked. Shook her head. "What?"

"I know it sounds crazy, but it's true. Someone is in our heads." He thought it was Five but the guy had been unconscious when he left him. *So how come Three was still intent on murder?* "The team and I—we can communicate telepathically."

Again, she shook her head.

"We're fucking dead men walking…*we can communicate telepathically.*" He used his hold to make her move with him. They had to get out of that place before the gas released. *Five minutes.* "But it's not just thoughts that we are sharing. It's emotions, too. Dark and…shit, twisted desires, okay? Things are wrong. I swear, it's like someone is pumping poison right in my brain. Trying to make me do things, terrible things." *I won't hurt you.*

"L-let me go, Sawyer."

His head turned toward her.

"You don't need to take me with you. Wherever you're going, whatever is happening, you don't need me."

That was what she didn't get. He let out a soft sigh. "You want to know why I'm not as fucking crazy as Five? As Three? Want to know why I got my shit back together in Landon's office?"

Her lips were trembling. He *hated* her fear.

"Because of you," he told her.

"Sawyer…"

"Something is between us. Something about you *gets* to me. And I can't hurt you. I won't hurt you. I'll also fucking never let anyone else so much as bruise you. There's danger here, all around us, and I don't know who I can trust and who I can't. I only know this—" His voice dropped. "I won't leave you alone. I have to protect you. I can't let you go."

"What if…what if you're the one I need to be protected from?"

He looked down at his ankle. "You disengaged it." He freed her wrist and bent to touch the band. He'd heard the lock disengage when he'd been in Cecelia's quarters. Beneath his fingers, the band pulled easily apart, and he tossed it aside. "You did that for me because you feel the connection, too."

"I didn't want you to explode, okay? I didn't want—"

"I want *you*." Flat. True. Dangerous. "I want you to stay alive. I want you to stay safe. I don't remember what we were like before. Hell, I wish that I did. And I don't have time to convince you that you'll be safe with me. I just—we have to go. Leaving you behind isn't an option. Protecting you—it's the only thing I can do. It's my mission. *You* are my mission."

She stared at him with her deep, dark eyes.

"We need to haul ass, baby. And we have to do it now."

She hesitated, but then gave a grim nod.

Fucking A. He pulled her into his arms, carrying her easily even when she gave a start of surprise. "I'm faster," he said. And he was. So much faster than he'd let on. Faster. Stronger.

The hallway disappeared in a blur as he ran. First, he went back to the cells because he needed to find the others. *Four. Six.*

But a fast glance showed him they weren't there. Their cell doors had been broken open, just like Two's. Sawyer sent out a fast, mental call...*Four? Six? Where in the hell are you?*

There was no answer. Only silence. He didn't know if that meant the guys were dead, if they were unconscious or if...if Three had been right. Maybe Four and Six weren't the men he'd thought they were. Maybe one of them was sending the poison into his brain.

We're running out of time. He sent out that fast mental call. *The gas is coming in less than five minutes. Get to safety.* He headed for the elevator, for the shaft that would lead him to his freedom. He just had to get there. Had to get up to the helipad. He kicked down any doors in his way, and the heavy metal was not a match for him. In moments, he could see the elevator waiting. Two was there, with Cecelia at his side. They were there, and...General Jamison was crumpled on the floor.

Sawyer caught the coppery scent of blood.

"We've got a problem," Two snapped.

The problem was that Jamison's throat had been cut, a long slash from ear to ear. The general's body was still warm and blood soaked his shirt-front.

"Not my kill," Two added darkly. "Someone beat us here."

Subject Four? Subject Six?

But..."The access keycard is still around the general's neck." Sawyer put Elizabeth down and yanked up the card, ignoring the blood that covered it. He scanned it, and then he typed in the code he'd seen the general use that day.

The elevator opened. "*Everyone…in.*"

But Two didn't move. "What about the others? The others on our *team?* We can't leave them behind. No man gets left, remember?"

"We can't trust them." He barely trusted Two. "Five was attacking Cecelia. He wanted to torture her, and you saw Three for yourself."

At the mention of Five, Two's face went hard, brutal. "He touched Cecelia?"

"Get in the fucking elevator."

Two grabbed Cecelia's hand and held her tight. "He was the one who hurt you? Five? He was—"

"Stop using the damn numbers!" The cry burst from Elizabeth as she jumped into the elevator. "You all have names. You're people, not numbers!"

Sawyer hit the button to take them up to the helipad.

"He's Sawyer, and your name is Flynn."

Flynn. Sawyer saw the other man blink slowly.

"Five is a man named Bryce King. I didn't know him before I came here, he didn't work with us back in D.C." Her words were coming fast now. A wild tangle. "Flynn, you and Sawyer were best friends before Lazarus. You went on every single mission together. You always watched each other's backs. You trusted each other then, and I-I don't know what's going on now, but the facility has gone mad. We have to think. We have to—"

The elevator dinged. The doors opened. Sawyer advanced first, making sure to keep Elizabeth behind him. The chopper waited up ahead, and no one was near it. The helipad was empty.

"That's our way out."

"Yeah, but I know someone beat us here." Flynn clenched and unclenched his hands. "I can smell the blood."

So could Sawyer, but they didn't have time to waste. "Get in the bird."

Flynn was already running for the chopper. Flynn. Had the guy really been Sawyer's best friend before the nightmare began?

"I sure as hell hope you remember how to fly," Elizabeth said.

He locked his hands around her waist and lifted her into the chopper. "I remember." Just as he remembered how to kill. But how to love?

He'd forgotten that.

They got in the chopper. He took a position in the pilot's seat. "Buckle up!" He yelled over the roar of the blades.

"They might try to shoot us down," Flynn warned grimly.

They might. If they stayed, Sawyer knew he was dead.

"The others..." Flynn stared at him. "Are you sure we can't help them?"

Elizabeth. Have to get her out. She's priority. "Three tried to kill her. And Five—fuck, Bryce—he went after Cecelia. We can't risk them."

Flynn nodded grimly.

"I can't reach Four and Six." Yeah, they had names—he didn't know them. *But I will find out.* "Can you? I try, but it's just darkness."

"Only darkness." Flynn's voice was soft. Sad. "Does that mean they're dead?"

Sawyer didn't know what it meant. The men should have met him at the rendezvous point. The elevator *had* been the rendezvous point. The gas would be spraying in that facility at any moment. If they didn't leave, there was no going back.

Attack. Destroy... The sinister thoughts shot into his head again, surging hard at him.

"Fuck!" Flynn snarled. "Someone is in my head!"

The chopper lifted into the air. Up, up, higher and higher. The higher they rose, the softer the voice in their heads became.

Sawyer could taste freedom. It was so fucking close.

They'd get out. And the Lazarus bastards would never find them again. He and Flynn would vanish. Disappear.

But what happens to Elizabeth?

His head turned so he could see back into the rear of the chopper. She sat with her shoulders huddled, still clutching that laptop in her hands. Still so beautiful it made him ache. He was getting her to safety, but after that, was he supposed to walk away from her?

Her head lifted. Their eyes met. There were a thousand things he wanted to say to her, but the helicopter blades were whirring at full force and it was too late.

Higher, higher.

Flynn let out a whoop of joy. "Never gonna be in a cage again!"

No, no, they wouldn't be. They'd be free.

Dead men? Hell, no. They were finally about to start living. The chopper flew away, heading into the growing darkness of the night. With every beat of the blades above him, the tension eased from Sawyer's shoulders. His thoughts settled. The rage and darkness eased. It was okay. They were going to—

Do you think you can come back from the dead again?

The voice blasted right into his head, rough and hard, mocking with laughter. A familiar voice. A voice—

An explosion sounded from overhead. The blades stopped spinning — half of the blades flew away, and the chopper plummeted. It just fell, like a stone sinking from the sky.

Sawyer heard screams and yells. Desperate cries. And he didn't realize some of those cries were his own. He didn't realize — *"Elizabeth!"* He wrenched free of the harness and belt and jumped from the seat. Piloting was impossible. They were going down, and they only had seconds left.

He grabbed for Elizabeth. He saw Flynn reach for Cecelia.

"I love you," Elizabeth said as her hands stretched toward Sawyer.

No, no, she hadn't said that. It was a dream. It was the past. It was a nightmare. It was —

Wind whipped around them. The chopper was plunging straight for the ground. They were all going to die. Just when he'd started to live.

Fuck, no.

"Hold tight," Sawyer told her. "Baby, don't ever let go."

She closed her eyes, and she held on. And he curled his body around hers, determined to hold her in his arms, to keep her safe, no matter what price had to be paid.

I'd die again for her. Over and over…for her.

When the helicopter slammed into the ground, he was still holding her tight.

CHAPTER NINETEEN

She hurt. Her whole body ached. Elizabeth let out a groan as her eyes slowly opened.

"Baby?" A rough hand pressed to her face. "Look at me, okay? *Look at me.*"

That voice—Sawyer's voice. Her head turned and she found him, leaning over her. Blood streaked his forehead, and his face was stained with dirt and sweat. He was staring at her, his face grim and scared. That was odd. Sawyer didn't get scared. She'd never seem him be afraid before. Why would he be—

The helicopter.

The crash.

They'd fallen out of the sky. *Out of the sky.* And he was still alive. *She* was still alive. Impossible. Insane.

Elizabeth jerked upright.

"No! Stop, just take it easy." He swore grimly. "You scared the hell out of me." His arms wrapped around her, cradling Elizabeth carefully. "Shit, doc, I thought I was losing you."

She'd thought they were all dying. "H-how?" That one croak was all she could manage right then.

He was warm and strong against her. "I tried to shield you with my body. When we hit the ground, I held you as tightly as I could."

"We *crashed*. We should be *dead*."

A gruff laugh came from him. "Yeah, you mentioned that to me before. You seem to think I'm always dead."

But they weren't dead. They'd survived a helicopter crash. If he was strong enough to survive and use his body to protect her during that kind of fall, then that meant… "You've been keeping an awful lot of secrets, haven't you?"

There was a faint cough from her right. Elizabeth's head whipped around, and she saw Cecelia, a bruised but very much alive Cecelia, standing at Flynn's side. "They've all been keeping secrets." Cecelia's clothes were torn and a bit bloody in spots, but she seemed okay. They'd all survived a crash that should have killed them.

Super soldiers.

"We all have different strengths," Sawyer said quietly. His fingers stroked over her arm. "Flynn and I…well, when we worked the second mission for Jamison, we found out that we were both damn near indestructible. And when we do get hurt, we heal very, very fast."

"I broke my left ankle and my right wrist in the crash." Flynn gave a shrug. "They've both healed already."

She blinked.

"Doc, we used our bodies to protect you and Cecelia, to cushion you from the impact. Wasn't sure it would work…" Sawyer's smile was weary. "But it was the only option we had, and I was desperate. I would have done anything to keep you safe."

"Same here," Flynn growled as his fingers slid over Cecelia's shoulder. "You weren't dying on my watch."

Elizabeth looked at the wreckage. It waited, about fifty yards away. A tangled mess.

"Are they going to think we all died?" Cecelia asked. She tucked a lock of hair behind her ear.

"That would be too easy." Sawyer released Elizabeth, but he didn't move away. And she liked having him close. Maybe he made her feel safe.

Maybe he scared her to death.

"A team will come out and search the wreckage. We have to be long gone from this site by then." He swept his gaze over her. "I can carry you. Every step of the way. But we have to get out of here."

She tried walking. Nothing hurt too badly, so she figured she had this. "I can walk."

"But not as fast as I can."

Yeah, okay, he had a point.

"We need to get moving. They'll be after us soon. The sooner we disappear from here, the sooner—"

Elizabeth grabbed his arm. "They aren't going to think you died. Not you." Her gaze swung to Flynn. "Not either of you. And it doesn't matter how fast or how far you run, they'll find you."

Flynn's shoulders straightened. "No, they won't. They aren't dragging me back into the ground, into their damn facility to be their attack dog. They *won't*—"

"They have a tracking device on you. On you both." She licked lips that were desert dry. "As long as that device is on you, they can figure out where you went."

Sawyer pulled her closer. "What device?"

"Wright said that a tracker was implanted on all of the test subjects, hidden beneath scars that you already had. The metal band that you wore for missions, that was just—it was a bomb. It was designed to be a back-up plan in case you ever went rogue."

"We're definitely fucking rogue," Flynn snarled.

Beside him, Cecelia flinched.

"You have to get the tracking devices out." Running would do no good while the trackers were under Sawyer's and Flynn's skin.

Sawyer stalked away from her, heading back toward the chopper.

She stood there, uncertain, and then she saw him scavenging inside. He pulled up a dark backpack. She caught the gleam of a blade. The rough form of a gun. And—

The laptop. Sawyer had just shoved it aside while he searched but she rushed forward. Her steps were uncertain at first and she felt a bit dizzy, but she staggered toward him and grabbed for the laptop.

"The thing is blown to hell," Sawyer told her as he turned away from the chopper. "Leave it."

It did look as if it had been to hell and back but… "I have a friend who might be able to retrieve the data on here. This is Landon's computer. Every secret he has could be on this machine." She wasn't just going to let it go. "It's important. We need it."

He stared at her a moment, then gave a hard nod. And he offered her a knife.

She clutched the laptop tighter as she eyed the weapon. "What do you want me to do with that?" But she had a sinking feeling in her gut.

"Find the tracking device. Cut it out of me." He pulled the laptop from her and shoved it into the backpack.

With shaking fingers, she took the knife from him. "But we don't know where the tracker is." Big problem.

"Then you'll just keep cutting until you find it."

Oh, no, she wouldn't.

They hurried away from the wreckage, moving to the shelter of a small patch of nearby trees. Narrow trees that had sprouted in the middle of that rough, red terrain. The night was lit by the full moon's glow. It hung, heavy and low, in the sky.

Sawyer dropped the pack and stripped off his shirt. He let it hit the ground. "Doc, you help me. Cecelia, you get the tracker out of Flynn."

Flynn already had a knife in his hand that he was offering to Cecelia. She stared at the weapon in absolute horror. "I don't like knives," Cecelia whispered.

"Yeah, well, I don't like having a tracker under my skin or being a freaking test rat for the U.S. government, so looks like we're both dealing with unfortunate shit today." He pushed the knife toward her. "Take it."

She didn't. Cecelia backed up a step.

"Come on," Flynn urged her. "Let's just check and—"

Cecelia was adamantly shaking her head. "I don't like knives."

When she was fifteen, she was taken right off the street. Elizabeth remembered what Landon had told her about Cecelia's past. Oh, damn. "I'll do it!" Elizabeth cried out. "I'll get it from both of you."

Flynn frowned at her.

"Don't make Cecelia do it, okay? I've got this."

Flynn focused back on Cecelia and finally seemed to notice that she was staring at the knife with a kind of numb horror on her face. "Cece?"

"The last time I used a knife like that...I killed a man."

Flynn's brows shot up.

"I just..." Cecelia's lips trembled. "I really don't like knives."

Flynn considered Cecelia a moment. "I can cut it out myself."

He couldn't just start cutting into himself. They had to think this through. "L-look for a rougher ridge in a scar you have. The tracker will be small, but near the surface of your skin so you shouldn't have to cut far to get it out." Elizabeth bit her lip. "If you guys heal as fast as you say..." And, obviously, they did. They'd just survived a helicopter crash! "Then Landon could have put the tracker in when he was doing another exam on you, and you never would have known."

Flynn flipped the knife in his hand. "I'll find it." He turned on his heel. "Think I'll get a little space while I do the job."

He walked into the darkness. Cecelia stared after him a moment, then she hurried forward as she called, "Flynn! Wait! I-I'll help, but just don't give me the knife."

Their steps faded away.

Elizabeth turned her head and found Sawyer staring at her. She swallowed. The knife was still gripped in her hand. "How long do you think we have—"

"Before a team comes after us? Not damn long, so we need to hurry. There's not a lot of cover in this desert, and they'll use an air team to do the sweep."

She was actually surprised that she hadn't already heard the sound of an approaching helicopter. But…

Sawyer lifted his hands and began sliding them over the scars on his chest. "A ridge, huh? I think that will be hard to find. I can—"

Her left hand flew out—the hand *not* holding the knife—and her fingers caught his. "I can find it." She *would* find it. He stared down at her. So big and dangerous in the dark. Maybe she should be running from him, but she wasn't. She'd gone to Lazarus with the express plan of freeing Sawyer. She just hadn't realized what a nightmare she'd find inside the facility.

I should have known, though.

His fingers slid away from hers. His hands dropped to his side. She eased out a slow breath, and then her fingers were sliding lightly over his skin. First over the scar that slid too close to his heart. She could feel the rush of his heartbeat beneath her touch. So fast and strong. Heat pulsed from his skin as her fingers drifted down. More scars slid over his ribs.

"I'm fucking covered in scars," he growled, voice deeper than before. "Don't even know where most of them came from."

Her touch stilled on the scars over his ribs. "You got these when you rescued a missionary off the coast of Africa. He'd been taken by a drug lord there, tortured, held for ransom. He'd been in captivity for forty-five days." Her fingers slid away from the scars. "You got him out within four hours of landing at the drop site."

He stiffened.

She touched the jagged line on his stomach. "This was a knife fight. Not one you got from a battle in some distant land. You got this when you were in high school, and a man in an alley tried to rob your dad."

"What?"

"You always fought back. That's just who you were." Her hand moved to the next scar. "And this—"

"Where is my father?" There was pain in his voice.

And it hurt her to tell him, "I'm sorry, Sawyer. He died last year. You were...you were with him when he passed." A long battle with cancer had taken his father. Sawyer had told her that story, when they'd been together one night, wrapped up tight in each other's arms.

"My mother?"

"She died when you were a child."

Elizabeth traced the scar right next to his belly button. Frowned. Traced again—

"Any other family?" Now his voice was flat.

"No. You were an only child." She could feel a hardness in that scar. Right at the tip. It was thicker there than it had been below. She *knew* this scar, too. Another reminder from a knife attack. He'd gotten this wound in Russia, during his early SEAL days, and she remembered that the scar had been thicker at the bottom. *Because the guy who'd attacked Sawyer had twisted the blade.* But the scar was different now. The bottom edge wasn't the widest point of the scar. The top was bigger, rougher. Was the tracker right there?

"No family." His muscles had tensed even more. "Then I guess there was no one to miss me when I vanished."

She looked up at him. "Someone missed you." *I did. Every single day.* "I...I think I found the tracker. It's going to hurt when I slice into you—"

"Do it."

Using the tip of the blade, she cut into his skin. The blood pulsed out and she clenched her teeth as she had to dig a little deeper, make the entrance cut wider. Then she pressed her fingers against the small opening, she caught the tip of the tracker...

"Get it out," Sawyer snapped.

She pulled it out. The device was covered in his blood and smaller than the length of her pinky fingernail.

Sawyer took it from her, and he dropped it to the ground. He smashed his foot on it, obliterating the tracker. Freeing him.

"Got mine, One," Flynn called. "The bitch is out!"

She didn't look over her shoulder at him. Sawyer was still in front of her, bleeding but not seeming to care about his wound at all. "Now they can't find you."

This was it. She was going to watch him walk away. He would be free.

She motioned toward the mountains that waited in the distance. "I hope the world is everything you want it to be."

He frowned at her. "What the hell does that mean?"

Uh, it meant… "Go. You and Flynn are far faster than Cecelia and me. You can disappear long before any search party arrives." She dropped the knife and it clattered to the ground. Elizabeth's shaking fingers—covered with his blood now—fisted. "I swore I'd get you out." She had to force herself to speak the words. "I wasn't going to leave you with them. I don't care about any video Landon showed me, I *know* you didn't volunteer. It wasn't your choice, and I wasn't going to leave you there." Locked away. She wanted to say so much more.

Instead, she turned away from him. It would be easier if she didn't see him leave.

"*Why?*" The one word was guttural.

She looked straight ahead and saw Cecelia staring at her. Was there pity on the other woman's face? Elizabeth couldn't tell, not for sure. That was good, though, she'd never liked pity.

But it wasn't the time for lies. Elizabeth didn't look back at Sawyer as she said, "Because I loved Sawyer Cage." She'd loved him and lost him.

Only now, finally, she might be able to sleep at night. Sleep and not wake up with nightmares over and over again.

Once, she'd had terrible dreams about her family. Her mother and father. Their deaths. Being trapped with them.

Then she'd lost Sawyer, and a new terror had claimed her nights. Twisted dreams of him, being trapped, experimented on, of him being on an exam table and calling for her.

Maybe that dream would stop now. Maybe not.

His hand closed around her shoulder. She felt his touch all the way to her core. "The man you loved died."

Her eyes closed. "Yes, and his death ripped out my heart."

He spun her toward him. *"I'm right fucking here."*

She could only stare at him. He'd jerked on his shirt and his blood dotted the front. He'd already slung the backpack over one of his shoulders.

"You think I'm not the same? You think because of the poison in my head, you think because of the things they did to me that I can't ever be that man again?"

"Sawyer—"

"Whatever I am now, *whoever* I am, know this…you are mine. I knew it from the first moment I saw you. I just have to prove it to you." He lifted her into his arms. "And I'm not leaving you behind. That shit isn't happening. You're staying with me. I'm not abandoning you in the desert. I'm getting you to safety."

"But you're faster without—"

"I will not be without you." Low, rasping. "I will…*not.*"

She stared into his eyes.

"Two — *Flynn,*" Sawyer corrected quickly. "Get your shrink. We're getting the hell out of here."

Elizabeth's head turned to see Flynn scoop Cecelia into his arms. "Hold on, Cece," he told her softly. "Things are about to move fast."

CHAPTER TWENTY

Elizabeth flashed a quick smile to the check-in clerk at the motel. She gestured toward Cecelia and held up two fingers. Then Elizabeth pushed cash across the desk. The young clerk swept the money away in a flash.

"You sure we can trust them?" Flynn asked as he edged closer to Sawyer. "One of us should have gone inside…"

"And then the clerk would remember our faces. When the search starts, he'd sell us out in a second." Besides that fact, he and Flynn both looked like shit. The run through the desert had been fucking hell, and sweat covered his body. They'd come across this little motel, and it had been like a sign from above. Their group could get shelter, shower, eat. And then plan their next course of action.

They'll be hunting us. No way would Wyman Wright just let them walk.

"I can't contact any of the others." Flynn's voice was threaded with tension. "I-I tried, man, after the crash. Just to see who was left standing, but the rest of the team is still dark."

Sawyer's head turned toward Flynn. "Don't reach out to them again."

"They're our *team*."

"You really want to risk Five getting close to Cecelia again?"

Flynn's face went ugly. "That bastard gets near her, and he's dead."

"That's what I thought."

"Five wasn't the only one we left behind. You know there were others—"

"I can think better now. More clearly." Sawyer tapped his temple. "The poison is bleeding away. Whoever was controlling our emotions—we left him back at Lazarus."

Flynn glanced toward the motel office.

"I can't risk losing control again. *We* can't risk it." If Sawyer ever did anything to hurt Elizabeth… "We can't go back for the others until we know more."

"You think that 'more' is on Landon's laptop?"

"I sure as hell hope so." But getting anything from that laptop wasn't going to be easy. When they'd been rushing through the desert, Elizabeth had said she had a friend who might be able to help them. A hacker.

"You really believe we were best friends?"

The women had exited the office. They were walking slowly and easily, as if they didn't have a care in the world—a great front—toward Sawyer and Flynn's place in the shadows.

"I mean, wouldn't I know if we were tight?" Flynn pressed, "Shit, not like we're wearing freaking matching charm bracelets for *besties*—"

"You're here," Sawyer cut through the guy's ramble.

"Uh, yeah, so?"

"I didn't bring anyone else from the team, did I? Not once I realized how many fucking secrets we all had." Secrets they'd even kept from each other. "You're here," he said again, "because you were different. I knew it from the start."

Flynn frowned at him.

"I knew I had to save your sorry ass," Sawyer added. "No matter what. Guess that was left over from our *bestie* days."

"Fucking asshole," Flynn muttered. But then he added, "I knew I had to save you, too."

Elizabeth flashed Sawyer a quick, nervous smile. "Got two rooms. It's a really good thing that Cecelia had some cash on her."

Cecelia wasn't smiling. She cast a nervous glance over her shoulder. "I didn't like the way that guy looked at us."

Elizabeth pushed back her hair. "Considering that we just walked out of the mountains with only the clothes on our backs, it stands to reason he'd give us some weird looks." She shrugged. "But the man did say he'd had plenty of other lost hikers stumble onto his motel, so I don't think we raised any suspicions with him."

"Let's get cleaned up," Sawyer said, glancing around the area. There was a small twenty-four-hour gas station down the road. They were going to need a car, and they'd probably be stealing it from that place because the motel's parking lot was deserted. "Shower, get the blood off, and we'll grab some food and maybe some fresh t-shirts from that place over there."

"I'll get the food and the clothes." Cecelia said quickly. She motioned to Flynn and Sawyer. "Since you guys are staying off the grid, you don't need to be running inside. There are probably security cameras in there."

"I'll come—" Elizabeth began.

"No." Flynn shook his head. "I'll go with her. I won't go in the store, but I'll keep watch. Make sure she's safe." He cut his gaze to Elizabeth. "Better for you two not to be seen together again. We need to mix up our interactions with the outside world, just in case folks come looking for us."

Elizabeth frowned at Cecelia. "That plan okay with you?"

Cecelia nodded. "Of course."

Her "of course" hadn't sounded very confident.

"Okay." Elizabeth straightened her shoulders as she held a key out to Sawyer. "You and Flynn are in room six. Cecelia and I will take room seven."

Sawyer took the key to room seven from her, and he tossed it to Flynn. Flynn caught it easily and fisted his fingers around the card. "Sorry, doc," Sawyer told her, not really feeling sorry at all. "But you'll be staying with me."

"And you'll be with me, Cecelia," Flynn added quietly.

Elizabeth's lips had parted in surprise.

"It's safer that way," Sawyer said before she could argue. "And despite anything else you believe, we don't want you two hurt."

She glanced down, not meeting his eyes. "I do believe that."

Good. That was something, anyway. He caught her hand in his and held tight. Flynn and Cecelia hurried toward the gas station. When they were gone, Sawyer and Elizabeth headed for their room. "You can shower first." He gave her a faint smile when they stopped in front of door number six. "See, I can be a gentleman."

"I never said you weren't."

He should let go of her hand, but he liked holding her. "I'm not just a fighter." He opened the door with his left hand.

"Sawyer, you're many things. I know that."

He wasn't sure how to take those words. Sawyer entered first and flipped on the light.

The room was small, the carpet was thread-bare, and the furniture looked as if it would break apart any moment. "Guess he didn't take you to places like this." Sawyer finally pulled his hand from hers and locked the door. The flimsy lock wouldn't keep anyone out. He dropped the key on the nightstand and set the backpack down on the floor.

"He?" She wrapped her arms around her body. "Who are you talking about?"

"The Sawyer you used to know." *The one you loved.* "Bet he took you to all kinds of fancy places. Expensive restaurants. Not shitholes like this room." And he wished he could remember. He wanted to know more about the life they'd had. He wanted to know more about the man she'd loved. *So I can be him again?*

Elizabeth swallowed. "We...we weren't supposed to fraternize." A faint smile pulled at her lips, but never reached her eyes. "Wright had rules about his team, and we were afraid if he found out that we'd broken those rules, he'd split us up." A tear leaked down her cheek. "So there weren't any fancy restaurants. They were stolen moments. Secret meetings. Promises for more."

Only those promises hadn't come true. "What did he promise you?"

"He?" Elizabeth shook her head. "*You. You promised.* And you promised that you'd come back." She licked her lips. "I think I will take that shower first. If you, ah, don't mind." Then she shook her head. "Screw it. I'm going in even if you do mind." She practically ran toward the shower, hurrying away from him.

The bathroom door slammed behind her. A moment later, he heard the rush of water.

Sawyer stood inside the motel room, his body tense. There were a million questions he wanted to ask Elizabeth, but every time she revealed more about his past—it just hurt. It hurt him. It hurt her. Her pain was the last thing he wanted.

The thing you want most…it's her. All of her. To own her. To bind her to you. To never let her go. The thoughts slid through his mind. They were dark and hard and…

This time, the thoughts are mine. Because he did want to bind Elizabeth to him completely. Irrevocably.

"Fucking hell."

He wasn't going to give in to the dark spiral. He was going to beat it. He could be more than a weapon. His mind could be more than madness. He'd gotten out of Lazarus. He would get his life back.

And that life included Elizabeth.

His Elizabeth.

Sawyer strode toward the bathroom door. His hand lifted, but he stopped. No, shit, no. She needed space. She didn't need him rushing at her like a starving man. Even though he was starving, even though he was desperate. Even though he craved her more than anything.

Even more than his own freedom.

Elizabeth.

Sawyer forced himself to step back. With his enhanced hearing, he could detect every single movement that she made. He could hear the hitch of her breath. The sigh that slipped from her. He could imagine the water sliding over her beautiful skin.

He wanted to see her completely naked. He wanted to touch every inch of her. Wanted to kiss her everywhere. When that chopper had crashed, he'd known real fear. For the first time since he'd woken at Lazarus, he'd been absolutely terrified. Not for himself. He'd been afraid Elizabeth would be taken from him. And if she'd died…

What would I have done?

The water turned off. The *drip, drip, drip,* seemed too loud. He took a few more steps away from the bathroom. The rustle of the towel teased his ears. The creak of the floor as she moved toward the door reverberated around him, and then that door was opening. Faint wisps of steam slid out and Elizabeth stood there, framed in the doorway, her wet hair sliding over her shoulders and a thin, white towel wrapped around her body. Her gaze met his. Red tinged her cheeks. "I…tried to hurry. I know you have to be feeling worse than I am. You're the one who ran all the way here."

Don't touch her. But he found himself being pulled toward her.

Elizabeth slipped away from the doorframe, clearing his path to the shower. She waved toward the bathroom. "Go inside. I, ah, saved you some hot water."

He didn't fucking care about hot water. In fact, what he needed was cold water. Ice cold. Because the sight of her in that towel was his undoing. No, *she* was his undoing.

He headed for the bathroom, yanking his shirt off as he went. He was at the door—

Her fingers touched his stomach. "You've already healed."

Only on the outside, baby. Inside, I'm broken beyond repair.

Her soft touch burned him worse than any fire. But what he wouldn't give for more of that burn right then.

Cold water. Icy cold.

He strode into the bathroom. He pushed the door closed behind him, but didn't shut it fully. He just—he couldn't shut her out. If she wanted to come in with him, hell, yes, he'd grab her and hold her tight. A yank of his hand had the shower thundering on once again. He stripped, shoving the rest of his clothes aside, before he climbed into the shower, moving beneath that icy water.

He put his head beneath the spray, closing his eyes as he tried to shut out visions of Elizabeth. Of what he wanted with her. Of—

Strawberries. How could she still smell like strawberries? But the scent was drifting to him, and he heard the soft creak of the door moving.

His eyes opened and his head angled toward the door. Elizabeth stood there, as if frozen. But he didn't want her frozen. He wanted her need, her desire, he wanted her to be wild for him. To want him so much that nothing else mattered.

"Sawyer."

He didn't try to hide his arousal. His dick was long and hard for her, and his body ached. A thin frame of glass separated them, and the glass was partially covered with steam, blocking his view of Elizabeth.

Sawyer grabbed that glass door and shoved it aside.

She stared at him.

I almost lost her. Lost what I had just found again.

Elizabeth let the towel drop to the floor. She didn't speak as she came toward him.

Fuck. Get the water warmer for her. His hand shot out and he cranked up the heat. He didn't want Elizabeth cold. He always wanted her hot.

Tense moments ticked past. Steam began to rise. A faint smile pulled at her lips as she climbed into the shower. As she stood less than an inch from him. The bathroom light was on, glaring down over them. His body was so much bigger than hers. Thicker, stronger, darker. He was covered in scars, marks that he would always carry. He felt too rough, too dangerous.

And she—she was slender, but curved. Her skin was a soft gold, her body absolute perfection to him. But she was so delicate. So vulnerable. So *breakable.* He never wanted her broken.

Her hand lifted and pressed to his heart. She still hadn't said another word. She had to feel his dick shoving against her. She was staring at him with her deep, dark eyes, and he wished, he wished so much, that he could be the man she remembered.

But I do remember one thing. I remember how to give her pleasure. I remember how to make her want me.

So he did.

His head bent. His mouth took hers. The water was still pouring on him, a hot bite on his back, and he didn't care. Her mouth was open, her lips parted perfectly, and his tongue swept inside as he pulled her closer. Her nipples were

tight, hard peaks. He wanted them in his mouth.
Wanted to lick and suck until she was moaning
for him. Until she was begging him to thrust into
her. Begging him for release.

Begging.

Her legs parted as she moved closer. She was
smaller than him, so much smaller. He lifted her
up, moving her into position so that his cock
pushed at the opening between her legs. She gave
a little gasp, and his eager cock jerked even more
for her. He turned, pushing her back against the
tiled wall of the shower as he kept kissing her. He
held her easily, even as one hand moved down
her body. Moved to tease her sex, moved to make
her moan.

Her nails sank into his back. He kissed his
way down her neck, stopping in the places that
made her tremble the most. Stopping and licking,
biting, then journeying down even as he lifted
her higher.

He licked her nipple. Pink and pretty and
perfect for him. He licked and he sucked and
when the dark urges inside of him told him
to *take, take, take…*

Sawyer thrust two fingers into her.
Withdrew. Thrust again. He worked her sex,
stretching her, making sure she was ready. They
hadn't spoken again, and he couldn't speak. Not
then.

Fuck her. Claim her.

His fingers withdrew. She was panting, her scent all around him. He positioned his cock, stared down a moment—down at their bodies as they pressed together. She was so perfect to him.

Mine.

He sank into her. Elizabeth's legs wrapped around his hips and she squeezed him so tight. With that first plunge into her, all control was gone. Lost. He was maddened, desperate, but not for his pleasure. For hers. He had to give Elizabeth pleasure. So much pleasure that she forgot the man he'd been. So much pleasure that she wanted *him*. Broken, damaged, dangerous—didn't matter. She would want him. Always, *him.*

The way Sawyer knew he would always want her.

He drove into her, tilting his body the way she liked, sliding down so that his cock stroked over her clit. Her nails sank deeper into him even as her sex squeezed him tighter. He thrust again and again, and when she came, when she exploded for him, it wasn't enough.

Not close.

He stilled inside of her, and her sex squeezed him, contracted, held him in a white-hot grip. He didn't want to come, not yet.

Not yet.

"Sawyer?"

He gazed into the darkness of her eyes.

His Elizabeth.

Without a word—because talking was beyond him—he lowered her until Elizabeth's toes touched the bottom of the shower. Then he yanked the faucet, turning off the water.

"Sawyer, you didn't—"

He had her in his arms again. He carried her out of that bathroom and to the bed. Still not speaking, he spread her out, pushing her thighs apart and staring at her. All of her. So beautiful. How could he have forgotten her?

You knew something was missing. All that time. A part of you was gone. That part—it was her.

Sawyer put his mouth on her sex. He was rough, too wild, too far gone as he tasted her. Her hands sank into his hair and her hips surged up against him. He needed her to come again, at least once more, come for him. To let go with him. To give herself fully to him. Always.

She tasted so good. They'd never given him wine at Lazarus. He knew what wine was, though, just as he knew about chocolate. He also knew those things didn't taste as good as Elizabeth. They couldn't.

Nothing could.

She came against his mouth. He loved it. *Loved* her pleasure. And he pulled back to lick his lips. To savor her and watch the pleasure slide over her face.

"You," Elizabeth gasped. "I need *you.*"

He surged into her. The bed rocked beneath him as he drove harder and harder into his paradise. The climax hit him, barreling through his whole body, gutting him, driving him absolutely beyond rational thought—driving him so hard that all he could think about, all he knew—

Was Elizabeth.

His heart raced too fast, a drumbeat in his chest, and Sawyer shoved his body up so he wouldn't crush Elizabeth. He propped himself up on his elbows and gazed at her even as his breath sawed in and out of his lungs. Her eyes were wide, her lips red, her smile was beautiful enough to break a man's heart.

"I missed you," she confessed.

And he knew those words weren't for him—not for the new Sawyer, not for the man who couldn't remember his past and was only designed to kill. No, those words, those soft tender words—they were for the lover she'd lost. The one she still loved.

He also knew something else. Sawyer knew he was fucking insane because he was jealous of himself. Jaw locking, he withdrew from her body. He *hated* to leave her. He wanted to stay inside of her and fuck her endlessly.

But they didn't have forever. They barely had the moment they were in. Sliding from the bed, his muscles were tense. He headed for the bathroom.

"Sawyer?"

He cleaned up and got her a warm cloth. He came back to the bed to find she'd dragged a sheet over herself. With a soft touch, he pulled the sheet away, and he slid the cloth between her legs. "Sorry if I was…rough."

"I didn't mind." Her words were halting. "And you…weren't."

She was lying. He didn't need enhanced senses to know that. He tossed the cloth onto the nightstand. His knuckles pressed to her throat. "I marked you here." His knuckles trailed down her neck, moved to the curve of her shoulder. "Here." Down, down he went, to the swell of her breast. "Here."

She caught his hand. "And I'm sure I marked you plenty. Do you want me to prove it with a body check?"

His jaw locked. "Was it always like this?" Why was he asking? Shit, what did he want her to say? That it was better now? Better with the *new* Sawyer?

"Like this?" Her head tilted. Her hair had already begun to dry. "Do you mean did we touch and go crazy?"

He wanted to kiss the faint marks he'd left on her body. He wanted to mark her more.

"Yes, it was always like this. I wanted you from the first moment I saw you, even though I knew it was wrong."

"Nothing about us will ever be wrong."

Her lashes flickered. "You…said that before. A long time ago."

"And I'm saying it again." He caught her chin in his hand and forced her to stare at him. "Nothing about us is wrong. I know I'm different, but give me a chance. I can be better, I can get better. The poison—those dark emotions—they're not going to rule me. They're not as strong. They're not—"

I'm going to find you. The words poured into Sawyer's mind. Only they weren't weak. They were strong and clear. Very distinct in a voice he recognized. *Five.* No, no, the bastard had a name. Bryce King.

I'm going to find you, and you're going to watch while I kill your precious Elizabeth.

"Sawyer?" Elizabeth curled her fingers around his wrist. "What is it?"

You're not the only one who's out. Bryce's laughter echoed in Sawyer's mind. *And I'm close, so close. The closer I get to you, the more power I'll have over you. I've been holding back. I won't hold back any longer.*

"Bryce," he snarled. He let Elizabeth go, and his hand rose to grip the headboard behind her. "The bastard says he's loose."

"What? What are you talking about?"

"I hear him," Sawyer felt the wood start to splinter beneath his grasp. "In my head."

You should have seen the fire. It was so beautiful. Burn, burn, burn...and the screams. God, they were so loud. The guards weren't all unconscious when I let the fire go.

Sawyer shook his head. *You fucking bastard, did you kill them all?*

Laughter came again. *We'll never go back. Because there's no place to go back to. They're all gone. Now I can hunt who I want, I can kill who I want, and no one will ever cage me again.*

Sawyer's temples throbbed.

And guess who I want to hunt first, One? It's you...because it's time for a new leader in this pack. I'm going to kill your precious Elizabeth, and then I'll kill you.

Rage washed over Sawyer. Dark, twisting, consuming. Making him want to roar his fury. Making him want to attack. To destroy.

Attack. Destroy. K —

"Sawyer?" Elizabeth was stroking his cheek. "Talk to me!"

How do you like that taste? Bryce taunted. *Just wait until you see what I can really do. I've been pulling strings you don't even know about, and it's time for you to see the truth.*

"Get the fuck out of my head," Sawyer snarled.

Elizabeth's eyes widened.

"*Now!*" Sawyer roared and he sent a blast of pure rage flying back toward Bryce. He didn't know if that trick would work, but he was too furious to stop.

And...

Bryce's connection to him winked out.

Elizabeth's breath panted in and out. "Tell me you're not having some kind of breakdown."

That would be easier to handle. "Bryce isn't dead. The sonofabitch was just in my head." He rose and paced away from the bed, his body full of desperate energy and his muscles tight with battle-ready tension. "He's coming after me." No, not just him. Bryce was doing something far worse. Swallowing, he faced Elizabeth. "He's coming after you. Because of what I feel for you, the bastard is using you as a target. He's going to hurt you so he can get to me."

She slid from the bed, pulling the sheet with her. "Why does he think I matter to you?"

"Because he's been in my head." *Because you do.*

"He can really do that? Slip into your mind?"

"I think he can do a hell of a lot more than we all realized." He whirled and stalked toward the backpack. He unzipped it and pulled out the damaged laptop. "Secrets are on this damn thing."

The floor groaned beneath her steps. "I told you when we were in the desert that I have a friend who can help us. If anyone can access the data on that machine, it will be Jay."

Jay. Her voice softened a bit when she said the other man's name. Did she realize that? Sawyer looked back at her. "But where the hell is this Jay? We need answers *now.*"

Her gaze darted to the phone on the nightstand. "Jay has some pretty incredible resources."

Well, wasn't he just fucking fantastic, this mysterious *Jay* that she spoke of so easily.

"If I call him…" She was still looking at the phone. "I know he can be here for us within the hour. He can take us out of here and put us in a safe place until we figure out our next move."

Be here within the hour. Eyes narrowing, Sawyer tilted his head and studied her. "How is the guy so close?"

"Because he's been working with me all along." The sheet trailed over the floor as she advanced toward him. "He didn't like me going into Lazarus alone, so he told me he would be close by, in case I needed him. I think it's safe to say that we need him now."

Something was twisting inside of Sawyer's gut. Something that made him feel… "Who is he to you?"

"A friend. An old friend."

"Just that?"

"Does it matter? We're kind of in a shit situation at the moment, and we need him. He's a phone call away."

"You're asking me to trust a stranger." A guy who could sell him out in an instant.

"No, I'm asking you to trust me."

Hell.

"There are things you don't know about me. Things I'm not proud of," Elizabeth said as her dark stare held his. "I'm the one who created Lazarus. I'm the one responsible for the formula. And it's because of me that you're even in the program now."

He didn't move. "Why do you say that?"

"Because Landon…he told me that Wright wanted you in the program because your involvement would be a way of controlling me. As long as you were in Lazarus, Wright knew that I couldn't walk away. I'd always come back when he needed me." She gave a hard, negative shake of her head. "No, not when *he* needed me. Fuck Wright. I would come back when *you* needed me."

And she had.

"Jay is my friend. I trust him with my life."

Sawyer trusted her. "Make the call." He nodded grimly. "Do it, now."

Her breath slipped out on a sigh. She hurried toward the phone and dialed quickly. He didn't move closer to her. Sawyer knew his enhanced hearing would let him hear every word of the conversation even from his position across the room.

The call was answered on the second ring.

"Elizabeth?" A man's voice. Rushed. Worried. *"I just saw the report on TV. Shit, baby, you scared the hell —"*

Baby?

"What report?" Elizabeth asked. "And how did you know it was me?"

"Other than West, you're the only person who has my private number." Again, he spoke in a rush. "And the report I'm talking about—it's the one that's blasting on every TV channel in the area. The one that says a government research facility was *bombed.* There are over twenty confirmed fatalities, and two female doctors—Dr. Elizabeth Parker and Dr. Cecelia Gregory—are currently missing. The reporters are suggesting that you two may have been kidnapped by the bombers, that we have some domestic terrorism nightmare going on—"

"I wasn't kidnapped. I'm okay. Cecelia's okay, too."

"I'm coming to get you." Flat.

"You don't even know where I am!"

"Oh, baby, this is me."

Again with the baby shit?

"I had a lock on you the minute you called this number. Stay where you are, and I'll be there to get you in thirty minutes."

Elizabeth glanced over her shoulder at Sawyer. "I'm not alone."

"Right, Dr. Cecelia Gregory. Don't worry, I'll get her, too."

"No, I mean, yes, Cecelia is here, also, but two men are with us. I need a safe place for them. And I need your computer skills."

Silence.

Sawyer found himself gliding closer to Elizabeth.

"You need me, huh?" The guy—Jay—gave a low laugh. "You know I'll give you everything you need. I'll get the transport. You just stay out of sight until I arrive."

"Thank you."

Jay had jumped to help her, no questions asked.

"Is he the man you remember?" Jay's voice was halting now.

Sawyer saw Elizabeth's shoulders tense.

"Beth?" Jay prompted.

Beth. A more intimate name, and the man's voice had held a tone...*they aren't just friends.* And the sudden emotion flooding through Sawyer's veins was heavy and ugly and angry. Jealousy.

"I'll see you soon, Jay," Elizabeth said, and she hung up the phone.

Let it go.

"He'll be here in thirty minutes." She gave Sawyer a weak smile. "Jay always keeps his word. I should, um, I should go get dressed." She took a step toward the bathroom and stopped. "Only I guess I don't have any new clothes."

"Flynn and Cecelia are in the room next door. I heard them return." But he'd been preoccupied at the time, so he hadn't cared.

Her eyes widened as she looked toward the wall that separated their room from Flynn's. "You heard…oh, no. *Tell* me that he didn't hear us, too."

Flynn probably had.

Her cheeks stained. "Wonderful."

"Why would you care if Flynn heard us having sex?"

"Because I do, okay? I just—"

"Have you had sex with Jay?" His voice was angry, and the darker emotions were surging in him, but he didn't let those emotions loose. He held them back with a stranglehold even as his hands clenched into fists.

She sucked in a sharp breath. "Does it matter?"

He stalked to her. Stopped only when he was right in front of Elizabeth. "*Yes.*"

Her chin lifted. "I did."

Fucking sonofabitch —

"Before I ever met you. Before a tough as nails SEAL headed into my exam room, and I found myself looking into a pair of blue eyes I'd never be able to forget." Her smile was sad. "Jay and I were before you."

"I was trapped in Lazarus hell for three months—" He stopped, unable to say more. His jaw locked as his teeth ground together. Had she been with someone else during that time? Had another man touched her, kissed her, made the pleasure tremble through her body while he'd been locked away? Had she turned back to that Jay asshole? *Don't want to know. Shouldn't have asked. Want to kill —*

"Jay was before you, and there was no one after you." Her gaze held his. "Did you really think I'd just go to someone else, when I knew what was happening to you? That I'd just turn my back on you that way?"

He'd hurt her. Shit. He could see it now. "I didn't mean—"

"I know that you don't remember me and that hurts. Because I remember it all. But try to understand me now, would you? Try to *know* me. I'm not the kind of person who'd do that. For me, you were...*it*." Her lips pressed together and she blinked quickly. "Being with someone else would have been wrong. Not that I ever wanted anyone else. Just you." She shouldered past him, marching for the bathroom.

He could only stand there, with his hands clenched, and with the image of her tear-filled gaze burned into his mind. "*Beth!*"

She stiffened. "You never called me that."

Jay called her Beth. Jay helped her. Jay remembered her. So why the hell hadn't she gone back to Jay?

"Why not?" he rasped.

"Because you got into the habit of calling me 'doc' when we first met." She reached for the doorknob. "And then, whenever we were together, you'd call me other things."

"Like what?" He should stop. Just — *stop.*

"Sweetheart. Baby." Her shoulders rolled back. "The endearments that lovers use."

"What did you call me?"

She looked over her shoulder. "Mine." She licked her lips. "Because you were mine, and I was yours, and then everything went to hell."

Yes, it had.

Elizabeth hurried into the bathroom and the door shut softly behind her.

Sawyer spun on his heel and strode for the motel room door. He wanted his past back. He wanted his life back.

I want Elizabeth.

He opened the door, making sure to check the perimeter to be certain there weren't any unwanted guests lingering around. Then he knocked softly on Flynn's door. The door was jerked open immediately, and Flynn stood there, looking slightly flushed, his hair raked back from his head.

"Clothes," Sawyer snapped. "I need them for Elizabeth."

Flynn lifted a brow. "Sure about that? From what I heard, didn't sound like you two were doing an activity that involved —"

Sawyer grabbed Flynn and shoved him back, surging hard until Flynn's shoulders hit a wall.

Cecelia gave a quick gasp and ran toward them. "Stop it!"

Sawyer didn't let him go. "You don't talk about her. Got it?"

Flynn searched his gaze. "Do *you* got your control, bro? 'Cause you seem a little unsteady to me."

Cecelia grabbed Sawyer's arm. "Let him go!"

He did, mostly to prove that, yeah, he still had his control. For the damn moment. Sawyer exhaled and rolled back his shoulders. "Give me the clothes." He didn't comment on the fact that Cecelia was wearing a towel and that Flynn was partially dressed. *How's that for control?*

"On the nightstand." Flynn caught Cecelia's hand and pulled her behind him.

A protective pose. Interesting.

"Elizabeth called her *friend.*" Friend, ex-lover, hell — he was going to have trouble being around that guy. The surge of emotion was not good. "Jay is coming for us. He'll be here within thirty minutes."

Flynn's brows rose. "Can we trust him?"

"Don't have any choice. He's not the only one coming for us." Sawyer snatched up the bag of clothing. "Got a little telepathic visit from our buddy Bryce. He's pissed as hell, and he's promised to hunt us down."

"He got out of the facility?" Cecelia cried. Fear flashed on her face.

Fury darkened Flynn's eyes. "He's a dead man."

"Aren't we all," Sawyer muttered. "The bastard said he was coming after Elizabeth. He thinks he's going to kill her and push me over the edge. *Not* happening."

Flynn nodded grimly. "We'll stop him."

I'll kill him, and he won't come back. That will stop him.

"Better turn on the TV." Sawyer inclined his head toward the dark screen. "Seems we've made the news." He strode toward the door.

"The news? What do you mean? Is Wright looking for us? Did the bastard say we're—"

"The whole facility is gone. Exploded. And Jay said the news reports are claiming that Elizabeth and Cecelia were kidnapped.

Kidnappers. Hell." He yanked open the door. "Add the crime to our damn resume."

CHAPTER TWENTY-ONE

The black SUV braked in front of the motel. Sawyer was peering out of the window, and he saw the two, armed men who jumped from the vehicle. Even without his enhanced vision, Sawyer would have been able to easily see the men. The light from the motel spilled onto their vehicle.

"Your friend came armed," he announced.

"Not like I invited him to a picnic," Elizabeth threw back at him. "Wouldn't *you* come armed to a situation like this one?"

Sawyer glanced back at her. Flynn and Cecelia were both in the room, too, but they were silent. Tense. They were all tense. If this meeting went south, if Jay wasn't someone they could really trust, then Sawyer would have to end him.

"Make sure it's Jay," Sawyer ordered quietly.

Elizabeth slid closer to him. Her body brushed against his, and her scent surrounded him. She peeked out of the blinds and the tension eased from her body. "That's Jay. The one with the too-long hair. The other guy is his bodyguard,

West Harper." Elizabeth gave a quick, decisive nod. "We need to go, now."

He caught her hand. "Stay with me."

Her lips parted.

"Bryce is coming after you. We can't get separated. I need you close at all times, understand?"

A shadow slid over her face. "Right. Bryce. Of course."

He'd said the wrong thing. Done something wrong. What?

But he didn't have time to question her. They had to move and move right then. He yanked open the door, and they rushed out.

The one she'd identified as Jay tensed even as his bodyguard—a tall, African American man dressed in khakis and a leather jacket—brought up his weapon and aimed it at Sawyer.

Sawyer's eyes narrowed on the guard. "You don't want to be doing that."

"No!" Jay's sharp voice. "West, it's okay. Lower the gun." Jay shoved his own gun into the holster at his hip. Then he was surging forward and grabbing Elizabeth, pulling her against him in a fierce hug. "You scared the hell out of me." He buried his face in her neck, but Sawyer could still hear his muttered words. "When I saw that news report, my first thought was that you were dead. And when the reporter continued, saying you'd been kidnapped..." He shuddered.

And he kept holding Elizabeth.

Enough of that shit.

Sawyer pulled her from the guy's arms. "She wasn't kidnapped." He wrapped his arm around her shoulders, keeping Elizabeth at his side. "I was keeping her safe. Leaving her behind wasn't an option."

Jay was tall, just an inch or so shorter than Sawyer, and his hair slid over his forehead. His features were even, the casual, handsome All-American look that some women might like. *Not Elizabeth. She'd —*

"Funny." Jay didn't sound particularly amused. "She said the same thing about you, Sawyer. Leaving you wasn't an option. That's why she's in this mess." He craned his head and looked at Flynn and Cecelia. He raised his brows. "Dr. Gregory, I assume?"

Cecelia nodded.

Jay's gaze swept over Flynn. "And you are —"

"Two —" Flynn began.

Cecelia stepped in front of him. "His name is Flynn."

Jay nodded. "Ah, right. The wing-man. I remember you now. Should have figured you two would still have each other's backs."

"Speaking of backs..." It was the bodyguard who spoke. His voice was low and gravel-rough, and his gaze kept sweeping the area. "I can't protect you in the open like this. Get your asses into the SUV."

I don't need protection. Did the guy have any idea who he was facing?

Jay gave a little laugh. "Don't get all offended, Sawyer. West was talking about me." He reached for Elizabeth's hand. "I guess some things don't change. Sawyer still has to be the baddest asshole in the group, huh?"

Sawyer caught Elizabeth's other hand. The guy kept talking as if he and Sawyer had met before. Maybe they had. *And maybe I disliked him just as much then.*

They jumped into the SUV, though, because they didn't have time for some freaking drama. West got into the passenger seat. It was a three-row SUV. "Bullet-proof windows," Jay announced. "And amped with every bit of bonus tech I could think of."

Flynn and Cecelia crowded into the rear, while Jay, Elizabeth, and Sawyer slid into the second row. Elizabeth was locked between Jay and Sawyer. The driver spun the SUV out of the lot, and then they were racing down the dark highway.

"I have a laptop for you," Elizabeth said to Jay. "It's screwed to hell and back, but it's got data on the drive that I need."

"I'll take care of it." The guy sounded absolutely certain. As if he could get the job done, no questions asked.

He was also still holding onto Elizabeth's hand. What was up with that crap?

Sawyer kept his hold on her, too.

"Sawyer and Flynn..." Jay cleared his throat. "I'll get new identities for you two. I have a private plane you can use for your escape, and I'll have my pilot drop you off any place you want to go."

"What?" Sawyer turned his head, frowning at the other man.

"Your new identities." Jay spoke as if what he'd said before had been crystal clear. "Not like you can just waltz back into your old lives, am I right? I mean, you're dead and buried to the rest of the world."

The hell they were.

"You'll need to get out of the country, especially with all the press that's happening right now about the bombing at the facility. No one knows just what kind of work was going on in that place, and I'm sure Uncle Sam is going to make sure the truth doesn't ever get out. Right now, the story is that all of the government employees—except for Elizabeth and Dr. Gregory—they were all killed and—"

"They weren't," Sawyer cut in grimly. "We weren't killing the guards. We knocked them out to escape, but Flynn and I didn't *kill* them."

"Someone did." Jay's voice was flat. "Because I've got a contact who sent me pictures of the bodies being removed. The reporters are being fed a line of bull about explosions, and, yeah, some fire rocked the place, but it was hardly the bombings portrayed by the media. Still, my contact saw the bodies. The guards who were *inside* are all dead."

Elizabeth's hand jerked in Sawyer's grip. "Who is your contact? You never said anything about having a man at Lazarus."

"I couldn't have you going in blind. You think I was going to risk you dying?"

He cares about her. There was so much tension in the guy's voice.

"I bribed a guard to keep me updated, but he was on outside duty at Lazarus, not given access to get to the lower levels of the facility. And he swears the folks inside are all *dead*."

Silence. The driver kept the vehicle surging through the darkness.

"Your contact is wrong," Sawyer finally said grimly. "Everyone isn't dead. I know for damn sure that another test subject got out. Subject Five—"

"Bryce King," Elizabeth cut in.

"He got out. And the bastard is coming after us."

"How do you know that?" Jay immediately wanted to know. "Did you see him escape? Was he with you all when you left—"

"Not hardly," Cecelia mumbled.

"If he had been," Flynn added in a voice that was hard with purpose, "I would have killed the bastard myself."

The front seat squeaked as West turned to look back at them.

"We know Bryce got out," Sawyer announced clearly. "Because the bastard *told* me he got out. Just like he said he was coming after Elizabeth."

"He *told* you?" Jay's voice rose. "He contacted you? Fuck, is he following us right now?"

"Uh, Jay, there are a few things you need to know." In contrast to his high voice, Elizabeth was oddly soothing. "Turns out my formula had a few side effects that I didn't realize."

"You brought men back from the dead, Elizabeth. Of *course,* there were going to be side effects—"

"The subjects can communicate telepathically."

Jay didn't speak.

"They have enhanced strength, healing abilities, senses—"

"Let's go back to that telepathic bullshit," Jay said. "And then go over things...slowly, from the beginning."

***

He didn't take them to just any safe house. With Jay, she shouldn't have been surprised. He spirited them away from the no-tell motel to what was basically a mansion, one that was totally walled off with top-of-the-line security and a giant gate that promised to keep the rest of the world away.

"Why do I feel like we're walking into another prison?" Flynn asked as he exited the vehicle.

But Jay just shook his head. "You've never been to a prison this nice." He jogged toward the sprawling stone steps. "I've got men watching the gate, but I'd still prefer to get our asses inside as soon as possible." He looked back at her. "And Elizabeth, you and I need to talk."

She caught the part he didn't say...*alone. You and I need to talk alone.* She'd felt the tension in his body as soon as she started discussing the enhancements that the Lazarus subjects had. Jay wasn't happy. Actually, she thought he might be on the verge of freaking out, and with Jay, that was never good.

"Jesus, man. Who the hell *are* you?" Flynn demanded as the group followed Jay inside. The interior of the house was as decadent as Elizabeth had suspected it would be. Gleaming marble floors. Glittering chandeliers. She was pretty sure she caught sight of a Monet painting. Typical Jay.

"Better question," Sawyer growled. He'd been silent for most of the trip to the safe house. She didn't think that was a good sign. "How do you afford this place?"

West was at Elizabeth's side. West wasn't just Jay's bodyguard. The guy was his best-friend, his closest confidant, and pretty much the only family that Jay had ever had. The two men had been foster brothers once, and when they'd grown up, West had gone into the military. He'd become part of Delta Force, sliding into danger every chance he got. And Jay...

Jay had found trouble. As he typically did.

"Glad you're okay," West murmured to Elizabeth. He pulled her into a quick hug, and the move surprised her. West wasn't much for emotion. Jay, on the other hand—the guy was always bursting with emotion. Barely holding his feelings in check. The two men were such opposites.

And they were her best friends.

"Thank you," Elizabeth squeezed him back. "I can't ever repay you and Jay—"

Sawyer snarled.

It was a rough, animalistic sound, and Elizabeth stiffened. She slowly lifted her head from West's shoulder and found Sawyer glaring at her. No, not at her, at West.

"Him, the hell, too?" Sawyer snarled. "How many exes do you have around this place?"

Her cheeks burned. No, he had *not* just said that to her.

"Watch yourself," West warned. "Super soldier or not, I will take your ass down if you use that tone with Elizabeth."

"Get your hands *off* her."

"His hands aren't on me." Elizabeth lifted her chin. "Mine are on him. Because West is my friend. Jay is my friend. They are helping us, and you—"

Sawyer let out a guttural cry. He put his hands on either side of his head and hunched his body. "Fucking trying to control…"

"Uh, Beth?" Jay cleared his throat. "Maybe do us all a solid and back away from—"

Sawyer's head had snapped up. His eyes had gone cold and lethal. "She's mine."

Her body iced.

"The only thing that got me through hell. A memory that snuck into my head while I slept. A dream I didn't think was real." He stalked toward West. "You won't take her from me. *No one will take her again.*"

"Sawyer!" Elizabeth jerked from West and put her hand on Sawyer's chest, stopping him. "What are you doing?"

He stared at her, and she saw the confusion in his eyes. He just looked...lost. Oh, dear God, was Bryce in his head again? Feeding him emotions? Driving up his rage? Was he—

"He's been living in a vacuum for months." Cecelia's steps seemed to echo as she crossed the marble entranceway. "Then you returned to his life, and you brought emotion back to him."

Sawyer squeezed his eyes shut. "Sorry," he rasped to Elizabeth. "So damn sorry."

"Emotions can be good," Cecelia continued in her soft, quiet voice. "There are good emotions like joy, love, and hope, but some emotions can be bad. I think Bryce has shown us that. When dark emotions take hold, I think they are particularly dangerous for the Lazarus men."

"Jealousy," Jay announced as he lifted his hands into the air. "It's a bitch for any man."

Sawyer's eyes flew open. His stare locked on Elizabeth. He didn't look as lost, but he did look...sad. So very sad. "I remember that you're mine," he told her, his voice still little more than a rough rasp. "And I don't want to lose you to another because you can't stand the idea of being with a fucking monster."

Her breath caught. And that foyer got very, very quiet. The silence lasted until she said, "I don't see you that way."

"Don't you?" His lips twisted in a humorless smile. "Warned you before, I can tell when you lie. Your heartbeat kicks up, your breath catches, and you—"

She took his hand in hers and Elizabeth lifted it, putting it over her heart. "I don't see you as a monster. I never saw you that way."

"I want my life back," Sawyer said, still rasping. "I want *you* back."

You have me. She was right in front of him. Didn't he see what she was offering?

"Okay." Jay cleared his throat. "This is getting weirdly awkward, so how about you two go upstairs and get some privacy? Or some sleep? Or whatever the hell it is you need. There are plenty of guest rooms upstairs." He lifted the laptop he held. "I'll get to work on this. If I can retrieve anything on it, I will. Then, Elizabeth, you and I need to talk."

Right. *Go upstairs.* She and Sawyer shouldn't have this conversation with everyone watching. The problem was that she didn't know what else to say to Sawyer.

But she had to say something.

She took his hand and she led him upstairs.

***

Cecelia watched Elizabeth take Sawyer up the stairs. He shadowed her movements, always staying so close to her. No one spoke, not until Elizabeth and Sawyer had disappeared. When the door shut upstairs, Cecelia released the breath she'd been holding.

"Will she be safe with him?"

Her head turned. Jay was staring at her—only Jay wasn't his real name. She knew him. She'd read news stories about the guy before, and she'd recognized him on sight. Jennings Maverick. *The* reigning tech king. Flynn and Sawyer had asked how the guy got his obvious wealth, and she knew the answer. He'd built a multi-billion-dollar empire by the time he was twenty-five years old. He'd blown the lid off cyber security, creating new technology that the United States government had been eager to snatch up. But Jennings hadn't wanted to work just with Uncle Sam. He'd gone private, and his wealth had sky-rocketed. He was known to be reclusive, brilliant, and definitely eccentric.

"Will she be safe?" Jennings—Jay—repeated. "Or do I need to take protective measures?"

Beside her, Flynn tensed.

"She'll be safe," Cecelia said quickly. And she thought her words were true. "She's the one person he remembers, the one link that Sawyer has to his past. He won't hurt her."

Jay didn't look convinced.

"He didn't hurt her back at Lazarus." And Cecelia knew the guy had been driven by demons. *No, by a particular demon – Bryce.* "He's uncertain of her when other men get close. It's a territorial thing. She matters most to him, and Sawyer wants to secure their connection." Because, as he'd said, Sawyer viewed himself as a monster. He didn't think the woman he wanted would stay with a monster.

"A territorial thing, huh? If you go by that, then I guess all men can be monsters." Jay's brown gaze was hooded as it swung toward Flynn. "And what's your story? You got the telepathic link thing going on, too? All the super soldier upgrades?"

Flynn stared back at him.

"I'm trying to *help!*" The words exploded from Jay. "Don't you see that? I'm the good guy here!"

"Get the files off that laptop. Give me intel I can use. Then I'll see how good you are." Flynn took Cecelia's elbow. "Right now, we're crashing." He guided her up the stairs. Since a bone-deep weariness pulled at her, Cecelia didn't argue with him.

"Uh, yeah, you're welcome!" Jay called out. "I risked my life for you all, but, hey, don't worry about thanking me. Just go right on up there, don't stop to —"

Flynn stopped.

Unease slithered through Cecelia.

He looked over the railing at Jay and West. "I'll pay back this debt. I'll find a way, you have my word."

And Jay's eyes gleamed. "I'll remember that."

He wanted that promise. Cecelia's stomach knotted. She had the bad feeling that they'd just been played. Not surprising because everything she'd read about the man had indicated that Jay was a master manipulator.

She'd just seen him in action.

They reached the top of the stairs. There were rooms to the left, rooms to the right. The place was huge. And it made her feel small.

"I'll…um…go this way." She pointed to the right and turned away from Flynn.

But he followed her. The carpet was thick and lush, swallowing the sound of his footsteps, but she could feel him behind her. She reached for the nearest doorknob and twisted it. Cecelia shoved open the door and hurried inside.

Flynn followed right behind her. Again, she could *feel* him. Cecelia spun around. "You don't need to—"

"I don't know the men downstairs. I don't trust them." He crossed his hands over his chest. "And I won't leave you unprotected."

"We are *safe* here."

But he just shook his head. "I won't leave you unprotected."

***

"Jay?"

He clutched the damaged laptop a bit tighter. "Double the patrols outside. If their story is true, and they're really being hunted by this Subject Five…" Jay glanced at West. "I don't want that bastard getting inside."

West nodded. "Neither do I."

Jay hesitated, but said, "And…I want you to remain inside, okay? Keep an eye on our new guests."

"You think they're a threat?"

"I think Elizabeth might not see Sawyer Cage as a monster…" His lips thinned. "But I sure as hell do." What else were you supposed to call a man who'd rose from the dead? A man who was far too powerful.

And dangerous.

CHAPTER TWENTY-TWO

Elizabeth leaned against the closed bedroom door. Sawyer paced around the bed, looking like a caged lion who was about to roar.

Then he just stopped. His head sagged forward as he stared down at his clenched hands. "I'm not him."

Elizabeth wanted to wrap her arms around him and hold tight. "Who?"

His head lifted. "I'm not the man you loved. I'm not the same."

"Sawyer—"

"I was Subject One for months. I lived in a void. I existed to hunt and to kill, and I don't know how to go back to being normal." He gave a bitter laugh. "But then, I'm not normal, am I? Far the fuck from it. I've got voices in my head—literal voices that aren't my own. I've got emotions that aren't my own. As for *my* feelings, they're wrong."

Her heart ached.

"I want you too much."

Elizabeth shook her head. Her lips parted. *That's not possible —*

"I want you fucking constantly, Elizabeth. Every moment I'm with you, I want you. I crave you, like — like you're a fire in my blood. I need you. And the things I want to do with you…" He exhaled. "The guy you knew before — he was the tender lover, right? The one who had dreams with you. Pretty promises about the future."

Her throat had closed on her.

"But he's gone." Sawyer took a step toward her. "You lost him, and you're just left with me. A man who wants to fucking own you. Who wants to keep you, possess you, always. Because I swear, you *are* my sanity. I feel whole when I'm with you, and the thought of losing you…" Another step. He was right in front of her now. His hand lifted and his knuckles brushed over her cheek. "That terrifies me. Nothing else scares me. But living in a world without you? *I can't.*"

She caught his hand. Held tight. "Now you know how I feel."

A furrow appeared between his eyes.

"I wasn't going to let you go, I wasn't going to —"

Pain flashed on his face. "I'm not the same man! I'm not *him!*"

"And I'm not the same woman I was before, either. But I am the woman who is standing before you, the woman who is saying…I want you just as much as you want me. I crave you." In her blood? Yes. He was in her very soul. "I don't care what name you go by — One, Sawyer — it's you I want. *You*. I would risk anything for you, don't you see that?"

"Elizabeth — "

"I want *you*. And you're not some monster. A monster doesn't risk his life for someone else. A monster doesn't fight so desperately to protect someone else." She brought his hand to her lips and pressed a kiss to his knuckles. "You know who does that?"

His eyes blazed at her.

"A good man," Elizabeth whispered. "*You* are a good man."

"Does a good man want to beat the hell out of two guys he just met? Two guys who did nothing but help him." His breath was ragged. "Because Jay and West — they've done nothing to me, but seeing them with you…when they put their hands on you…"

"Jealousy is normal."

"I'm *not* normal, and emotions like that aren't safe for me."

"Then trust me."

He blinked at her.

"*Trust* me. Because you're not trusting me. You're looking at me with them and thinking…hell, what are you thinking? That I'd want to be with them? That I'd choose them over you? Look, they're both great guys, don't get me wrong. But it's you that I want. *You.* I'll say it as many times as you need to hear it. Until it sinks in. I'm not running from you. I'm running *with* you. Because you're the one I choose. It will *always* be you."

His eyes widened. She thought she saw the faintest flicker of hope in his gaze. But in the next moment, his head lowered toward her. His mouth crashed onto hers. The kiss was rough, wild, and desperate.

And she didn't care. Her hands rose and locked around his shoulders. Her nails sank into his shirt. He kissed her with such need. Like he was starved for her. Like he'd never get enough of her.

She'd never get enough of him.

His hand slid between them. He yanked up her shirt and shoved her bra out of the way. His warm, callused fingertips stroked her nipples. Teased. Tugged. Arousal flooded through her. Sawyer had said that he always wanted her. Didn't he get it? She always wanted him, too. She always would. He wasn't a monster.

He was her man.

Show him. She pulled her mouth from his. Her hands slipped from his broad shoulders and pushed against his chest.

"Elizabeth? *Baby?*"

"You're a man. Mine." She gave him a smile and then she let her hands drop to his waist. She unhooked his pants, slid down the zipper—

"Elizabeth."

"I want you. I want to do this." She'd always loved to drive him wild this way.

He shuddered.

And he let her hands go. He wasn't wearing underwear, and that just made things easier. Elizabeth lowered to her knees before him. His cock filled her hands, long and stretching, with moisture already gleaming on the broad head. She put her mouth on him. Licked the tip lightly and his hips jerked against her.

"Baby…"

She opened her mouth. Took him inside. Sucked. A shallow suck, not too deep. Teasing.

He growled.

She took him in deeper. Licked him more. Pumped his cock with her hands even as her mouth slid over him. He was warm and hard. And she loved the feel of him. Her hips rocked even as she took him in her mouth once more. She'd suck him, then go back to lick the tip—

His hand sank into her hair. "I can't…control…*Can't…*"

She let him go. Licked her lips and stared up at him. "That's what I want. I want you to let your control rip away. I want you to see that with it gone, you won't hurt me. I can take what you have to give." *I always could.* "I want everything you have."

She put her mouth back on him. Licked. Sucked. And she—

He gave a guttural cry and lifted her up. He moved fast, and she found herself dropped onto the bed. She sat up, but he was yanking off her shoes, pulling down her jeans and her underwear. He'd stripped her so fast, and there was no stopping him. She didn't want to stop him. She wanted to drive him wild.

He dragged her hips to the edge of the bed. Her legs splayed open. He sank into her. No tender touches. No seduction. Just raw, savage need. Exactly what she wanted. He thrust into her, withdrew, then plunged deep with hard, driving strokes. Her legs locked around his hips as she bucked up against him.

She didn't want him to slow down. Didn't want him to go softer. She wanted faster. Harder. She wanted oblivion.

Her nails didn't bite lightly into his back this time. They raked down his back in a frenzy. She was as savage as he was. His hands were too tight on her hips, and she didn't care. She wasn't afraid of rough. She wasn't afraid of him.

He dragged his cock over her clit as he thrust, and Elizabeth came, erupting with pleasure. Her sex spasmed around him as the climax went on and on, pounding through her body. He drove

into her, not stopping and making the climax all
the stronger. He grabbed her legs and lifted them
over his shoulders, opening her fully to him. She
couldn't control his thrusts, couldn't limit him,
and she didn't want to.

I want everything.

His eyes were stark, filled with lust, his face
locked into tight lines. "Again."

Her breath heaved from her lungs.

"Want to feel you come around me…*again.*"

He plunged deep into her. She was swollen
and sensitive from her climax, and Elizabeth
gasped out his name. She wanted him to find
release. Wanted to see the pleasure on his face.

He kissed her. Rough. Demanding. His
tongue swiped into her mouth even as his cock
sank into her body. She was lost in sensation.
Lost so completely in him.

He withdrew from her. Pulled out
completely.

No!

Sawyer flipped her over on the bed. Her
hands flew out and grabbed the sheets, bunching
them in her fists. He caught her hips in his hands,
lifted her up, and drove into her. She couldn't
limit his thrusts, couldn't stop him, didn't want
to stop him. A second release was closing in on
her. Elizabeth tossed back her head. "Sawyer!"
She was moaning and gasping and being too
loud. She clamped her lips together.

He bit her. Right on the curve of her shoulder. The bite made her sex clench around him as she came once more.

And he was with her. She felt the hot tide of his release inside of her, and he held her even tighter. His body surrounded her. So strong and powerful. He held her, held her so close.

Monster, man—*hers.* Always.

***

"*Don't!*" Elizabeth's voice was sharp. Desperate. Terrified. "*Don't die! Don't! Don't leave me!*"

Sawyer's eyes opened. He was in bed with Elizabeth. They'd both crashed hard, and, even in sleep, he'd held her close.

Now, her body was tense against him, and when he turned his head, he saw that her face was twisted in fear, even as her eyes remained closed. Keeping his voice gentle, he soothed, "Baby, it's okay. Just a bad dream."

"*Sawyer!*"

He stiffened. She was calling his name, but he knew she was locked in a dream. "Elizabeth?"

"*Sawyer! No! Stay with me! Don't die! Don't leave!*"

The pain in her voice gutted him. Sawyer shook her. "Elizabeth, wake up. It's a bad dream."

She gave a gasp and shuddered. Her eyes finally opened as her head turned toward him. "Sawyer?"

"Right here, baby. I'm right here." And this scene—it was so familiar to him. *Elizabeth has bad dreams.* And he didn't like it when she had to wake from those dreams alone. He worried about her waking up alone and being scared.

She's not alone now.

"I had a bad dream." The words were oddly familiar to him.

"I know." His voice was still gentle. He pulled her closer, held her cradled against him.

Her desperate breathing evened out, but her body remained tense. "Sawyer?"

"Yeah?"

"It…wasn't a dream."

He swallowed and kept his hold on her. "I know."

"You died. You were on the exam table, and Landon was going to bring you back. He wanted to put you in Project Lazarus. I couldn't—the formula wasn't ready, and I never wanted it for you. *Not you.* You weren't supposed to die. You were supposed to stay with me."

His hand was on her back. He stroked her spine. *I am with you.*

"He had a guard drag me out of the lab. I saw Landon give you too much of the formula. *Two doses.* You didn't wake up, and Landon thought something was wrong. He was blaming me, and..." Her words trailed away. He heard the painful little click of her swallow. "Then you woke up."

There was so much pain in her words.

"Part of me was so happy." Shame slid into her voice. "You were awake. You were back..."

"I don't remember that." He didn't remember anything before he'd opened his eyes to find himself in a cell at the Lazarus facility. And when he'd woken, Landon had immediately shown him a video, proof that Sawyer had "volunteered" to be in the government program.

"You woke up," she said again and gave a little shudder.

He realized her hand was on her chest, tracing the red line of her scar.

A cold wind seemed to fill the room. "Elizabeth?"

"Promise me, tell me that you'll always come back."

Did she think he was going to walk away? Cut and run, vanish with some new identity because of what Jay had said? *No.* Not without her. Not ever without her.

"Promise me," she said again, and it was almost as if she were begging him.

He would have given her any promise she wanted. Didn't she see that? He would give her anything. Everything. "I promise." Sawyer held her, keeping her close against him, cradling her, until Elizabeth fell asleep once more. When the tension finally eased from her body, he pressed a kiss to her temple.

He heard the faint sound of footsteps on the stairs. At first, he figured someone was just heading to one of the other guest rooms, but those soft steps headed toward *his* room. His head turned as Sawyer stared at the door. His eyes narrowed on that door. He could hear the faintest of rustles…

Sawyer slipped from the bed. He dressed quickly. Silent, he stalked across the room and he yanked the door open just as Jay was lifting his hand to knock.

Jay's eyes widened. "How did you—"

Sawyer pushed the guy back into the hallway. When they were both clear of the doorway, Sawyer pulled the door shut behind him.

"Right. Enhanced senses." Jay nodded. "Just takes a little getting used to, you know?"

"Elizabeth is sleeping. She had a bad dream, and I don't want—"

"Still has them, huh?" Sadness flashed on Jay's face.

The bastard has been with Elizabeth at night. In her bed. He's held her when she cries out.

"Guess she'll never get over the death of her parents."

Elizabeth hadn't been dreaming about her parents this time. *She was dreaming about me.*

"She was trapped with them, you know." Jay rubbed his hand over his jaw. "Not that Elizabeth ever told me that part. Don't think I got past her wall far enough for her to reveal that bit about herself." He flashed a quick smile. "But I have this terrible habit. I always have to know everything I can about the people in my life. And with a computer, I can find anything. *Anything.*"

Sonofabitch. "You dug into her past."

"I wanted to know what demons drove her." Jay turned away and headed down the hallway. He kept his voice low as he said, "She was like a woman possessed. She never told me specifics about Lazarus, not while we were together, but I figured it all out. She wanted to stop death. She never wanted to lose anyone close to her again."

Slowly, Sawyer followed the other man down the stairs. He didn't want to leave Elizabeth. What if she had another bad dream? But he needed to clear the damn air with Jay.

When they reached the landing, Jay sighed. His gaze raked over Sawyer. "She didn't want to lose someone she loved, and that's why it must have hurt her so much when she found out that Landon and Wright planned for you to be the first test subject."

You weren't supposed to die. You were supposed to stay with me.

"Do you remember her at all?" Jay asked, pushing.

"Yes." And what he didn't remember...*I think I'm falling for her again.*

"There are some videos you need to see." He looked back up the staircase. "Some that she needs to see, too, but maybe it will be better for you to see them first."

"I don't have secrets from Elizabeth."

"You sure about that?"

No, actually, he wasn't.

"Come on." Jay waved to the left. "My office is this way."

Eyes narrowing, Sawyer followed. When he entered the office, he wasn't particularly surprised to find West standing near the window. West had his arms crossed over his chest, and his back was against the wall that bordered the window. When his gaze fell on Sawyer, West lifted a brow. "We gonna have a problem?"

"Not if you keep your hands off Elizabeth."

West's lips twisted. "Known her for years. If we were interested in fucking each other, it would have happened by now." He pointed at Jay. "I would have stolen her away from this asshole."

Jay frowned at him. "If you weren't family, that line would piss me off."

"I am family, and it still pisses you off."

Sawyer shook his head. He didn't understand these two men. "I'm living in a damn nightmare right now, so can you both save your shit for someone else?"

Jay gave a brisk nod and headed for his desk. The laptop was there, but it was still closed. Wires ran from it, though, wires that connected to the two giant screens set up behind Jay's desk. "Took me all of five minutes. Hardly a challenge." Jay tapped on a wireless, black keyboard and a video appeared, stretching to cover both of the two screens. "This is the first one we need to talk about."

Sawyer saw his own face staring back at him from those screens. The image was frozen. "Play it," he bit off.

"Here we go." Jay tapped a key, and the video played.

On the screen, Sawyer's face tightened. "Why the hell do you need to record this?"

"For the record." That was Landon's voice. No mistaking that smug asshole's identity.

In that video, Sawyer rolled his eyes. "This is such bullshit. Fine. Okay. I, Sawyer Cage, volunteer to be part of Project Lazarus."

The video stopped. Thirteen seconds.

"I've seen this shit before." Sawyer knew an edge had entered his voice. "When I woke up in my cell at Lazarus, it was the first thing that Landon showed me. He wanted to prove that I'd agreed to be in the program, that I'd volunteered—"

"Did he show you the rest of the video?" Jay cut in.

The rest?

"Right. Judging by your expression, I'll say he didn't. He'd separated the files, but once I got into the system, I found the rest of your, um, volunteer reel, shall we say?"

"*Play it.*"

Jay did.

Sawyer saw himself lean forward, his hand clenched on a metal table. "Are we done? Because this is such bullshit. I've been involved in the program here for over a year."

"The program is going through some changes." Landon's voice was mild. "This is just a new protocol that Wright wants the Pack to follow."

"It's a waste of my time. I have a mission to get ready. I need to be with my men." He shoved away from the table and rose.

"You'll get to keep working with Dr. Parker now," Landon assured him. Landon still wasn't on camera. "That's the most important thing, isn't it?"

On the dual screens, Sawyer tensed. "Are you threatening to separate me and Elizabeth?"

"No, not at all. On the contrary, I've just assured that you'll keep working with her for as long as you want."

"Yeah? Well, here's a newsflash for you. This is my last mission. After this, I'm done. Getting out of this program, and starting a new life." He spun on his heel.

"A new life with Elizabeth?"

Sawyer threw an angry glare over his shoulder. "What I do on my private time is none of your concern. I've got a mission to run." He stormed out of the small room.

The video kept filming. The camera lens was locked on Sawyer's empty chair.

"It will definitely be your last mission." Landon's words were a low whisper.

The video ended.

Sawyer realized he wasn't breathing.

"Yeah." Jay cleared his throat. "Based on that little parting shot *and* the documents I found on the guy's laptop, it's safe to say he was involved in getting you killed."

Sawyer's gaze jumped to Jay's face.

"The mission was a success, you see. I found documentation of that. The hostages were rescued. There were no reports of enemy fire on the ground. No reports of friendly fire, either. The mission was logged in Landon's computer as being a complete success."

Sawyer shook his head.

"Yet, somehow," West didn't leave his seemingly relaxed position against the wall as he spoke up, "both you and your buddy Flynn wound up dead *after* you came back to the facility in D.C."

"And you were both immediately placed in preservation per Lazarus protocol." Jay looked at him with pity in his eyes. "You never had a chance. They wanted you for the program, and they made sure they got you."

Sawyer forced himself to take a deep breath. "What the fuck else is on his laptop?"

"There's a tape of your buddy Flynn basically saying the same thing you did. I don't believe he had any idea about what Lazarus truly was. He just thought it was some new pre-mission BS that Landon and Wright were swinging his way."

Sawyer heard a faint creak from upstairs. His gaze lifted to the ceiling.

"And then there's this…" Jay's fingers tapped on the wireless keyboard. "I believe you mentioned Bryce King? Subject Five?"

"He's the, uh, sadistic bastard who thinks he's gonna get his hands on Elizabeth." Fury battered every word.

"Not happening," West announced flatly.

"No, it's not." Sawyer stared at the screens and fought to regulate his breathing. "So Bryce was tricked, too?" Maybe the bastard had been normal, once, before Lazarus.

"No, not at all. He wasn't tricked."

A new video began to play. Bryce was smiling—that smug, twisted smile that never reached his eyes.

"*State your name.*" The voice came from off-camera. Landon's voice again.

"Bryce King." He lifted a blond brow. "What? You want my rank and serial number, too?"

"No, I want you to state that you are willingly offering yourself as a participant in Project Lazarus."

"Hell, yes, I'm in. I've seen the results, and I want that power boost myself." His eyes shone eagerly. "I willingly volunteer."

Jay paused the feed.

I've seen the results myself. "He came into the program a few weeks after Flynn and I were there. At first, it was just the two of us." Sawyer's shoulders tensed when he heard the creak of the stairs.

"Yeah, well, turns out the guy knew *exactly* what he was getting into." Jay resumed play on the video.

And the camera zoomed out. The video had just been focused on Bryce's face, but now Sawyer could see the exam room around him. Bryce was sitting on a reclining hospital bed. An IV fed into his arm. "How long will it take?" Bryce asked.

Landon walked into the frame. "Just a few moments. It's not going to hurt, I assure you."

Bryce was wearing a paper hospital gown. He gave a rough laugh. "I don't mind pain. Never have. Never will."

"You'll be out for a few moments. When you wake up, well, the other test subjects have no memory of their past lives."

"Some memories are better forgotten anyway. If I can do the things those other bastards can, it will be well worth the loss."

Landon gazed down at him. "You'll be able to do more than they can. I'm improving the formula with every new experiment."

"And folks always wake up? I mean, they always come back?" His voice had grown sluggish. His eyelids were falling shut.

"Usually." Landon checked the beeping monitor on his right. A moment later, he moved to strap down Bryce's right wrist, then his left. "Though we've had a few failures."

The beeping turned into a steady drone of sound. Sawyer realized what he was watching. "He just flat-lined." Sawyer shook his head. "Landon *killed* him."

There was a flurry of activity on the screens then. Men and women in green scrubs rushed in. Landon picked up a large syringe, and he plunged it straight into Bryce's heart.

Sawyer's hand rose and pressed to his own heart even as he heard the soft creak of the door opening behind him. He didn't look back, not even when he heard Elizabeth's swift intake of breath.

Landon is plunging another needle into Bryce — this time into the back of his head.

Sawyer's hand fell away from his chest.

"Come on," Landon urged as he stared at Bryce's still form. "Wake your ass up. The faster you wake up, the stronger you'll be. Come the hell—"

Bryce's eyes flew open as he roared. He jerked upright, ripping right through the straps that had locked down his wrists.

"Tranq him!" Landon shouted. "Tranq—"

The video ended.

Sawyer didn't move. "So that's what it looks like. When a man dies and comes back. And Bryce *knew* what was going to happen." Fucking hell. "Landon documented it all, didn't he? Because he's a scientist, and this is all his grand experiment. He documented every transformation."

"Yes." Unflinchingly, Jay met his stare. "Every one. The successes and the failures."

Elizabeth slipped to Sawyer's side. He didn't touch her, but Sawyer could feel her warmth near him. Her sweet scent wrapped around him. "How many failures were there?"

"Four."

Four dead men. Sawyer unlocked his jaw. "Were they like me and Flynn? Dead first, then given the formula? Or were they — "

"They were like Bryce. Landon gave them some sort of IV cocktail that stopped their hearts. They died, and he tried to bring them back with Lazarus. Only he was doing something wrong with them."

Elizabeth's fingers brushed Sawyer's. "How many successes? There were, um, six men in the Lazarus facility — "

"And one of them is dead. I killed Subject Three." Sawyer's voice was cold. He couldn't let emotion get to him, not then.

Jay licked his lower lip. "Ten subjects made the transformation."

Ten?

"But the exam room was different for the last four test subjects. The background was off. I think Landon must have kept them in a different location."

Where the hell were those men?

"I also saw some files that made me think Landon changed up your original formula, Beth. He wanted to *increase* the aggression that you feared. Only I don't think he ever told you that he was stirring up the cocktail even more."

"Sonofabitch," Elizabeth breathed.

Yes, Landon was a damn sonofabitch. "I want to see my transformation." The words burst from Sawyer. Still cold, still emotionless, but a demand nonetheless. "Show it to me."

Jay glanced at Elizabeth. "I don't think that's the best idea…"

"Show the fucking video to me."

West stepped in front of the screens. "Why? You know what happened. You were dead. You were injected, and you came back. End of story." West crossed his arms over his chest. "Let it go."

"I want to see it. Show—"

"Just show him," Elizabeth cut in quietly. "He has a right to see it."

West glanced at Jay.

Jay's face tensed. "But I don't like seeing your pain, Beth. I never did."

"Neither the hell do I," West muttered, but he stepped aside.

"Show him." Elizabeth reached for Sawyer's hand. She laced her fingers with his.

Jay bent to tap on his keyboard. It took a moment, but then another scene loaded.

Elizabeth squeezed Sawyer's hand.

The video began…

"What's happening? Why are they here?" On the screen, Elizabeth was in a cold, sterile-looking exam room. She was staring at several guards who crowded in the room. Two sheet-covered bodies waited on exam tables.

Landon picked up a chart. "Because in case any of that *aggression* that you mentioned manifests with these test subjects, I want to be prepared." He gave a brisk nod as he seemed to scan the notes in the chart, then he focused on her. "This is your moment, Elizabeth. Don't back away now."

Her hands clenched at her sides. "There can't be any degeneration to the tissue. The subjects—"

"Their bodies were protected," Landon responded at once. "Exactly per your protocol."

She stepped toward the nearest exam table, her movements stiff and jerky.

"Glad to see you're getting on board," Landon murmured.

Elizabeth's hand lifted and curled around the sheet. She pulled it away from the test subject's head. "*S-Sawyer?*" There was so much pain and shock in that gasped name. "*Sawyer!*" Now she was yelling. Her face had gone chalk white.

"He was killed on the mission." Landon's voice was brisk. "Both he and operative Flynn Haddox didn't survive. Wright knew these two men would be prime candidates for Lazarus, so he immediately ordered the preservative process to be utilized with their remains."

Elizabeth's body hunched, as if she'd been punched in the gut.

"Flynn's…dead. *Sawyer's*…dead."

"Obviously, they're dead." Now Landon sounded annoyed. "But if Lazarus works, they won't stay that way. We'll start with Sawyer first—"

She whirled to face him. "Sawyer...*no!* We can't use Lazarus on him!"

"Why not? He's the perfect specimen. His body is strong, he's a warrior, exactly what Wright wants in Project Lazarus. Sawyer is the ideal candidate. With his background and training, he'll be the alpha for this program."

She was crying. Elizabeth swiped her fingers over the tears on her cheeks. "Lazarus isn't ready. You can't—you can't do this to him!"

"Do this?" he repeated. "He's dead, Elizabeth. We can either let him stay that way, or we can try and bring him back. You're crying. Look, I get that it's...difficult...because this is someone we both know—"

"*Difficult?*"

"But you had to realize the men here would make perfect subjects. And if they died on a mission, well, isn't this the natural next step?"

She didn't speak.

Landon edged closer to her. "He's dead. What we're doing...we're bringing him *back*."

"What if he comes back wrong?" Her voice was rasping, so weak with pain and grief. "The Lazarus formula is not perfect and it's—*it's Sawyer!*" More tears slid down her cheeks. "No, no, this is not happening. I can't do this to him! I won't—Sawyer isn't some lab rat. He's—"

The video stopped.

Jay let out a long sigh. "I really think that's enough. Obviously, you were given the formula and you—"

"*Play the fucking rest,*" Sawyer snarled.

Jay opened his mouth.

"You heard him, Jay," West growled. "Just play the rest. You can't start it and then stop. At this point, he deserves to see the end."

"But she doesn't." Jay was staring at Elizabeth. "She doesn't deserve that pain again."

"It's okay." Her voice was soft. "Play the rest. It's a scene that I see in my head every day. Seeing it now isn't going to hurt me more."

"Sonofabitch…" Jay tapped the keyboard.

The video resumed.

Landon's gaze was on Elizabeth. "I thought you might respond this way. Once you saw it was him. Unfortunate, but…it is what it is." He motioned vaguely with one hand. "Guard, escort Dr. Parker out of the lab. She's done here."

As he watched, Elizabeth tensed. A guard grabbed Elizabeth and pinned her arms behind her back. The guard yanked her across the lab, hauling her toward the lab's door.

"Stop it!" Elizabeth yelled. "Let me go, right now!"

But the guard didn't let her go. And Landon reached for a syringe.

"Don't!" Elizabeth screamed. "Not to him!"

Landon put the needle over Sawyer's body. Then he pierced Sawyer's chest.

The guard had dragged Elizabeth to the door. *"Sawyer!"*

Landon reached for the second needle. He moved behind Sawyer, placing the needle at the back of his head. But Landon paused and glanced over at Elizabeth. "Don't you want him back?"

Before she could answer, Landon gave Sawyer the injection.

"Stop! Let me go, please!" Elizabeth begged the guard.

Landon frowned down at Sawyer. "Nothing is happening."

The guard hauled Elizabeth into the hallway. A nurse slammed the door shut behind them. More needles were brought to Landon. The bastard grabbed one and injected the formula into Sawyer's heart again.

And Elizabeth was there. She'd ripped open the door to the lab. "Don't give him too much!" Elizabeth yelled. "Don't—"

Landon administered another dose to Sawyer. "He's not fucking moving. This doesn't work." Sweat covered his forehead. "I have to tell Wright this doesn't work!"

The guard grabbed her again. And once more, she was physically pulled out of the lab. A nurse shut the door.

Then…

In the video. Sawyer sat up. Landon started smiling. He reached out his hand to Sawyer.

Only I threw the bastard across the room. Sawyer felt his eyes widen as he watched the scene. He'd just tossed the bastard a good ten feet. Landon's body smashed into a glass viewing window. Elizabeth's horrified face was on the other side of that window.

The guards inside that lab room immediately pulled their weapons. They aimed at Sawyer. They fired.

But Sawyer didn't stop. He jumped off the table. He ran right at them. He attacked, punching, kicking, taking their weapons —
firing on them.

The nurses were racing for freedom. They screamed as they fled into the hallway.

Sawyer kept attacking the guards.

Watching that terrible scene, Sawyer could only shake his head. He'd been so out of control. Dangerous. *A monster.* "Who stopped me?" The question ripped from him.

But then he saw — on those two freaking monitors — he watched as Elizabeth rushed back into the lab. Landon was on the floor, trying to crawl for the door. And Sawyer had taken a gun from one of the guards.

"*Sawyer!*" Elizabeth yelled his name.

At her call, his head lifted. He still held the gun in his hand. His eyes immediately locked on her.

"Sawyer, put down the gun," Elizabeth told him, her voice shaking. It sounded as if she were begging him.

He looked at the gun in his hand.

She crept closer to him. Behind her, Landon kept crawling toward the door.

"Put it down," Elizabeth pleaded. "I know...I know this is confusing and scary, but I can help you. I *will* help you."

He glanced back at her...and he...he *aimed* the gun at her.

"*No!*" The video was still playing, but Sawyer had just shouted that denial. No, no way would he hurt Elizabeth. "*No!*"

"This is why I didn't want this fucking video shown," Jay muttered as he raked a hand through his hair.

On the screens, Elizabeth had frozen, seemingly rooted to the spot. "Sawyer? It's...it's me."

But on the monitors, he was staring at her with no recognition.

"Shoot him!" Landon thundered.

Elizabeth looked over her shoulder. A guard stood near the doorway, and he held a gun—one that was aimed right at Sawyer. "No!"

The guard's finger began to squeeze the trigger. Elizabeth threw her body forward, placing herself between the guard and Sawyer.

The bullet hit her in the chest, and as she fell… "*Sawyer!*"

He stared down at her, watching as the blood covered her body.

A fog—no, a gas—began to fill the lab. The gun fell from Sawyer's fingers. He staggered forward, and then he sagged to his knees, right beside Elizabeth.

And then Sawyer reached out to her. His hand pressed to her chest as he shuddered. For an instant, pain—*grief?*—flashed on his face, but he collapsed, his body falling on top of hers.

A few moments later, the lab door opened again. The people who rushed in were wearing masks that covered their faces. They dragged Sawyer away from Elizabeth, but he roused enough to fight them. To fight them and try to reach for her once more.

The video ended.

Sawyer's chest was tight. His muscles were locked with tension. With fury. With fear. *Elizabeth.*

"I swear," Jay cocked his head as he studied Sawyer now. "I swear, it seemed like you recognized her at the end."

Sawyer's head turned toward Elizabeth. "You took that bullet for me."

One of her shoulders lifted in a shrug that wasn't casual. "I'd lost you once. I wasn't going to let someone kill you again."

"You loved him that much?"

"No." She gave a hard, negative shake of her head. "I love *you* that much. It's not him, it's you. You're the same. No matter what happened with Lazarus, you are the same. You are the same strong, brave man I always knew."

A brave man who'd attacked guards? No, no, he was—

"I see it when I look in your eyes. Landon gave you *twice* the dosage. Yes, when you woke up, you were out of control, but you fought your way back. Because you are strong. And you are fierce, and you will always be the man I love."

An alarm began to sound. A shrill shriek that had his body immediately going into fight mode as he pulled Elizabeth closer. "What in the hell is that? What's happening?"

Jay was already typing on his keyboard once more. "Security footage, I need a live feed from outside now...*Shit*." The live feed appeared on the monitors. The feed showed several guards slumped near the entrance gate. Dead? Or unconscious?

"On my way," West immediately barked as he headed for the door.

"If a Lazarus soldier is out there, you won't stop him." Sawyer was certain. "You need me. I'll go." He stared down at Elizabeth. "Stay inside. I won't let anyone hurt you. Not ever again, I swear it."

Her eyes were wide. "You think it's Bryce? But…do you feel him? Has he contacted you again?"

Actually, Sawyer hadn't felt anything on their psychic link. But he sent out a message now—not one to Bryce, but to Flynn. *We've got trouble. Guards outside are unconscious, maybe dead. I need you to keep Elizabeth safe while I take care of the threat.*

Immediately, Flynn's voice was in his head. *I'm coming, too. You need me —*

I need you to keep her safe. Her and Cecelia. If something happens to me, you make sure no one so much as touches them, you got me?

"There's a safe room in this house," Jay announced. "One of the reasons I decided to make it my base while I was in Arizona. I can keep Elizabeth and Cecelia there. No one will get in."

Elizabeth shook her head. "Sawyer—"

He kissed her. Had to do it. "I won't lose you again. No one will take me from you ever again." He pressed his forehead against hers. "I'll come back. I swear, I will always come back to you."

Then he let her go. Sawyer glared at Jay and West. "You keep her safe—or I will kick your asses."

West handed him a gun. "Take this."

"You keep it for—"

"I have another. And I get that you're all enhanced and shit, but nothing beats a bullet. Take it."

He didn't wait any longer. Sawyer took the gun. And as he slipped from that house, he let the shield in his mind lower as he began to hunt. *Bryce, you fucking bastard…are you here?*

There was no answer. Just a thick, heavy silence.

And then Sawyer found the first body. A guard who was lying in a pool of his blood. His neck had been broken, and he'd been stabbed, again and again.

CHAPTER TWENTY-THREE

"This way!" Jay called, voice sharp. "The safe room is just under the stairs. It's reinforced with steel. There is no way anyone is getting inside once we seal that door. Super solder or no—"

Footsteps clattered on the stairs. Elizabeth looked up to see Flynn and Cecelia rushing toward them. When they reached the landing. Flynn ran toward her, his hand tight around Cecelia's wrist. "Bryce *doesn't* get her." His eyes glittered. "He doesn't get near either one of you, Elizabeth. I swear it."

Her stomach twisted in fear. "Is he here? Do you feel him?" And, even worse, if he was there, what if he started influencing the others? Just what could he do? She didn't know the limits of his power. Didn't know what she'd made when she'd played Frankenstein.

"I can't feel *anything*." Flynn shook his head and urged Cecelia inside the open safe room. "It's like someone put up a wall. I don't know where the threat is coming—"

Gunfire exploded. It burst out sharp and fast and Flynn jerked when the bullets slammed into his back. His eyes were on Elizabeth, and they'd flared wide. *"Get...safe..."*

She wasn't going in there without him. West was at her side, and he bent, aiming and firing at whoever had attacked them. The blasts were so loud. Elizabeth grabbed Flynn's arm and dragged him away from the gunfire. West kept firing—

West went down. Blood splattered onto the wall behind him.

"Oh, the fuck, no," Jay yelled. He rushed back out of the safe room, grabbed West, and heaved him over his shoulder. He was running back toward them when—

A bullet hit him. It slammed into Jay's leg, going in the back of his thigh and bursting out of the front. His leg immediately crumpled, and he hit the marble floor.

***

The guards were all dead. They'd been lying face-down, so Sawyer hadn't been able to see the blood in their video feed. Blood that covered their torsos. They'd all been killed in the same manner. Broken necks first—then stabbed. *Fucking overkill.*

There were at least seven dead bodies.

It takes time to kill seven men. The killer had been out there, going through the men one at a time, and Sawyer hadn't known. He hadn't heard anything, hadn't sensed anything.

Gunfire blasted.

His head jerked at the sound, whipping toward the mansion. Bullets flew in a fast thunder, an exchange of gunfire, and he leapt forward, fear nearly choking him. He'd left Elizabeth in that house. She should have been safe.

Elizabeth. Elizabeth! Rage and fear poured through his veins, and he ran fast, so fast. He'd destroy whoever was in that house. Whoever had fired at Elizabeth would be dead.

Attack. Destroy. Kill…

The sinister, twisting thoughts burned in his mind. They were the only warning he had that Bryce was close. Because in the next instant, gunfire was thundering again. Only this time, the gunfire didn't come from the house.

It came from behind me. The bastard was out here, waiting for me. Waiting for me to lower my guard. To turn my back.

Sawyer threw his body to the left, and the bullet burned over his side.

***

"Get in the safe room!" Jay bellowed. "Go! The door automatically locks when you close it— *go!*"

No, she wasn't going to leave him and West out there. She scrambled toward them. She—

Elizabeth.

The voice stilled her. It was a voice that filled her mind. *Only* her mind. Because no one had said anything out loud. That voice was so familiar. And utterly terrifying. Without a word, Elizabeth immediately spun around. Cecelia had been surging after her, obviously determined to help, too.

Elizabeth shoved her back, sending Cecelia tumbling into the safe room, and then Elizabeth yanked the door closed, sealing Cecelia inside.

But keeping myself out.

Laughter echoed around her. Her shoulders stiffened as she turned back to the face the shooter. She found him standing just behind Jay, with a gun pointed at her former lover's head.

Sadly, Elizabeth expelled a long sigh. "You just had to try the formula for yourself, didn't you, Landon?"

And Dr. Landon Meyer—arrogant asshole, government pencil pusher, and now Lazarus soldier—slammed the gun into the side of Jay's head. Jay slumped on the marble tile, blood dripping from his head, even as Elizabeth lunged toward him.

"No, Elizabeth, dear, you stand right there." Landon lifted the gun and pointed it at her. "And, of course, I tried the formula. Got a trusted associate to help me. I mean, seriously, did you truly believe I'd let all of that power go to waste?"

***

Sawyer's body rolled and he came up in a crouch, the gun West had given him gripped tightly in his hand. His gaze scanned to the right. Bryce was there. *Why hide, Five? Come out and I'll kick your ass.*

Bryce didn't answer, but a dark pulse of rage filled Sawyer's mind. Sawyer eased out a slow breath. His eyes narrowed as he stared into the darkness. Dawn was due soon, but the night still reigned. So very close.

But Sawyer didn't need light to find Bryce. He just let his senses out, sending them surging into the dark. He listened, so intently, for the faintest of breaths, for the weak beat of a heart— *got you.*

Sawyer fired into the shadows just as Bryce lunged forward. The bullet found its target, sinking deep into Bryce's right shoulder. The gun dropped from his suddenly useless fingers as Bryce bellowed his fury. Sawyer fired again, and the second bullet hit the bastard in the chest. Bryce fell, his body twitching on the ground. In an instant, Sawyer was on him. He put his gun right under Bryce's chin. "Make another move, and it will be your last."

Bryce froze.

Rage beat at Sawyer, making his temples throb.

Attack. Destroy. Kill.

Sawyer gave a grim laugh. "That shit doesn't work now. I think I've built an immunity to you...see, once I knew the thoughts and feelings weren't mine, it got easier to beat them back. I'm not some puppet on a string. You don't control me."

Blood poured from Bryce's wounds.

"How the hell did you find us so fast?" Sawyer demanded. "I cut out my tracker."

Bryce's eyes widened. "T-tracker?"

"Yeah, the fucking GPS tracker that Landon shoved into us so he could always find our team. I cut mine out. Don't know how the fuck you found me, thought you—"

"F-followed him..." Bryce jerked. His skin had gone stark white. "M-made me...f-follow..."

"Him?" Sawyer thought of the gunfire he'd heard in the mansion. Bryce couldn't have fired those shots, not when the asshole had been lying in wait *outside*. "Who's in there? I killed Three. The bastard was out of control. Probably because of *you*. Who else have you screwed in the head? Is Subject Four up there? Is he the one who helped you kill all those guards at the gate?"

"N-not me…" Blood dripped from Bryce's lips. "Not…g-guards…didn't kill…th-them…"

"Right. Like I believe your bullshit." His finger wanted to squeeze the trigger. "You're done." He had to get to Elizabeth. And he had to make sure that Bryce never threatened her again. "You think you're going to take Elizabeth away? Hell, no. You're just going to die. You will just—"

"L-Landon…" Bryce could barely speak. His breath came in rough, slow pants. "He's…one…killed…"

"*What?*"

"F-followed h-him here…he…he's the one…wants Elizabeth…made me…made me t-taunt you…wants…you…weak…"

Landon? Landon Meyer?

But Bryce wasn't saying anything else. His body had gone still, and when Sawyer put his hand to the guy's pulse, there was no beat. No weak flutter. Nothing. *He's gone.*

Fuck. Sawyer shoved to his feet and ran for the mansion. Bryce's final words kept playing in his head, over and over again. Landon was a scientist, not a super soldier. Wasn't he?

Sawyer burst through the front door of the mansion, the gun gripped in his hand. The door flew back and banged into the wall, and the scene before him made Sawyer's heart stop.

West was on the floor, a pool of blood beneath him. Jay was unconscious next to him, his body in a heap. And Landon—Landon stood just a few feet away from Elizabeth. A gun was in the doctor's hand. A gun that he had aimed right at Elizabeth's head.

When Landon glimpsed Sawyer, he lunged forward. Landon grabbed Elizabeth and hauled her in front of him, using her body as a shield even as he put the gun to her head. "You should be *dead!*" Landon spat. "What the hell use is Bryce if he can't get one job done?"

Sawyer's gaze was on Elizabeth. She was afraid. He could see her fear, and he hated it. "Let her go."

"Do I *look* stupid? Hell, no. I release her, and you'll shoot me. That's not how this is going to work. You drop your gun, and then we'll talk about letting Elizabeth go free."

Sawyer's jaw clenched.

"Don't," Elizabeth's voice was soft. Her dark eyes were on Sawyer. "Don't drop your gun. If you do, he'll shoot you."

Yeah, Sawyer figured that would happen.

"If he doesn't drop it," Landon snapped as spittle flew from his mouth. "I'll shoot *you*, Elizabeth. The hero over there can watch you fall, just like before. Only this time, the bullet will be in your head. You'll die, and he won't be able to bring you back. What do you think that will do to him? You're the only emotional connection the guy seems to have.

Losing you…" He laughed. "I bet it will rip his world apart."

It would. Sawyer knew it. She was his center. No, she *was* his world, and Landon couldn't take her away.

"You won't shoot me." Elizabeth lifted her chin and her gaze never left Sawyer's. "You need me. I'm Lazarus, remember? Not you."

"I've already improved your formula, I made it better! I don't need—"

"You. Need. Me. That's why Wright came to me in D.C., isn't it? Because you told him I had to get back in the program. You messed with the formula, and something went wrong."

"*Drop your weapon, Sawyer!*" Landon screamed. Only the scream wasn't just out loud. The scream *echoed* in Sawyer's head, a hard, psychic blast. The compulsion that came with it was so strong that Sawyer's hand trembled. But he didn't drop the gun.

"The test subjects get different psychic powers, don't they?" Elizabeth's voice was so cool. As if she weren't afraid at all. But that was a lie. Sawyer could see the fear in her eyes. "Another side effect that we didn't anticipate. Bryce could push his emotions onto others and you…you do something a little different, don't you?"

"*I can get into people's heads. Make them do what I want…*" Landon boasted as his mouth came closer to Elizabeth's ear. "I can make them attack! I can make them destroy. I can make them *kill!*"

Attack. Destroy. Kill. Those dark orders had come from Landon?

Landon laughed again. "You thought I was so weak at Lazarus, didn't you? When you pushed me into my office and tried to make me release the band on your ankle. You thought you held the power then, but you were wrong!"

"I still knocked your ass out, didn't I?"

Landon's laughter faded. "I was only out a few moments. I heal fast, maybe not as fast as you, but I heal."

Elizabeth still had her eyes on Sawyer. "You woke up to find your precious laptop gone, didn't you, Landon? Bet that freaked you the hell out."

"I knew you had it. Knew I had to find you. But that was going to be easy enough." And his left hand moved down to her chest.

"*Stop!*" Sawyer snarled.

"Easy…just showing dear Elizabeth where *her* tracker is located. You had to wonder how I found her so fast, right? Well, while Elizabeth was being sewed up after her little incident with the gunshot, I took the liberty of having a tracker implanted in her. I knew it would come in handy."

"You're a fucking bastard," Elizabeth said, her eyes hard with fear and fury.

"No, I'm not a bastard. Thanks to you, well, I'm pretty much a god among men now."

"You're insane," she fired right back.

He pressed his nose to her cheek. "I can make you do things, too, Elizabeth. So many things."

No, he fucking wouldn't. "*Let her go.*" Sawyer's words were a roar.

"I can make you do things," Landon said again, as if he hadn't heard Sawyer. "I just have to be close enough to my prey. Within five feet. And I'm plenty close enough to you now." Landon's face had gone smug. His head lifted and he smirked at Sawyer. "I want you to take the gun, Elizabeth." His voice had turned low, soothing. "Take the gun from me…and *you* fire at Sawyer."

Her eyes widened. Elizabeth shook her head.

"*Take the gun and fire at him!*" Landon bellowed. "He won't shoot at you. Never at you. He's been obsessed with you the whole time. When you were shot back in D.C., he went wild when we took him away from you. He started screaming your name when he was pulled down the hallway. I killed him again. Did I ever tell you that? I killed him again because he was so out of control and desperate to get to you. I killed him, and I took him back in the Lazarus facility for more experimentation. He woke there, but he'd still dream of you. I'd see him at night, that's why I had all of those cameras—"

Sawyer took a step toward the bastard.

"The subjects remember more when they sleep. They call out for people. They whisper their secrets. Bryce—he was a freaking killer. He loved torturing women. I knew that, though, before I brought him in to Lazarus. Wanted someone with a killer edge."

A tear leaked down Elizabeth's cheek.

"Take the gun!" Landon blasted. "Take it and shoot—"

Sawyer fired his weapon. The bullet hit Landon in the side of his neck, and blood poured from his wound. Landon's eyes were wide and desperate as he staggered back.

Sawyer yanked Elizabeth from the sonofabitch's hold. Landon had put his left hand over the gaping wound, and his right was swinging up the gun—

Sawyer knocked the gun out of Landon's hand. "You fucking killed me. *Twice.* It's your turn to die." And he fired, almost a point-blank shot. The bullet slammed into Landon's heart, and the man fell immediately, just crumpled on the floor.

Elizabeth's breath panted in and out. Sawyer pulled her into his arms, holding her tight. *His* Elizabeth. She was okay. They'd both made it. And he was never, fucking ever going to let her go. "I love you." The words were torn from him. He needed to say them. Needed her to understand. There were parts of him that were gone. Missing. Gaping holes inside, but there was one thing he knew with utter certainty. "I love you." His head lifted because he had to stare into her eyes. Had to make her see what he felt was real.

When he'd rushed into that house and seen the gun at her temple, everything had become utterly, crystal clear to him. Elizabeth couldn't die. Elizabeth *was* his world.

Elizabeth was his.

"I love you," he said again. He'd say it a thousand times. Forever, if she'd let him.

Her smile came. Slow, unsteady, but it made his heart feel lighter. The threat was gone. Elizabeth was okay. They'd both made it. They had a chance at forever.

They —

Horror flashed in her eyes. "Flynn! Oh, God, Flynn!" She pulled out of Sawyer's arms and rushed to Flynn's side.

Sawyer hadn't even seen his friend at first. He'd seen Jay and West, and he'd detected their heartbeats so he knew they still lived. But now he saw Flynn, sprawled in a pool of blood behind the staircase. He'd fallen down, face-first, and bullet holes littered his back.

Elizabeth reached for him. Her hand went to his neck. "Flynn? Flynn!"

Sawyer focused on his friend. Tried to hear breathing. A heartbeat.

Nothing.

Grief wrapped around Sawyer even as his hands went to Elizabeth's shoulders. "Baby, he's gone."

Her head lifted. Tears slid from her eyes. "He was protecting me. He...Landon shot him in the back! Flynn didn't deserve this—you and Flynn never deserved this!"

Sawyer heard a frantic banging. Wild. Desperate. His head turned toward the right.

"The safe room," Elizabeth whispered. "It's Cecelia, I-I locked her inside—"

Sawyer focused hard, and he could hear Cecelia's cries. *Let me out! Get me out! I can't be locked up again—I can't!*

"I'm so sorry, Flynn." A sob burst from Elizabeth. She'd rolled Flynn over and her hand was on his cheek. His eyes were closed. His face was slack. "I wanted to help you and Sawyer, I didn't want—"

Flynn's eyes opened. They flew open at the exact same instant—

Thud. Thud. Thud.

At the exact same instant that Sawyer heard the guy's heart start beating. Sawyer's jaw dropped.

Flynn let out a low groan. "Oh, man…feels like I was hit by a…a truck…" He licked his lips. "Wh-what the hell happened?"

Elizabeth gaped at him.

He was dead. His heart stopped. He was dead.

But wasn't Project Lazarus all about bringing men back from the dead? All about them rising again? Stronger, more powerful than ever before? What had Landon said before…

"I killed him, and I took him back in the Lazarus facility for more experimentation. He woke there, but he'd still dream of you."

Holy shit.

They could come back from death. How many times? How many?

Sawyer could see the same thoughts whirling in Elizabeth's head. Her eyes grew wider and she suddenly yelled, *"Landon!"*

He'd had the same realization. If Flynn could come back, then Landon could, too. Sawyer whirled, and he scooped up the gun he'd discarded when he grabbed Elizabeth. He bounded toward Landon just as the guy's eyes started to crack open.

A sly smile was already curving Landon's lips.

But that smile froze when he saw the gun right over his face.

"No!" Landon croaked. "N-not my head…n-need brain to f-function—"

Sawyer fired. One shot right into Landon's head. The doctor jerked back. Then he was still. Completely, ominously still.

"Is he going to come back from that?" Sawyer demanded. He didn't lower his gun. He spared a quick glance toward Elizabeth.

She was still on the floor, with Flynn sprawled half on top of her. Her face was stark white. "I sure as hell hope not."

Yeah, so did he...but how about, just to be safe...

Sawyer fired again and again until the gun was empty. Until Landon's brain was full of bullets.

Just to be safe.

Payback, bastard. Payback.

CHAPTER TWENTY-FOUR

"I can't find any trace of Wyman Wright." Jay sat behind his desk, his fingers poised over his keyboard. "I looked, Elizabeth, and I looked hard. If I can't find him…" He glanced up, his jaw set. "Then no one can."

They were back in D.C., well, technically, they were just outside of the city. In yet another of Jay's houses. He'd been released from the hospital and so had West—though West was on strict orders to take things easy. *Her* orders.

Currently, West was stationed near the door, and a glower was on his face.

There were a few more occupants in the sprawling office. Flynn Haddox stood next to West—his body in the same, falsely relaxed pose. Cecelia Gregory sat perched on the edge of the couch. While the last member of their little group—Sawyer—

He stood right beside Elizabeth.

"From what I can tell, Wright never made it out of the Lazarus facility alive." Jay rolled back his shoulders. "Landon wanted to cover all of his tracks there. I think he set the explosions to destroy the place. I think he blew the place to hell and back because he wanted the formula for himself." He nodded once. "I found plans on his laptop. Logistics that showed the facility's entire layout. Places that would be perfect for explosive devices. He mapped out the facility, and then he just waited for the perfect moment to strike."

"What about Bryce?" The question came from Cecelia. Quiet. Hesitant. "Is he…?"

Elizabeth glanced at her. She could feel Cecelia's fear.

"No sign of him, either," Jay confessed. "But unlike Wright, we know that Bryce is enhanced. And all indicators say that he slipped away from my house in Arizona, then the guy went completely off the grid. I'm pretty sure Bryce cut his tracker out long ago. Hell, that's probably how he was able to slip into Cecelia's quarters so often. He must have left the tracker in his room while he went to see her—"

A low, menacing growl came from Flynn. "He should be *dead*."

"Dammit! I didn't know he could get back up after I shot him in the chest!" Sawyer said, voice flat. "If I'd known it took a bullet to the brain to stop him, trust me, I would have made sure the bastard didn't rise again."

Because, unfortunately, Bryce *had* risen. By the time they'd realized that Lazarus subjects could come back from the dead — apparently, multiple times — he'd already been long gone. Only a pool of blood had been left to mark where he'd been at Jay's Arizona safe house. Both Sawyer and Flynn had tried to track the guy, but he'd just vanished.

"He's going to come after me." Cecelia squared her shoulders. "I know he will."

Flynn stalked toward her. "Then he'll find me waiting for him. I'll finish him."

Elizabeth bit her lower lip. She was afraid of Bryce, too. Afraid that he was hunting both her and Cecelia.

Sawyer caught her hand in his. "Doc, you don't need to be afraid. Not ever again."

If only that were true. She had Sawyer back, and when he looked at her, she could *see* the love in his eyes. He was going to stand by her, she knew it, just as she would stay by him. Always. But there was plenty to fear.

Landon had created ten Lazarus test subjects. Ten subjects that they knew about. What if there were more?

They had to find them. Maybe those men were good, maybe they were like Flynn and Sawyer — warriors who wanted to protect. That was the best-case scenario. The worst-case?

They were like Bryce and Landon. Monsters who wanted to kill.

She'd poured through all of the notes and files that Jay had been able to retrieve from Landon's computer. He'd been brutally honest in those notations, ever the cold, unbiased scientist. And he'd realized some truths about himself. "The Lazarus formula amplifies your personality traits. The good ones and the bad." She swallowed. "Bryce was a sadistic predator even before he got the dosage." An Army Ranger who'd been dishonorably discharged — he *never* should have been a candidate for Lazarus. But then, Landon had been so curious about what would happen to a subject like him. "The formula made Bryce into even more of a threat." Her gaze slid to Cecelia.

"He *won't* get to either of you," Flynn swore.

Some promises were easy to give. But what happened when the monster you hunted could slip so easily into your mind? Into the minds of his victims?

"We have to find them all," West said, stirring from his position. "If they're threats, we eliminate them. If they're not, if they're like Sawyer and Flynn…"

"We aren't exactly the perfect image of *good* guys," Sawyer drawled, voice rough.

She thought he was. To her, he was better than perfect.

"Landon was a killer before he took the formula," she said. "He was killing test subjects."

Wright had said Sawyer was deliberately killed so that her lover could be brought into Project Lazarus. Now, Elizabeth couldn't help but wonder just how involved Landon had been in Sawyer's death. *Because Sawyer was close to me.* That pain would always be there. "The formula just made him worse. He lost his grip totally and was consumed with the idea of getting more power, of being able to control others." To her, he'd become the real monster.

No, he'd *always* been a monster. He'd just hid his evil beneath the skin.

"I think the authorities and the media bought our story." Jay flashed a broad smile. "*My* story. It was, after all, pure genius the way I got access to those security videos from the Lazarus facility. The videos that clearly showed Landon setting the explosives. We were able to prove to the world that he was batshit crazy, while explaining that Elizabeth and Cecelia were never kidnapped—they just managed to escape the mad doctor's clutches."

Pure genius? Not so much. Turned out…when she'd installed his little virus into the computer system at Lazarus, she'd opened a back door for him. Jay hadn't told her about that part, not until later. Once she'd uploaded the virus, he'd snuck into the system and sent the video feeds to himself. He *had* caught images of Landon planting the explosives. And, he'd also gotten a video of Landon killing Hugh Cleston.

That wasn't Bryce. The guard's blood had all been on Landon's hands.

Jay reached into his desk and pulled out a manila file. "Sawyer and Flynn, I've got new social security numbers for you." He put the file on top of his desk. "Since the world thinks you're dead, no one is looking for you. I mean, there are graves out there for you two. When you went into Lazarus, Landon and Wright took care of burying you both—literally."

Elizabeth had once visited Sawyer's empty grave. And she'd been gutted.

"You can do anything you want," Jay continued earnestly. "Go anywhere you want—"

"I'm staying with Elizabeth," Sawyer said flatly.

"Right." Jay coughed. "Like we all didn't see that shit coming."

Elizabeth shook her head. "Jay, thank you. I'll never be able to repay what you've done for me."

"I'm sure you'll find a way, one day." He just shrugged. "We've got plenty of time to work everything out later."

They did have time. Time to hunt the bad guys, time to find the good guys. Time to fix the mistakes of the past. Time to dream about the future.

A future that she'd have with Sawyer.
Finally.

They left Jay and the others. Headed out into
the D.C. night. Flynn escorted Cecelia home — he
seemed to always be with her these days. A light
flurry of snow had started to fall. By the time
Sawyer and Elizabeth reached her apartment, a
soft coating of white littered the ground. She
slipped from the car and Sawyer took her hand.
A snowflake slid across her nose.

He stopped her on the sidewalk, and her
head tilted back as she stared up at him.

"Are you sure about me?" Sawyer asked her.

She knew he still worried about the darkness
he carried inside. He might never get his
memories back completely, they both knew that.
But she also knew that they could make new
memories. "I've never been more certain of
anyone."

He pulled her close. His lips pressed to hers.
His lips were cold, but he still warmed her. He
heated her, from the inside out. Banished her
fears and made her feel alive. He made her hope.

"I love you, Elizabeth," Sawyer whispered
against her mouth. "Always."

Just as she would always love him. They
headed into her building, shutting out the night.
They'd fought death and won, they'd fought
killers and *won*. They could face anything else

that would come their way, as long as they were together.

And they would be together.

Because she would never give up on him, just as he wouldn't give up on her. They'd stay together.

They'd never let go.

EPILOGUE

"You shouldn't have lied to Elizabeth."

Jay turned at West's low words. The others had left. He'd been staring at the light snowfall, thinking about how life could be so strange. All of the twists and turns that it could take. He hadn't even realized West had come back into his office. Frowning now, he said, "I didn't lie to Elizabeth." She was one of the few people in the world that he valued. Not his lover any longer, but he still cared for her. She and West were his family. The only family he had.

"You never told her that *you* were one of Wright's biggest backers. That *you* gave him the money to turn Lazarus into reality."

No, he hadn't told her that particular bit. "Once, Lazarus was her dream. I simply supported Wright to give her the chance—"

"Bullshit." West's voice was low and angry. West didn't usually get angry with him. "I know you. You saw an opportunity, and you took it. You realized what kind of things could happen with Lazarus, and you jumped on board, didn't you?"

"I did it for her."

"You lying to me…or to yourself?"

"I didn't *know* what Wright and Landon were doing. I didn't *know* – "

"You helped her get Sawyer and Flynn out of that place because you wanted to atone for your sins."

Jay clamped his lips shut. West knew him too well.

"You going to atone with the others? The ones who might be psycho killers? The ones who might be *good* soldiers, trapped in some other facility? You going to atone with all of them?"

He would try. That was the plan.

"You wanted Elizabeth and Sawyer — hell, even Flynn — to owe you. Why? What's your end game? From where I stand, you owe *them*. That's what atonement is, right?"

Yes, it was, but he did need them. "It's not over yet." He wished that it was. He wished the nightmare would end. But…

When you knocked down the wall between life and death, there were no easy endings. There couldn't be. More danger would come. More fear. More pain.

And they had to be ready for those threats. So, hell, yes, he wanted two super soldiers to owe him. Two super soldiers and the woman with the most amazing mind he'd ever known. He'd use them all.

Because the story wasn't over. Not yet. There was a price for cheating the grim reaper, and the price had to be paid.

The End
###

ABOUT THE AUTHOR

Award-winning author Cynthia Eden writes dark tales of paranormal romance and romantic suspense. She is a *New York Times, USA Today, Digital Book World,* and *IndieReader* best-seller. Cynthia is also a three-time finalist for the RITA® award. Since she began writing full-time in 2005, Cynthia has written over eighty novels and novellas.

HER WORKS

Romantic Suspense

Lazarus Rising

- Never Let Go (Book One, Lazarus Rising) - Available 09/26/2017
- Keep Me Close (Book Two, Lazarus Rising) - Available 10/24/2017

Dark Obsession Series

- Watch Me (Dark Obsession, Book 1)
- Want Me (Dark Obsession, Book 2)
- Need Me (Dark Obsession, Book 3)
- Beware Of Me (Dark Obsession, Book 4)
- Only For Me (Dark Obsession, Books 1 to 4)

Mine Series

- Mine To Take (Mine, Book 1)
- Mine To Keep (Mine, Book 2)
- Mine To Hold (Mine, Book 3)

- Mine To Crave (Mine, Book 4)
- Mine To Have (Mine, Book 5)
- Mine To Protect (Mine, Book 6)
- Mine Series Box Set Volume 1 (Mine, Books 1-3)
- Mine Series Box Set Volume 2 (Mine, Books 4-6)

Other Romantic Suspense

- First Taste of Darkness
- Sinful Secrets
- Until Death
- Christmas With A Spy

Paranormal Romance

Bad Things

- The Devil In Disguise (Bad Things, Book 1)
- On The Prowl (Bad Things, Book 2)
- Undead Or Alive (Bad Things, Book 3)
- Broken Angel (Bad Things, Book 4)
- Heart Of Stone (Bad Things, Book 5)
- Tempted By Fate (Bad Things, Book 6)
- Bad Things Volume One (Books 1 to 3)
- Bad Things Volume Two (Books 4 to 6)
- Bad Things Deluxe Box Set (Books 1 to 6)

Bite Series

- Forbidden Bite (Bite Book 1)
- Mating Bite (Bite Book 2)

Lazarus Rising

- Never Let Go (Book One, Lazarus Rising)
- Keep Me Close (Book Two, Lazarus Rising) - Available 10/24/2017

Blood and Moonlight Series

- Bite The Dust (Blood and Moonlight, Book 1)
- Better Off Undead (Blood and Moonlight, Book 2)
- Bitter Blood (Blood and Moonlight, Book 3)
- Blood and Moonlight (The Complete Series)

Purgatory Series

- The Wolf Within (Purgatory, Book 1)
- Marked By The Vampire (Purgatory, Book 2)
- Charming The Beast (Purgatory, Book 3)
- Deal with the Devil (Purgatory, Book 4)
- The Beasts Inside (Purgatory, Books 1 to 4)

Bound Series

- Bound By Blood (Bound Book 1)
- Bound In Darkness (Bound Book 2)
- Bound In Sin (Bound Book 3)
- Bound By The Night (Bound Book 4)
- Forever Bound (Bound, Books 1 to 4)
- Bound in Death (Bound Book 5)

Made in the USA
Coppell, TX
25 March 2020

17677403R00233